First published in 2018.

This edition published in 2022 by Sharpe Books.

To Stuart and Miranda

CONTENTS

Note on Roman names

Roman men had two or three names at this time: unfortunately, for first names, everyone tended to use one of a very short list one of about ten first names. You will therefore find a lot of people with the first name Marcus or Lucius or Quintus whenever you read about ancient Rome. Girls were given a feminised version of their father's second name, and if there were more than one daughter in a family, the family would use nicknames to distinguish the daughters. In the Sestius family therefore, the two daughters were officially both called "Sestia", but I have decided that the elder daughter also took on her mother's name, "Albinia", and the younger was known by her nickname, "Tia".

In this novel, many of the characters are based on real people and I didn't feel I could change their names too much. I have used a number of ploys to help the reader to identify characters, such as using the standard Anglicised version of their name: the historian in this novel was called Gaius Sallustius Crispus, but is usually referred to as Sallust, for example.

There is often no logic as to which name we use for a Roman nowadays: Cicero, Caesar and Brutus are known by their third names, Publius Sestius by his second. I have followed this lack of logic (if that is possible), wherever I thought that it helped to clarify the narrative.

Prologue

The crowd in the Forum falls silent as the Consul comes down the hill, towards the Speaker's Platform. He looks at the ground as he walks, a thoughtful expression wrinkling his brow, as if he imagines posing for a statue of himself at this critical moment. The young slave, who has been posted near the Senate House steps, straightens up and shifts nearer to the platform, along with everyone else, and tiny noises of movement swell to a whisper that runs through the crowd then dies away as the Consul faces the people of Rome and opens his mouth to speak. Torches – for it is nearly dark now –hiss and spit and light individual faces which seem to spring out of the crowd, eyes narrow with concentration or wide and frightened. The Consul seems about to speak but checks himself and takes a deep breath.

The slave is now at the front of the crowd and hopes that everyone will keep calm. He wishes the Consul would get on with it, instead of dramatising the occasion still further. He watches the lines across the Consul's brow as they deepen slightly, and waits, wondering briefly how the Great Man could possibly deliver yet another memorable speech at the end of this year of speeches. He knows what news the Consul has to deliver – everyone knows it. It is a question of how he says it, and the slave concentrates, knowing that he will have to repeat as much as he can remember when he gets home.

"Vixerunt," says the Consul very clearly, and pauses. The crowd sigh, and then hush again, and the slave shivers. But the Consul is turning, going down the steps once more. The crowd begin to talk excitedly and the slave feels his mouth open in surprise. "They have lived!" A single word – didn't the occasion demand more? Surely Marcus Tullius Cicero, greatest orator in Rome, could have dredged up a few florid phrases to commemorate the most important day in his career? No – so perish all enemies of Rome and not even their epitaphs are allowed to commemorate their deeds.

It takes the slave a long time to get out of the Forum, because of the numbers of people moving slowly, as if no one wants to leave. Once on the road up the Caelian Hill, however, he moves quickly and even runs along the little side street leading to the Sestius house. Young Lucius is waiting in the atrium, of course, and so, to his surprise, is the master's new wife, Cornelia. They both run up to him – there isn't much unnecessary ceremony in the Sestius household.

"Decius!" cries Cornelia. "Is it...?"

"Are they dead, Decius?" says Lucius, looking very serious.

"Come into the study," says Cornelia. "There's some water there for you."

The woman and child lead him in and fuss around him, making sure that he is comfortable. They sit patiently while he drinks, the only sign of their eagerness the fierce way in which the five-year-old Lucius swings his legs as he sits on a couch that is too high for him.

"They've just been executed," reports Decius. "Cicero has just announced it in the Forum."

"What did he say?" demands Lucius.

"He just said, "Vixerunt," says Decius.

"They have lived? That's a funny thing to say when you've just executed someone," says the boy scornfully.

"It's the traditional way of announcing an execution," says Cornelia. "It's bad luck to mention death itself."

"Only for Lentulus and the others," says the boy cheerfully. "And they deserve it for plotting against us all. That's what Father would say."

"I'm not sure that your father would say that – not quite. And anyway, you mustn't think about it anymore," says Cornelia. "They were wicked men, but now they've gone, so we don't have to worry."

"But Catilina's not gone, is he? And Father will have to fight him before he goes," says the boy. "My tutor says there will be a big battle. Do you think there'll be a battle, Decius?"

"Yes, I do, Master Lucius," says Decius. "But I don't think your father will enjoy it. It isn't a glorious thing, Romans fighting Romans."

3

"I don't think Father would enjoy any battle," says Lucius sadly. "He's not really a fighting sort of person, is he?"

"Your father will do his duty, and that's what matters," says Cornelia. "Now you have heard the news, have something to eat – only a snack, mind – and go to bed."

Obediently, Lucius jumps down from the couch and takes Decius' hand.

"Have you ever seen Catilina, Decius? Is it true that he really looks monstrous?"

"He is certainly not a monster," says Cornelia, firmly. "He's an ordinary man, just like your father, except that Catilina wants to take over the country, which is wrong. Now go to the kitchen and tell Melissa I said you could have a snack. And I don't want to hear that you've been pestering Decius with questions."

The boy and the slave leave, and their voices and the light patter of their sandals die away as they go off to the kitchens. Cornelia puts her hand on her belly, and sighs. What a time to be having a baby! She thinks of her husband, who has spent the last three months patrolling down in Capua and returned to Rome a week ago only to set off immediately for Etruria where Catilina and his troops are mustering. She crosses to the small shrine in the corner and puts a pinch of incense into the burner, whispering a prayer that the gods will protect Publius Sestius and bring him safely home to his family.

Chapter One

The Lady Claudia, whose husband is, she would have him know, Extremely Concerned, is the only curse of Lucius Sestius Quirinalis' existence that morning, as he struggles over a pile of wax tablets filled with unhelpful notes. Claudia is convinced that her next-door neighbour is trying to poison her. She does not know how she is being poisoned, or why, and she has not been able to give him details of any symptoms she has suffered, but that hasn't stopped her accusing an extremely rich Greek freedman of conspiracy to murder. So far, she has convinced no one; even her husband will commit himself to nothing more than Extreme Concern. It will not be too long before she provokes the poor Greek into threatening to sue her for malicious allegations. Lucius wonders why he has taken on such a bore of a case, especially early on a beautiful September morning, when from his seat in his study he can see shafts of delicate sunlight stirring the dust to dance in the atrium. He needs a leg stretch, he thinks, and in two strides he is standing in the doorway of his little room and thinking of escape: just across the atrium the main door is within reach, and he can hear a commotion in the street outside, voices, bumps and curses and laughing. He turns away and sighs hopefully at Decius. The secretary sits very straight on his little stool, looking as always proper and respectable. His face takes on his "If I may make a suggestion" expression, and Lucius' heart lifts, for once more Decius has a solution.

"Go on then," he invites, trying not to sound too eager.

Decius looks down at his tablet. "It strikes me that we are not going to get very far on this, are we?"

"No, we're not," Lucius agrees. "But we've known that since she first opened her mouth yesterday. We could advise her to stop before her accusations get her into trouble, maybe. What do you think we ought to do?"

"Nothing," says Decius firmly. "Why don't you become very ill for a few days? The Lady Claudia is, I would imagine, quite impatient. She will soon turn to someone else if you don't show wild and frequent enthusiasm."

His tone on the last phrase puts a horrible thought into Lucius' head.

"Decius," he says pleadingly, "she doesn't – er – like me, do you think?"

"Undoubtedly," says Decius calmly. "She offered me a surprising amount of money and the use of her husband's library if I made sure that I delivered messages to and from you myself. Discreetly."

Lucius gazes at him in a mixture of horror and sympathy.

"It sounds like she's after you as well. The offer of the library is a very nice touch, though. What did you say?"

"I told her that I am not allowed out on my own, for fear of my running away," says Decius. "She seemed to accept that."

"Oh. And she believed you? Decius, she'll think we're slave-beaters!" Lucius exclaims, and adds, "Not that I blame you, but if she meets Mother and starts talking to her about it..."

"I have already warned the Lady Cornelia," says Decius. "And if you quietly do nothing, the matter should go no further than that."

He is right, as ever, and Lucius thinks of all the times over the last day and night that he has wished he had never met the Lady Claudia. Being polite is one thing, but this is no time for courtesy. All he has to do is summon up enough courage to explain to his father, and the Lady Claudia herself – and her Extremely Concerned husband as well, no doubt. Inwardly he wonders whether he can do it. Lucius is not used to letting people down, and he doesn't enjoy conflict. Sometimes, in these moments of frustration, he wonders if he should really be a lawyer, but in the courtroom he relishes the procedure and the drama of the speeches, and he loves the work beforehand – building the case, preparing the witnesses, watching a structure grow, ready to pit it against that constructed by his opponent. But he cannot see a way of getting anywhere with the Lady Claudia.

"It's awkward because her husband knows Father – no, you're right, Decius. I should have gone about this differently. I'll talk Father out of it and we'll find some way of backing out gracefully. I don't suppose you could write a polite refusal letter for me...?" he asks hopefully, knowing full well that this is one letter he must write himself.

Decius is saved from the painful reply this request demands (for whatever he does, accept or politely decline, will pain him) by the entrance of Lucius' father, Publius Sestius.

"We have a visitor," he announces. Sestius senior (may all the gods bless him, thinks his son) loves visitors.

Visions of a furious Roman matron sweep in front of Lucius' eyes, then sense takes over. Not even the sensitive ears of the Lady Claudia can have picked up on the proposed rejection. So – it is someone else. Well, as it is early in the morning and as the more desperate half of Rome is still engaged in trotting around the less desperate half, this is scarcely surprising. But the Sestius family have already seen their modest group of clients that morning and his father is waggling his eyebrows excitedly, so Lucius tells Decius to carry on (he merely nods, not a trace of any expression crossing his face), and Lucius follows his father obediently across the atrium to his study. It is diagonally opposite to Lucius', a lot quieter as it is well away from the front door and the street. It is bigger too, of course.

"Here he is," says Sestius senior, waving a hand first in the direction of his son, then towards the man in the visitor's chair. Lucius and the stranger stare at each other, unsure as to which is being shown off, but the stranger solves the problem by introducing himself.

"Gaius Sallust Crispus. Your father says you're a good lawyer."

Despite the almost-compliment, this is barked out in an abrupt voice, and Lucius wonders for a moment if he has ever come up against Gaius Sallust Crispus in court. Lucius hasn't yet handled so many cases that he can't remember all the main speakers and he would surely have remembered this man – but has Sallust been a witness or given a character reference? He certainly looks annoyed with something, but that may be his usual expression: the lines at the corners of his mouth pull it down. Apart from that, thinks Lucius, Sallust has what should be quite a friendly-looking face, round and with plump, little-boy cheeks and large eyes. His nose is impressive without being beaky, and his hair is cut in a no-nonsense, straight-all-round fashion, suggesting that his cook cuts it in the kitchen with the aid of a bowl. He is looking like a very bad-tempered baby at the moment.

"I am Lucius Sestius. My father is very kind, but biased," Lucius replies, put off by Gaius Sallust Crispus' expression even if the stranger can't help it. Lucius' father frowns at him but he waits quietly, feeling slightly irritated by being here at all. Other people, he thinks, have also had a frustrating morning. The visitor stares at the floor and does not seem inclined to talk again, but Sestius senior, who loves to smooth everyone's path, starts bustling. Soon they are all equipped with large cups of well-watered wine, ready to start again.

"Now we can begin, Sallust," says Sestius senior with satisfaction. "Lucius, I really do think you're going to find this interesting."

"If not, this has all been a waste of effort," says their guest bitterly. This time, the surprise must show on Lucius' face, although he makes an effort to hide it, and even decides that the rudeness is not directed at himself or his father. Sallust tries to smile at him and waves a hand apologetically, if not energetically.

"You'll have to forgive me. I am puzzled and, to be honest, worried. Here is my problem: I've just returned from governing the province of Africa Nova, and I have found out that someone is about to bring charges against me. I don't really know why. I have the support of Caesar and so I ought to have fewer enemies than most. I haven't done anything out of the ordinary, or so I thought. The charge will be provincial corruption, I presume, but I don't know who is bringing the charges. I haven't even been officially notified by the praetor's court. Anyway, I can see that I shall need a lawyer. I can speak for myself, of course, but I want you and your father working for me as well. I'll need you to speak in court, but I also need someone who can dig around. I want to find out exactly what is going on."

This is delivered quickly, and Lucius is hard put to take it all in. He sits for a moment and counts up the unknowns – unknown client, unknown charge, unknown prosecutor – and his initial thought is that they should not touch this case. He takes a quick look at his father, but he is beaming as though he cannot wait to start snooping around in the less than lovely world of provincial corruption. He is not going to be of any help.

"Why us?" Lucius asks, wondering how to back off gracefully. Maybe the Lady Claudia isn't such a bad idea after all.

"Connections, Lucius Sestius. Your father has very good connections, as well as speaking ability."

Speaking ability? This is mere flattery as his father has not spoken in court himself for years. But the visitor has not finished.

"You, I'm told, can keep your mouth shut, as well as spin lawyers' tales with it. And I can offer you experience and support in turn. You are young and presumably ambitious, and the quaestorship is looming, I would have thought. If I get off this charge, I may be able to help there. And of course, Marcus Tullius Cicero thinks highly of you both."

"My father and Cicero have been friends for years," Lucius says, wondering how this sour lemon of a human being and the pompous, well-meaning Cicero have ever exchanged enough words in conversation for the Sestius connection to come out.

"Ever since the year of Cicero's consulship, eh?" Sallust's tone is tart. "The Glorious Year! The end of the conspiracy – and the conspirators."

"The Catilinarian Conspiracy! I remember it very well," says Publius Sestius happily, and with irritation his son realises that his father is settling down for a long story, which is all too well known. The Catilinarian Conspiracy had been put down, with thoroughness and efficiency, in Cicero's consulship nineteen years previously. A dissolute and dissatisfied aristocrat, named Lucius Sergius Catilina, had tried to seize power in a rebellion at Rome and at a town called Faesulae north of Rome. He had some initial success in attracting those who, like him, didn't think they were being fairly treated by the system, but the government were very well informed about the whole movement from its inception, thanks to the Consul's intelligence-gathering network. Cicero had kept his eye on

Catilina's progress and had stirred up a lethargic Senate into action when necessary. The leader of the rebellion had fled, while those left behind in Rome to lead the revolt there, had been arrested and brought before the Senate. After a debate, the Senate had decided that the emergency demanded their execution, and Cicero had ensured that this was carried out. Catilina himself had died a couple of months later, in battle.

Lucius shoots a look at Sallust. He does not look like a man who needs to be reminded of one of the best-known political crises of recent years.

"But back to you," he says hastily. "May I ask you how you discovered that you were going to be prosecuted?"

"A friend," says Sallust. "He overheard some criticism of me in the Senate. He thinks he was meant to overhear it. He said it was clear that a prosecution was being planned."

This is not unusual for anyone coming back from governing the empire on behalf of a thankless people and Senate. You have to make money out of your governorship to pay the debts you have run up getting that far; but it is a wonderful opportunity for your enemies when you get back. A stirring speech about what Rome owes her dominions, a few witnesses to swear that you've bled the province dry, and there you are in exile. Lucius started off his illustrious career in the law with a few prosecutions, though not in this particular law court. But he knows the pattern.

"Well, it isn't unknown," he says. "You have made it far enough up the ladder to make enemies. Does anyone come to mind? Or can this friend of yours find out anything more?"

"He made it clear that any involvement on his part ended with him being kind enough to warn me. He is going to remain civil but at a distance until he sees how things work out. I can't really blame him, but the thing is, this shouldn't be happening at all!" says Sallust, and the last few words come out with increasing force. "I've had my problems, of course I have, but I have been Caesar's supporter for years, and everybody knows that! Anyone who prosecutes me risks Caesar coming into the case to speak for me, and who is going to do that? It's not really worth anyone's time and effort, and I don't think this is just the work of a foolish youth just back from his year abroad in Greece and dying to try out his rhetorical skills on the establishment."

There is a pause while Lucius tries to think of another question.

Sallust sighs. "I really enjoyed my stint in Africa Nova. Decent weather, bit hot in summer, nice enough people, not too whiny. The hunting is good, and it is pretty peaceful, though I had to keep the legions up to scratch and make sure they weren't bored. It wasn't a difficult job, but like everyone, I needed money! And I only took so much because I was sure I'd be safe. Of course, I'm guilty of the actual charge – but that's not enough! I need to know what is really going on!"

His voice rises again, and Lucius looks appealingly at his father. He is now sure that the two of them should not commit themselves, for, like Sallust's nameless 'friend', he does not want to be involved in a dodgy and possibly highly political case at this point in his career. If Sallust is indeed still in the Dictator's good books, the defence will have to call on that connection. If he isn't, then it is a hopeless case, as Sallust himself has just admitted. Lucius is not very ambitious and certainly not a risk-taker. The longer he goes without encountering the Dictator, the happier he will be. Until he needs Caesar's approval to get into office, of course. But to Lucius' horror (and to that of Sallust himself) his father is already patting Sallust's shoulder. Lucius speaks quickly.

"Clearly, we shall have to discuss this between us, my father and myself and – er – make some preliminary enquiries. When shall we let you know our decision?"

Sallust gives him a hard look but then smiles in genuine amusement. Lucius isn't sure he likes it any more than the sour expression, but Sallust replies courteously, "Would it be convenient if I call after dinner this evening?"

It is convenient, if unusual, and Publius Sestius escorts Sallust to the door. The new client (Lucius realises that this is a fight he has already lost) leaves the house amid a flurry of soothing noises more suited to one who has been recently bereaved, and who cannot contain his overwhelming grief. Sallust might be in trouble, but Lucius thinks that he looks equal to it as he strides down the little street with two slaves in tow.

Once Sallust has gone, Lucius takes his father into his own study for a serious talk. He wants Decius to hear what has just happened. Perhaps Decius can come up with another plan to wriggle out of another awkward case. He quickly explains what has happened, then turns to Sestius senior.

"Father, I really am not sure about this – this sort of thing is way too political for us, you know. And he admits that he is guilty, and can you imagine that face of his in court, totally useless at appealing to judge or jury?"

Lucius stops. His father is looking at him with an apologetic expression on his face. In his hand is a small wax writing tablet, which he holds out to his son. When Lucius opens it, he finds an uncharacteristically brief message:

"I have recommended you both to this man, safe in the knowledge that I can ask and trust you to help him. Marcus Tullius Cicero."

And Lucius resigns himself to the knowledge that he and father will be on Sallust's defence team.

For years, Lucius Sestius has known that he wants to be a lawyer like Marcus Tullius Cicero. He has practised the art of pleading and arguing inside his head at every opportunity – for example, if an argument breaks out over dinner, he constructs speeches for and against in his head. "My mother, a woman who normally exhibits all the true virtues of a Roman matron, on this one occasion, goaded by the cruelty of her spouse..." "Gentlemen, imagine the horror of finding out – at your own family dinner table as well! – that your beloved children have broken their mother's heart..." That sort of thing.

And he has been brought up in a family that idolises Cicero. During the crisis caused by the Catilinarian Conspiracy when Lucius was small, Cicero saved Rome. He had then nobly gone into exile when a hostile city turned against him, and on his triumphant return, he had successfully defended Publius Sestius on the one occasion when the Sestius family had been seriously threatened by political infighting. Cicero is a leading politician, a distinguished author and lawyer, and the best public speaker Rome has ever known. The letters written to Publius Sestius by

Cicero are in a special box in the big study. So, if the Great Man wants the family to play a part in the defence of Sallust, then they will, even if neither Lucius nor his father can imagine why Cicero should want such a thing.

"We'd better have a meeting with Cicero," Lucius says. "Decius, could you organise an appointment to see Marcus Tullius Cicero?"

"Oh nonsense, I'll pop round for the morning greeting," says his father. "Maybe I can wangle an invitation to dinner as well. It will give us both a chance to have a good chat."

"You'll not need Decius then," says Lucius quickly.

"My dear Lucius," says his father, a little ruffled. "Decius is my slave. Decius, I'll take you along with me."

Decius, the perfect secretary, keeps a straight face as he gathers together writing materials. Lucius starts to think about what they now need to do.

"I'll check to see if any formal charge has been laid against Sallust before the praetor. Maybe one of the clerks knows something. Father, what are we going to do if a charge has been brought and Caesar refuses to support Sallust? The man is guilty – he admitted it himself, and it sounds as though there is going to be good evidence against him."

"If the Dictator won't stand by him, then Sallust won't stand a chance," says his father briskly. "We'll just have to rely on Caesar to be the great man when it matters for Sallust. After all, people have to stand by their own – it wouldn't look at all good if Caesar ignored Sallust now. Although, I can't help wondering – Sallust has been in some trouble before, you know. I don't remember all the details, but I think something went wrong about half a dozen years ago and he has only just been let back into the Senate. Yes, this could be tricky, Lucius. I'll go around to see Cicero, and you go and find out what you can in the Forum."

"Right," Lucius says. "Decius..."

"Decius is going to be busy," says his father in his Head of the Household voice.

Like a dutiful son, Lucius sets out without Decius.

Chapter Two

It is good to get out. He and his father – and Decius, come to that – make an excellent team, but every now and then Lucius has to get away, leaving behind the chat and the fuss. His sister Tia, who is five years younger, once said that he would learn to tolerate his father, just as his father has learned to tolerate him. He thanked her in heavily sarcastic tones for her unasked advice and has brooded about it ever since.

Lucius walks along the little street leading down to the main road into the heart of Rome. The Sestius family own a two-level block which would be fashionably high up the hill if the Caelian Hill were in the least fashionable. It is too built-up to be desirable to those who hanker after a big villa but is too classy for the lowest strata of Roman society. The family live comfortably on a row of senatorial and equestrian households, having owned a house on the site for nearly two hundred years. They live on the ground floor, and along with the rest of the street, have not let out any space to shops. They do, however, let out the upper floor to family friends from the Bay of Naples, who use it as their town flat. The street is usually one of Rome's quieter thoroughfares – thanks in part to there being no shops or businesses, thus limiting traffic and the inconveniences of bad smells and litter. As Lucius treads the worn stones, he descends into an increasingly malodorous, noisy and crowded environment, and he pushes his way through with patience and some nimble footwork. This is second nature: Lucius has come this way nearly every day of his life from the age of seven when he was sent to Aristides' school near the Forum to learn his basic reading and writing. After that, he had tutors at home, then a series of friends and acquaintances of his father, who took him on to show him the ropes of a career in the law. In return, he and his father put up with a couple of utterly gormless teenagers on the team when they went out to the eastern province of Cilicia where Publius Sestius was governor for two years. This sort of reciprocal back-scratching is perfectly normal in Lucius' world, and as he walks he thinks about something which Sallust has brought to his attention: Sestius senior has an amazing network of contacts. For some reason, which Lucius Sestius has never understood, his father knows everyone, and the only people Publius Sestius avoids are the men who prosecuted him ten years ago. Even in this one case, Lucius feels it is because his father feels terribly hurt, rather than that he is angry. Lucius knows his father to be one of the most honest and honourable senators Rome has had in a long time, and yet this honest and honourable man was prosecuted for bribery and violence. His father is usually remarkably calm about it, pointing out that at the time, everyone who was anyone was being prosecuted, but at the time of the trial and for some time afterwards, he had been upset and afraid, and had not been able to rise above it as other people going through similar situations had done. It was then that the link with Cicero was of great use, of course; the support Publius Sestius had given the Great Man during the Catilinarian Conspiracy, and later, was fully repaid in information, introductions and, of course, the small matter of a speech that had freed him from the courts. It was a terrific speech, as Cicero's speeches usually were, and it managed to ensure Publius' acquittal without mentioning him very much, or indeed the charges against him. Cicero had even used Lucius himself to make a point: Lucius was still in his boyhood toga when Cicero made him stand up and speak a few words in court, in an effort to win sympathy from the jury. Lucius had been proud and excited to be part of the team but also very embarrassed at these moments of attention. He remembers the earnest conversations about whether or not his voice would break during the course of the trial, and whether or not he should be trained to appear even younger than he was. There was even talk about letting Lucius' younger sister into court, but in the end it was decided not to take the risk. She wasn't a baby – Cicero is good with babies in court – and she was only a girl. Tia, aged six and confident of her ability to charm a jury of middle-aged, middle-class family men, had been furious.

The road leaves the Caelian Hill and heads towards the Forum. The buildings get a little larger, and the homes, shops and small businesses of the Caelian give way to more and more official buildings. When he passes the Regia, home of the Chief Priest of Rome, Lucius knows he has entered the Forum, and he cuts straight across the square, heading for the Records Office.

The Forum, despite the early hour, is warming up. The buildings are surrounded by little groups of people, who all want something.

"Hear my prayer!"

"Buy my goods!"

"Free my client!"

"Approve this bill!"

In the Forum, you only hear imperatives and entreaties. Rome's system of patronage means that favours flow up and down chains of human beings, and in these buildings the favours are sought and granted: even the Romans' gods have a duty to assist when asked – why else do they get those sacrifices? But this constant need to get something done is what makes the Forum so interesting, and there is always a mixed air of achievement and disappointment and looking ahead. It is never boring.

Despite the usual crowds, nothing too unusual seems to be happening; the loiterers around the Rostra, who can always be seen there in good weather, like flies around a soldier's sponge-stick, are not being bothered by any golden word escaping the lips of the Republic's leaders. As he passes the front edge of the Rostra, it strikes Lucius, not for the first time, that the jutting bits of wood which stick out of the wall are rather daunting. They are supposedly the beaks of ships captured in war hundreds of years ago, but Julius Caesar has just rebuilt the Rostra and these adornments are too new-looking to be believable. He thinks of the many times a crowd has been stirred by a speaker on the platform of the Rostra, or the steps of a Forum temple – how often have those waves of emotion turned to breakers which hurled people upon those jutting beaks? Politicians are not interested in the minor side-effects of their speeches; if a law they support is passed, what does it matter if the incidental violence results in a few injuries or deaths? Violence has been part of the political life of Rome for too long, and one of the things that could be said for the Dictator is that he has put an end to it. Well, mostly.

Not all speeches made in the Roman Forum are so emotional, anyway. He remembers the story Decius told him about the Catilinarian Conspiracy. Decius had been sent down into the Forum for the news by Lucius' mother, and arrived in time for an important announcement. After a nervous and temperamental Senate debate over the fate of the captured rebel leaders (not including Catilina himself as he had already fled the city) it had been decided to carry out the ultimate punishment. Cicero had broken the news of the executions to the silent and still crowd with the simple announcement, "Vixerunt". It wasn't much of an epitaph – "They have lived" – but it avoided the unlucky mention of death itself, and its simplicity appealed to the sombre mood of the crowd. Or so Decius said. After the Consul had climbed down from the Rostra, the crowd had parted to allow him to cross the Forum to the Temple of Concord, where the Senate were waiting. People then had drifted into smaller, muttering groups. A few nonchalant youths hung around the state prison, the Tullianum, in case any bodies were carried out, but they were frustrated. The Consul had seen to that, and the conspirators were already on their final journey home.

But today is a warm golden day in early September, so Lucius shakes off the dark and cold of a winter long ago and looks up at the building on the slopes of the Capitoline Hill ahead, with its zigzag of steps. He starts to climb.

Once inside the Records Office, it takes a few minutes of browsing through the last few years before he finds out just how interesting a career Sallust has had. Lucius has not yet allowed himself to speculate too much about Sallust, although he has noticed that he is already biased against him a little because of the unfortunate start to their relationship. Lucius, however, is a conscientious person and always does his research, finding out the facts before reaching the conclusions. If only Sallust's face didn't work against him...! Honestly, with those cheeks and big eyes he should have looked like a baby – it is just that miserable, downtrodden mouth. The first piece of information he gathers though does nothing to convince him of Sallust's innocence.

You have to work pretty hard to get expelled from the Senate (unless you're a bankrupt of course), but Sallust had already managed it, just five years before. The precise handwriting of the censor's clerk reads "Dismissed for immorality". Lucius tries very hard not to speculate on the immorality concerned and fails. Without realising, he whistles a happy little tune as he reads the rest of the record. It is a terrible thing to be so intrigued at the thought of another man's downfall. An equally fascinating, but equally curt entry for the year of Caesar's second consulship, informs him that Sallust was allowed back into the Senate, working up through the junior offices again. Lucius can't help feeling slightly envious. When the Dictator considers him qualified for a stab at public life, he will have to do lots of smiling and promising to become the most junior of officials, a quaestor. Then, if he and his family can stand the expense and effort, and if Caesar approves, he will try to climb the ladder of offices, becoming aedile, praetor and finally consul, fulfilling roles for which he will not be paid, and yet will cost him large amounts of money. If Lucius makes it to the top, it will take him years. Sallust though has shrugged off the disgrace of his loss of rank and has made quaestor, praetor, then governor of Africa Nova in three years, and no doubt a consulship will soon beckon. And with that thought, Lucius is back to the troubles of the day and the threats of prosecution; he wonders if the Dictator's enthusiasm for Sallust is waning.

Several frowning clerks now brush past him looking busy, and he realises that the whistling has not gone down well. This venerable edifice has not been constructed so that he can be cheerful among the carefully compiled lists of consuls, priests and generals. He decides that he needs to talk to someone and heads off back down into the Forum.

It doesn't take long, once he starts looking. Outside the Hall of Aemilius, he finds his regular newsmonger, Sextus Cornelius Rufus. No need to be impressed by the fancy name: ever since Lucius Cornelius Sulla the Fortunate freed thousands of slaves, who all took his name in the hope that some of the good luck would rub off, the name of Cornelius does not necessarily mean very much, and they were wrong about the luck as well. Sulla used up any luck going by managing to marry a beautiful young woman and die in natural circumstances, despite being a bloodthirsty dictator and murderer of thousands. Cornelius Rufus is about forty, and a born-and-bred Subura rat, who makes his own luck. The family had been introduced to him in the year after Cicero returned from exile, when the Great Man was kept busy with a great deal of defence work. Everyone who had worked for Cicero's recall in the teeth of opposition from Cicero's fiercest enemy, Publius Clodius Pulcher, could expect to be prosecuted on some made-up charge. In the case of Sestius senior, the charges were bribery and violence, and there was some juicy and vivid story-telling from the prosecution. "Once upon a time, there had been rioting at a public meeting of the tribunes, one of whom was Sestius. Sestius whipped up this violence with his inflammatory calls for Cicero's return from exile! Now he must pay!"

During the preparation for the trial, Cicero and his brother Quintus had put together a group of – what would you call them? – bodyguards? Enquiry agents? People who went around beating up other people as needed? Maybe that is a little unfair. With Clodius controlling large gangs of thugs throughout Rome, more and more people were forced to keep bodyguards. Cornelius Rufus was in this elite circle and Cicero assigned him to keep an eye on Publius Sestius as he prepared for the trial. Cornelius Rufus at once made his home in the kitchen and got on very well with everyone, of course. Even their cook, Melissa, tolerated his presence, and Lucius knows that his father and mother had found it comforting just knowing that he was around. Tia had been too young to understand what was going on, and Cornelia had kept her away from the main part of the house whenever possible, frequently taking her on visits to friends and family to get her out of Rome. But Lucius had been approaching the time when learning about the legal system was a vital part of his education, and it had been decided that he was to play a small role in his father's defence. He had listened as his father and Cicero worked on the speech, and they had drilled him in how to stand, how to look and even how to cry. Cicero is not above the use of a carefully concealed slice of raw onion to help bring on the tears. At the age of twelve, this had all seemed exciting enough – well, apart from the crying – but to find a genuine Subura heavy in the kitchen was thrilling. Cornelius Rufus had seemed to him to be omniscient and told him more about how the lower classes lived than he was able to believe. He could play the game Little Robbers well enough to beat Lucius on a regular basis – and, on one memorable occasion, Decius. He had come in useful as well, finding out a couple of choice items about the almost unknown figureheads who were going to make the prosecution speeches. After Publius Sestius' trial, Cornelius Rufus had faded back into the Subura, used on occasion by Lucius or his father, but never again reaching the point of sitting and gossiping in the kitchen. Maybe it is the difference in status which means that the family can only allow him near during a crisis.

Lucius greets Cornelius Rufus with a handout as usual, and as usual, Cornelius Rufus takes it with a barely suppressed sigh and stows it away somewhere in the folds of a rather flashy and definitely new tunic. He has terrible taste, and his girlfriend, a dealer in cloth who runs the business on behalf of her aged father, does not seem to be able to restrain him. The pair of them have now reached that stage of the relationship where the girlfriend is in the process of making her decision about settling down, and Lucius, despite quite liking Cornelius Rufus, wonders if she might benefit from a longer period of reflection. In appearance, Cornelius Rufus is tall and thin and scraggy around the neck, and his hair is thinning on top as he gets older. He wears an expression of weary respectability, but Lucius has no idea how he makes a living beyond the money the Sestius family give him – which is not enough to live on, and certainly not enough to buy tunics like the one he is wearing. Presumably, he is an information-gatherer for other people, but Lucius sometimes wonders how – well, legal – Cornelius Rufus is. In the end, however, he has no proof that Cornelius is guilty of anything more than gossip and gambling. And he did once introduce Lucius to a quiet, pretty and discreet flower-seller, called Lydia. She had been independent enough to suit him and he had been wealthy enough to suit her. She has moved on, but Lucius has good memories of her.

"Hear you're on Sallust's side," says Cornelius Rufus with a certain amount of gloomy satisfaction. Lucius has long ago given up outraged denials or demands along the lines of "How did you know?" Now, he knows to keep quiet and wait.

"Friend of mine knows the bloke who delivers the bread from the local bakehouse back to Sallust's," says Cornelius Rufus after a suitable pause to see if Lucius would rise to the bait. "My friend says that this morning, the baker overheard the slaves in the kitchen talking with some sort of secretary-type. Secretary's a bit fed up because Sallust hadn't actually told him that you were going to get called in. He'd just heard his master talking about it to someone else. You know how narked these high-class slaves get. Anyway, you owe me for the drinks."

Cornelius Rufus' tactics for the extraction of information are never painful. He usually homes in on the nearest wine jug and lets his victims talk, while appearing to be concentrating totally on the alcohol. Why he doesn't suffer from a perpetual hangover, Lucius doesn't know, but it costs him less than outright bribery and isn't illegal. There is always 'a friend' involved who garners the information first-hand, then gets it to Cornelius Rufus, and Lucius admits to being impressed at the speed with which Cornelius Rufus has worked to get the story from the baker via the friend. He makes a point of checking that the sun is only just approaching noon, before handing over the money. Cornelius Rufus pockets his expenses with a slight shake of his head.

"Nice tunic," Lucius remarks. "Did your source say who was with Sallust when the secretary overheard them talking?"

"She reckons it suits me," says Cornelius Rufus confusingly. "No, he didn't, though I should think the secretary definitely knows, and the rest of the household soon will, I dare say. I'll get my friend to work on it if you like."

Lucius wonders if it was Sallust talking to Cicero, but there is no harm in checking. Now, though, he needs to know about the actual prosecution.

"I'm going to the praetor's office," he says. "I doubt if I'll get anywhere, so if you find out anything..."

"All right," says Cornelius. He pauses, then says seriously, "Why are they doing it, do you think? I mean, everyone screws their province, it's only natural. Most people, though, only get prosecuted for a reason."

Lucius gives him a look.

"All right, then, another reason," he says. "An ulterior motive, as you lawyers would say. Like some young hotshot straight from a fancy law school on Rhodes, showing off his litotes, or whatever. You know?"

Cornelius Rufus is not stupid.

"I don't know," Lucius says. "I mean, I don't know the real reason why Sallust is being prosecuted. Do what you can."

Cornelius Rufus nods, and turns away towards the Subura, that part of Rome where respectable young men do not venture. His walk is almost jaunty; he is interested in this case, and will no doubt enjoy presenting Lucius with some juicy little morsels, if he finds any. He has always tried harder for the Sestius family, mainly because of those days sitting and gossiping in the kitchen.

Lucius tramps back up the Capitoline Hill and finds the office of the praetor in charge of the law court of provincial corruption. No luck. The praetor himself is in a meeting ("Long lunch," thinks Lucius), but his clerk has no hesitation in denying any knowledge of a prosecution for mismanagement and/or corruption in Africa Nova. With the official denial ringing freshly in his ears, Lucius goes back home for lunch with his father, who is in a buoyant mood.

"Oh, we had a lovely chat," says Publius Sestius, chomping on dates with serious pleasure. "Cicero doesn't have the visitors he used to in the mornings, and so he had time for me. In fact, I think he was pleased to see me. And he is definitely eager that Sallust is acquitted, because Sallust is writing an account of the Catilinarian Conspiracy, you see."

"What!" Lucius is amazed. "You don't really believe that that dried-up, sour old...prune of a has-been is writing history!"

"It did occur to me that he may have been flattering Cicero for his own ends," confesses the ever-trusting Publius, "but

Cicero is convinced that he really is interested. Sallust even offered to show him the opening chapters."

"I don't believe it," declares Lucius, rash youth that he is.

Dinner that night is an informal family affair with Lucius' mother and sisters. Cornelia is not actually his mother (who died when he was born), so Tia is his half-sister. His full sister, Albinia, is married and lives near the Forum with her husband, but tonight she has come to dinner minus the likeable Apuleius, who has a prior engagement. The family don't mind. Sometimes it is good to have Albinia to themselves. She shares a dining-couch with her brother, and they present their identical profiles to the rest of the family - noses long rather than beaked, and determined chins. They also share their mother's large dark eyes and very dark, slightly wavy hair, thinks Publius Sestius, as he looks at the wispy tendrils escaping from the knot of hair at the base of Albinia's neck.

Tia is in the throes of wedding preparations. While her mother and father have spent three years discussing a possible future husband and worrying about her, Tia has solved all problems by falling in love with the son of the family who rent the upstairs floor of their house. Caecilius will never be a politician (the family's main residence is on their huge estate down south near Campania, and the flat is just their town house), but he will be rich, so everyone is very pleased and relieved at Tia's choice.

Naturally, they have all found out about the Sallust job and want exhaustive updates. Publius Sestius, as do many men of his class and background, believes strongly in educating his women, and so they are up to date with politics and personalities. The conversation is allowed to stray all over the ramifications of the problem once Publius Sestius has given his usual strong warnings about not breathing a word to anyone outside the family, even Caecilius.

"The really peculiar thing, I think," says Tia, once her elders have all had their say, "is why Uncle Marcus is so involved. I know you all say it's because Sallust has taken him in with this story about writing a book about Catilina, but even so, why should he help someone he doesn't like, someone who has done something wrong? You know how much Uncle Marcus hates it when governors mistreat their provinces. When he was in Cilicia, he says, he was so restrained that..."

"Not a single penny was wasted!" Albinia and Lucius chant, having heard of Uncle Marcus' adventures in Cilicia many times.

"Well, not a single penny was wasted," says Tia. She is Cicero's favourite. He says that she reminds him of his beloved daughter Tullia, who had died earlier in the year.

"How do you know that Cicero dislikes Sallust? Apart from the corruption in the province question – which is, of course, still to be proved," Lucius asks.

"Uncle Marcus couldn't like him," says Tia firmly. "Not if Sallust was expelled from the Senate, which has already been proved."

Sestius senior coughs loudly to remind his son not to go into the question of Sallust's expulsion from the Senate. He is afraid that Tia will ask what the "immorality" concerned was. Lucius is not sure that there is any need for worry as neither of them know anyway.

"Well, what was Sallust doing before he was thrown out of the Senate?" asks Tia, and they automatically turn towards the head of the family, fount of all political wisdom.

"He was doing rather well in an unspectacular way," says Publius, and frowns off into the distance as he gathers his facts. "He became quaestor in the year Cicero went into exile. I can't remember what job he did, but he was Caesar's man from the start. He even put himself forward to be tribune of the plebs, that was in the year Clodius was murdered, because he helped the prosecution at Milo's trial. Do you remember that, you two?"

Lucius and Albinia do remember the great trial of Milo; it was a high point in a very exciting few years in Roman politics. The Sestius family had a special interest as well, for the murder at the heart of the case was that of Publius Clodius Pulcher, Cicero's enemy and the power behind the prosecution of Sestius senior. When the news arrived in Rome that Milo, Cicero's ally, had killed Clodius on the Appian Way, the rioting had grown to unprecedented levels, which in the Rome of that time was quite something.

"I didn't attend the trial," says Albinia. "Too dangerous. The Clodians were completely out of control. I couldn't believe that you and Father went!"

Lucius says to his father, "You would only let us stand at the back, so that we could get away quickly if things started to take off. Everyone thought that there would be some sort of violence, and Pompey had ordered the court surrounded by soldiers. It was the first time I had ever seen soldiers on official duty in Rome. And it was the only time I saw Cicero deliver a bad speech – he was terrible."

"He completely folded, didn't he?" says his father cheerfully. Tia looks as though she is about to cry, so he quickly adds, "And I don't blame him, he was in such danger himself, just for defending Milo."

"I can't remember Sallust though," says Lucius. "Do you think Caesar was also helping the prosecution, long-distance from Gaul?"

"Oh, Caesar will have known what was going on and have been involved somehow," says Publius. "He was partly responsible for Clodius' rise, and I am sure that Sallust wouldn't have done anything he thought would be frowned on by Caesar. Though, I think you are right, I don't remember seeing Sallust actually up there on the platform during the trial. And then, as you discovered this morning, Sallust was removed from the Senate by the censors just before the civil war." Publius nods an acknowledgement at Lucius. "He joined Caesar, of course, and got reinstated. Made his way rather nicely too, until this business, of course."

Cornelia thinks the girls have had enough of politics and trials for the evening and is preparing to take them out of the dining room, just as Decius enters. They are of course expecting to see Sallust, but at Decius' quiet announcement, Tia cries, "Uncle Marcus!" and runs to give their visitor a hug. Sallust has persuaded Cicero to come around to show off the first draft of the account of the Conspiracy of Catilina, and Albinia decides that she must stay for this.

Chapter Three

Marcus Tullius Cicero is about sixty years old and has been suffering at the hands of his beloved Republic ever since the day he slipped away from Rome and into exile, fifteen or so years earlier. He came back from exile with those two extra lines dug in between his brows and they have not disappeared. In fact, combined with the wide forehead (growing wider, despite his attempts to comb forward every last strand of his widow's peak), more attention is drawn to his large deep brown eyes, which one can see as an advantage. Cicero uses his eyes a lot when declaiming. He is fortunate, for his tall frame makes him stand out at a distance, and his eyes keep his audience's attention when he is closer.

Cicero brings with him a flurry of good wishes from his family and Tiro, his devoted secretary of many years, and a thick little scroll, containing Sallust's first draft of The Conspiracy of Catilina. Everyone sits down again, fruit and wine appear for their guest, and there is general conversation along the lines of everyone catching up with everyone else. But Cornelia does not want Tia around when the talk turns to Sallust, as she knows it will, and soon she shepherds Tia off to her own sitting room. The men and Albinia realise that they have been given permission to go ahead, and so more wine is poured as Publius Sestius asks Cicero how he knows Sallust.

"I didn't really know him until a few weeks ago, when he came to see me about this book he is writing," says Cicero. "I knew he had been governing Africa Nova of course, and I knew him as one of Caesar's faithful, but I had no idea that we were friends." (Lucius is reassured by this piece of sarcasm. Cicero is not taken in by Sallust's literary pretensions.) "He had read all my speeches of course, and we had a good talk through the events, and I was pleased that he was interested – but I didn't see him again until he came round this morning to tell me of this case being brought against him. I don't know why he came to me, but he asked about hiring someone who would be knowledgeable about the courts, and who would be prepared to do some investigative work as well. So I recommended you, Lucius."

"And is that the work itself? The account of the conspiracy?" asks Albinia, nodding at the scroll. Albinia is a writer herself, and she is clearly keen to hear what Sallust has to say.

Cicero reads the first few pages to them, and Lucius finds it revealing.

"Any man who wants to stand out from the animal kingdom should put all his energy into making sure that he does not live a life of obscurity like the beasts of the field, who, thanks to Nature, are grovelling and think only of their stomachs."

Great gods above, thinks Lucius, this is supposedly an account of the Catilinarian Conspiracy and its downfall – instead, Sallust has started off by having an all-embracing moan about The State of Things Today and The Decline of Moral Standards. By the end of the passage what he seems to be saying is that modern politics is a corrupt business and he has been picked on and it is all very unfair. Needless to say, there is no mention of the little matter of Sallust's own expulsion from the Senate. Lucius cannot fathom what Caesar's interest might be in such a miserable piece of writing.

"Of course," says Cicero, "he's right. I've been saying things like this for years now."

"You are doing yourself an injustice," says Albinia firmly.

She is right. Cicero has never descended to the bitterness of Sallust, even during his months of exile, his dark time. He has been distraught and bewildered, but his complaints were backed by his love for his country and his sense of justice – and to be honest, a certain amount of self-pity. Other people complain about Cicero's vanity, and pomposity, but Lucius thinks that he has a sort of nobility about him that Sallust lacks. Of course, the Sestius family are all biased in favour of Cicero.

"We must help," declares the Great Man decidedly. Deliberately he looks around the table, stopping to hold first the father's gaze, then the son's. Albinia drops her eyes before he can get to her, but Lucius doubts that this is from modesty. Albinia has a vibrant sense of the ridiculous. Knowing what is required of them, both Lucius and Publius wait respectfully, and try not to notice Albinia's shoulders twitching. Lucius feels amused that Cicero should try out this trick on friends, who know him so well, in the family's little dining room. He also feels great affection for him. But he is still worried about Sallust.

"Do you really think he wants to write this book for its own sake?" he asks. With an air of having just thought about it, he adds, "Or could it be a ploy to get your favour?"

"If he wants favour," says Cicero, his eyes now fixed on his wine cup, "he's far better off cultivating Caesar. I'm a bit of an old has-been now; the Republic is fading, and we have a Dictator. I can still make speeches, yes, but Sallust has not asked me to plead at this mysterious trial – which for all we know, might never take place."

"You're not an old has-been," says Publius. "Caesar stills respects you and who knows, even Dictators don't last for ever, especially as a dictator is supposed to be a temporary measure! Anyway, the point is that your country may yet call upon you, Marcus Cicero."

Publius Sestius is really a very nice man. He couldn't have said anything more likely to appeal to his guest. To a man like Cicero, the idea of being needed by his country is everything. His fondest memories are of the year of his consulship, when he guided the state through the Catilinarian crisis, and he never tires of talking or writing about it. Even now, his eyes grow a little wet as he smiles. Lucius interrupts this beautiful moment, however, for his father's words have given him an idea.

"Why not ask Caesar himself? See if he's going to support Sallust. You could very easily – as Father says, he respects you. You could find out if he knows who is behind this lawsuit business. I know he will have better things to think about, but he might have heard something from one of his... em... well, you know – they say he has a spy service..."

Lucius' voice trails away; instinctively he looks around to make sure one of Caesar's spies hasn't cunningly disguised himself as a lamp stand. Albinia winks at him and he pretends to punch her. Cicero's eyes, however, gleam as he grows enthusiastic.

"Excellent idea!" he exclaims. "I'll ask for an appointment in the morning."

And the dinner party breaks up.

Chapter Four

Lucius wakes in the middle of the night, suddenly shooting up and off his couch. It is second nature even in the dark to work his way through the house to the atrium once more, and there is a single oil lamp burning on the family shrine. Paulus the kitchen-boy fills it with a carefully measured amount of oil every evening, just enough to keep it alight through the night. Lucius borrows this lamp and in his father's study he goes through the tidy line of papyrus rolls. He finds what he is looking for almost immediately – the draft of Sallust's history, read in part to them by Cicero over dinner. Why has he not thought of this before? It has to be read in full and carefully, and he knows just the person to read it. Albinia had not commented on the short extract Cicero read last night, but he had noticed the way her jaw tightened slightly as Sallust's self-pitying prologue came to an end. He doesn't think she will be that eager to read the rest of the work, but she is the best person for the job.

In the middle of the next morning he is in his own study, when Decius comes in to tell him that Cornelius Rufus is in the atrium and asking to see him. Cornelius Rufus? It has been years since Cornelius Rufus was at the house.

"He says it is important," says Decius with a very slight emphasis on the "says". Lucius guesses that Rufus has patronised him.

"He's useful," Lucius says soothingly, for Decius is too valuable a slave to leave with his feathers still ruffled.

Rufus is admiring the daring simplicity of the Sestius atrium decor when Lucius arrives. Lucius realises belatedly that he is still holding his breakfast, a chunk of bread, and quickly and nonchalantly breaks off a piece, and pops it into his mouth as if he eats in front of morning callers every day.

Cornelius Rufus, needless to say, does not bother with niceties. He is in a hurry to impress.

"I think I know who's behind the prosecution," he

announces, his tone a mixture of smugness and genuine satisfaction at his success. "They say that Publius Sittius is back in Rome."

"Publius Sittius?" The name is definitely familiar, and Lucius takes a few moments to place the man. Cornelius Rufus looks ready to burst, but Sestius senior comes hurrying in, echoing him in tones of outrage.

"Publius Sittius? That scoundrel? Gods above! Good morning, Sextus Cornelius Rufus." Rufus nods respectfully as Lucius turns back to him.

"Are you sure?" he asks Rufus.

"Pretty well. Look, I was down at the docks with Rubria early this morning, seeing to this load of linen. It's from Egypt, costs a packet, and she likes to be there when it comes in. The barge loaded it up at Ostia and a couple of passengers got on as well, the master said. Anyway, I recognised one, can't remember his name but I know him. And the most interesting thing I know about him is that he went off to serve under Publius Sittius in Mauretania a couple of years ago when the fighting in Africa was just about to kick off – before you got wounded there, young Lucius. He was with another bloke who was all wrapped up in his cloak, so I couldn't get a proper look, but I reckon it could be him, Publius Sittius. He'd have to cover up well – who'd want him in Rome again?"

"No one!" says Lucius' father earnestly. "Really, I never knew such a rascal. He is totally untrustworthy, and I don't know why we let him stay on in Mauretania. The man's whole life is a disgrace."

"Yes, but he was very useful to Caesar on the African campaign," Lucius says, as memories drift back into his head.

"You were useful in Africa, but Caesar didn't give you a huge chunk of land as a thank you," says Cornelius Rufus.

Sestius senior snorts in derisive agreement. "And I was useful in Cilicia. We don't get anything from the Dictator, but Publius Sittius gets given – given! – a Numidian town! Which Caesar had no right to give, even if it had been land belonging to Rome in the first place."

"I got wounded – not very useful," Lucius says gloomily,

31

and finds himself scratching at the scar that stretches up his right arm above the elbow.

Decius has managed to steer them all into the main study by this time and they settle down on stools with some watered wine and a plate of fruit.

"But he did do some good work during the African campaign," Lucius points out. "He could have joined with Scipio and the others easily, but he chose Caesar at a time when it was not too clear that Caesar was going to win."

"He should not have been in Mauretania in the first place," says his father. "He was Catilina's man, through and through, and wanted cancellation of debts because it would get him out of a hole. His business affairs were in tatters, and he was all set to join Catilina when the conspiracy was under way. Once he realised that the attempt to take Rome was a complete failure, and that Catilina was going to have to fight a pitched battle, he ran off to Africa, made a home in Mauretania, and has stayed there ever since. If you ask me he chose Caesar because he saw a kindred spirit."

Lucius looks at his father with respect and curiosity.

"You know a lot about him considering he hasn't been in Rome for years."

"Well, of course I do," says his father briskly. "During the year of Cicero's consulship, we kept a close eye on everyone connected with Catilina. I was up in Etruria at the end of the year, chasing Catilina around until we could force him to make a stand. I learned about Publius Sittius then, when our spies reported that he had stayed in North Africa and was saying that he never intended to raise troops for Catilina there. After the battle, the Senate ran quite a thorough investigation to check that all the supporters of Catilina were accounted for, and Sittius decided to stay where he was."

Lucius thinks that Sittius has done rather well for himself, despite this unfortunate tie to Catilina. He had worked out that as long as he was outside of Rome's official boundaries, nobody had the time or inclination to do anything about him. Then the civil war started, and it was clear, once Pompey lost to Caesar at the Battle of Pharsalus, that the fighting would eventually reach Africa, so, twenty years after Catilina failed, Publius Sittius decided that Caesar was worth the risk. He was right. Like the Sestii themselves, Sittius has chosen the correct side in the civil war, ending up in charge of a sizeable amount of land in Numidia, next to the province of Africa Nova where Sallust was such a beloved governor. In fact, Sittius, it turns out, is in just the right place to be able to get his hands on first-class evidence against Sallust.

"He must be very confident about Caesar," Lucius says. "But then he helped considerably – he drew off a lot of the reinforcements sent by Juba at a crucial moment, and he sank Scipio's ship when Scipio was trying to get away. Caesar isn't likely to forget that sort of contribution. That's why Sittius was granted, more or less, the town of Cirta as a thank you. Cirta is just west of Africa Nova in Numidia, so Sittius and Sallust could well have met, but what I don't see is what he could gain from attacking Sallust."

"He'll have been hired by someone," says Rufus.

"Africa does seem to be cropping up a lot recently," says Sestius senior thoughtfully. "It's a pity that you weren't out there longer, Lucius."

Lucius remembers being very glad to make it out of Africa.

Sestius senior goes on, "I think I might know someone who could be of use here..."

He would. As he bustles off, Lucius turns back to Cornelius Rufus. "Concentrate on the Sittius angle," he tells him. "See if you can get the man you saw identified as Sittius beyond all doubt. Pity you didn't know to follow him – but if you catch his trail..." Lucius stops at the look Cornelius Rufus is giving him. If he looked smug before, now he looks as if he has just achieved a life's ambition.

"Actually," he says, "there is this bloke from the barge. Works for my lovely Rubria, so I got him to follow the pair of them and then get back to me. I'll let you know, shall I?"

Then – incredibly – Cornelius Rufus winks at him and strolls out of the door. He has forgotten to ask for any money – or perhaps he is so elated that he is letting it go. Lucius stares after him.

As he wanders back to his study it occurs to him that there is nothing he can usefully do at that moment. His father will set up enquiries into the African side of the affair using his huge acquaintance, Cornelius is looking after Sittius, Cicero is talking to Caesar. What is left? For a few moments, he wonders about returning to the case of the Lady Claudia, but he remembers his nocturnal rummaging in the study, and finding Sallust's book. And so, he persuades himself that a walk and a relaxing visit are just what is needed.

Albinia, his full sister, is three years older than him. Their mother died when Lucius was born, and Publius Sestius married Cornelia two years later, so as far as Lucius can remember, Cornelia is his mother. Albinia has a few memories of their real mother though, and when the two of them were children she would tell him about her: highly dubious tales, Lucius now realises, but Cornelia proved her wisdom by never intruding on these memories. That is one of many reasons why Lucius and Albinia get on so well with her and their half-sister. Lucius is very fond of Cornelia and Tia, but he counts Albinia as his closest family member, and they have managed to maintain the closeness formed in childhood now that she is married to Marcus Apuleius and living in her own house. Her husband is a nice chap from a decent family, who has also chosen wisely when it comes to the civil war, and he has just entered the Senate as quaestor. Lucius thinks, not for the first time, that his acquaintance now falls into three neat groups of people – those who had chosen Caesar at the start of the civil war, those who hadn't, and those who had chosen wrongly at first then reconciled with the Dictator. The last group is surprisingly large and nowadays its members are likely to be found close to the Dictator. Cicero, for example, found himself welcomed back into the folds of Caesar's toga with little fuss, and a genuine welcome, and decided to live out of the political spotlight as a sign of his gratitude. It also means that he feels free to express the occasional gentle criticism of the Dictator, thus ensuring that Caesar looks more accountable. Lucius sighs. He lives in a pragmatic age.

The journey from the Caelian Hill to the Velia is an easy one this morning, though as usual the crowds slow him down as he approaches the Forum. He turns off the Sacred Way and goes up the slight rise and meets Marcus Apuleius bustling out of the front door as he arrives.

"Lucius! Good to see you! I'm just on my way to the Treasury. Don't imagine you want to come, do you? You could explain what that awful clerk of mine tells me."

Of all the highly educated and intelligent young men elected to the quaestorship that year, Marcus Apuleius is possibly the worst choice to be quaestor to the Treasury. He has a brain and is a sociable creature and got on very well in the army, but he has no patience with detailed reports of income and expenses. He was fortunate to enter the position just as it was vacated by a highly competent official and he has an equally competent chief clerk. He is also completely trustworthy and thinks that Caesar is the best thing ever to happen to the Republic. He thinks Albinia is the next best thing, so Lucius likes Marcus Apuleius, even though he doesn't understand him.

"I'll let you handle all that on your own," Lucius replies heartlessly. "Is Albinia in?"

"Yes, she is in her study. Something to do with dactylic hexameters, as usual," says his brother-in-law, who is very proud of Albinia's writing.

Apuleius sails off down the street, and Lucius goes into the house. The door-slave knows him well enough to let him make his own way through the traditional atrium, and then through to the tiny peristyle garden at the back. Albinia's study is much nicer than his study back in the house on the Caelian. It looks out over the garden, if you pull the door back, and Albinia has had it painted in light bands of colours, decorated with tiny pictures of flowers. There is a comfortable couch as well as a chair and desk, and one wall is taken up with book cubbyholes. Albinia is seated at the desk, and looks up as he knocks on the doorway and comes in. Her face breaks into a grin. She hugs her brother, sits him on the couch and calls for fruit juice and wine, before getting herself settled at the desk again, angling the chair so as to be able to face him.

"I hope you have news or gossip or something interesting,

Lucius," she begins. "I'm as bored as Hades, and this new work just won't go where I want it to."

Albinia is a pretty good poet, and she is well known among the serious literature set. She was even friends with the great Catullus before he died, and he had written a witty and insulting little poem to Publius Sestius as a compliment to the family. At least, Albinia says it is a compliment, and her father has shown nothing other than delight and pride at being insulted by the darling of the literati. Every now and then, she and Apuleius hold a small dinner party, and she reads a poem or two, but she has never made any more of her talent than this. She says she doesn't need to make a living, doesn't want to attract a literary patron and doesn't feel inspired to educate the masses through verse, so just knowing that her work is valued by family and friends is enough. Lucius thinks that if she were a man, her work would be much better known and more widely appreciated. She once wrote a little poem based on some Greek poet or other – it was about Cupid being stung by a bee.

> The naughty little love god tries to steal honey,
> and gets a sharp sting on the hand in return.
> He jumps up and down, blowing on the sting, and crying.
> The wailing boy-god runs to Venus,
> Arm extended, finger pointed,
> The bee falls in the grass and dies,
> But the boy doesn't notice and cries still –
> how can such a tiny creature cause so much hurt?
> His mother laughs. "Aren't you just like the bees?
> So tiny and yet capable of so much hurt."
> And mankind goes on feeling the sting of love.

Lucius has always had a horrible feeling that the love god's whining may have been inspired by himself. He can remember being stung when he was very small, and he is sure that he made a huge fuss over it. And of course, it never occurred to him then that the bee in stinging him, brought about its own death. But that is the sort of thing Albinia notices – she looks for the effects of events on unexpected people. And of course, she denies that she was thinking of anyone in particular as she wrote that.

"Honestly, Lucius, I was just translating! Not everything is about you!"

But she definitely did write one poem with Lucius in it:

Brother, we live with a ghost you cannot remember.
She spun while rocking your cradle.
The spindle bobbed up and down,
And her foot trod the rocker,
And my eyes followed the movements
Until I fell asleep, safe on a warm lap.
She fell asleep too, but her shade soothes me
To sleep still, as the spindle and foot move
Up and down. Always rocking.

Lucius cannot remember their shared mother, but that poem makes him wish that he did. When he first read it, he strained his ears for the sounds of the rhythmic movements of spindle and cradle, but what he remembered was Cornelia doing the same thing for Tia. The thread on the spindle made the lightest of whispers as the cradle made a heavier roll, beating out the unevenness of the floorboards.

Albinia has a way of looking at Lucius while tapping the end of her pen against her bottom lip. He usually finds it irritating, because it is as if she is mentally listing every little detail about him, and he is always wondering what will pop up in a poem. But today, he just sits and grins at her while she looks at him thoughtfully.

He begins with an update of what Cornelius Rufus has discovered. They are just beginning to discuss the possibility of the notorious Publius Sittius being back in Italy, when the wine and juice arrive. Albinia makes an observation, which echoes Lucius' uneasy feelings about this case.

"Why is everything about this story involved somehow with Catilina?" she wonders out loud. "Don't you think it's funny, Lucius, that a failed rebellion from twenty years ago, should be hanging around now in The Case of the Dishonest Governor?"

"Yes, exactly!" Lucius says, thankful that she gets it. "Catilina was never going to succeed, you know, and everyone who followed him has died long since. Or has successfully lived down their indiscretion."

"Perhaps they haven't though," says Albinia thoughtfully. "Is there any chance that something from that time is still – I don't know – hanging around? Someone like Publius Sittius, once of Nuceria, now of Numidia?

"It is surely significant that Sittius turns up just as Sallust is back in Rome, and there are at least two connections there, firstly that both of them have just been in Africa, secondly that Sittius is involved in the Catilinarian Conspiracy which Sallust is writing up as a scholarly little monograph. But we keep coming back to why Sallust is being prosecuted," Lucius says. "It can't be because of the Catilinarian Conspiracy – he's going to write a history of it, that's all, and it's hardly controversial material. Everyone knows what happened and the only thing that's ever come out of it is the question of the executions. Oh, and that brings me to this – keep it quiet though, would you? Sallust doesn't know I'm lending it out."

His sister looks at the scroll and pulls a face.

"I really had enough last night, you know, Lucius..." But she takes it and begins to unroll it. He puts out one hand.

"Don't start just yet – wait until I've gone at least!"

"So funny, you lazy toad," she observes, eyes still fixed on the scroll. "Oh well, once he gets onto the conspiracy itself, I shall enjoy seeing how Sallust handles the material. As you say, it is a well-known episode, so how does our author make it seem new to the reader?"

Lucius shrugs. "You are the literary one. To me it is just history."

"Cicero was exiled because of it though," Albinia points out. "The executions were illegal, because a Roman citizen has a right to a trial in a law court. So, the Catilinarian affair is Cicero's downfall as well as his proudest hour, just like a Greek tragedy."

"I can't see how that could affect Sallust though," Lucius says. "Sallust wasn't in the Senate during either the rebellion or the fuss over Cicero later on. I don't think he and Cicero have anything in common, especially as Sallust has always supported Caesar."

ROME'S END

"And Cicero hasn't?" asks Albinia ironically.

"Not supported exactly – just been careful to keep on friendly terms with him, once the fighting is over. He's going to dinner with him tonight to try and get information out of him, and I wouldn't be surprised if he succeeded."

"And who are you dining with tonight?" asks Albinia. "Anyone interesting? Or do you want to come here?"

Lucius grins at her. "No, thanks. Your husband might want me to explain his job to him. It's just a family dinner tonight. I expect there will be a lot to discuss. Tia and Cornelia want to be kept up to date with what is happening."

"I wonder who could this strange man Sittius be seeing?" asks Albinia, with uncharacteristic inelegance. "I suppose you think Caesar?"

"I can't think who else it would be," says Lucius. "But I can't think why, unless, and I really hope this isn't it, Sittius and Caesar are working together to punish Sallust for something. And so, Caesar has decided to get Sallust prosecuted. Father, of course, doesn't want to think that anyone could have anything to do with Sittius. Since the Catilina business, he has definitely been persona non grata, skulking in Mauretania. And then in the last two years, he came right by picking Caesar's side when the civil war went to North Africa."

"I'm sure that any good done by Publius Sittius has already been published when our beloved Dictator updated his war memoirs. Have you read the account of the African War yet?"

"No. Fighting in it is enough for me, thank you. And I don't want to get annoyed by all that third person "Caesar did this and that" style he has. I tried the Gallic Wars and just found myself shouting "It's you! You're Caesar! Stop talking about yourself!" I expect he thinks he has dealt with Publius Sittius, by allocating him that land in Numidia, making his position official, and giving him a good reason not to come back to Rome. I can't imagine that Caesar will be too pleased to see him, but," Lucius shrugs, "who knows what goes on in Caesar's brain?"

It is as he is leaving that Albinia says to him, "What did Caesar do during the Catilinarian crisis?"

Lucius has to think about this. "Nothing, I suppose. He wasn't even consul then. I'll have to ask Father."

In fact, it occurs to him that Caesar had been elected High Priest at around that time, so it seems very unlikely that he would have taken any great interest in the rebellion. The rather tedious duties of the chief of Roman religion ensure that he has a busy time of it, especially at the beginning of his lifetime's office. However, you do get the rather nice house in the middle of the Forum, and the authority does you no harm at all. At the time, Caesar could probably have done with a house – his debts in his younger days were legendary.

That night at dinner, the family settle down to another enjoyable rehash of the Sallust case, and Lucius' father brings his womenfolk up to date with the arrival of the notorious Publius Sittius of Nuceria. He also announces that he has heard from Cicero, who has travelled out to the Dictator's estate and expects to be invited to stay the night there.

As he is speaking, voices can be heard in the atrium, and Decius appears at the door looking slightly perturbed. Lucius and his father realise at once that it is not some domestic crisis, and, at a nod from his father, Lucius excuses himself, and goes out into the atrium. The first thing he sees, seemingly filling the place, is Cornelius Rufus, striding about the atrium and looking fiercely at the floor as if searching for signs of the groove he is wearing in it. As soon as he notices Lucius he changes course straight for him.

"That bloke I told to follow the men from the Tiber – he's dead, murdered. I mean, murdered for Jupiter's sake! What sort of case are you working on, young Lucius Sestius? And you tell me why Sittius has to murder some poor Tiber-rat rather than let him see where he's going. Why can't he use bribery like everyone else? It's not as if the poor sod knew who he was or would have cared that much if he had known. I just hope you can deal with these people. Hercules in Hades! What am I going to tell Rubria?"

It takes some time before Lucius realises what is going on, since he is so stunned to be shouted at by Cornelius Rufus. Then he begins to understand the words and wonders if he can really take it all in. Someone he doesn't know, and never met, is dead, and for a reason he can't explain. A horrible heat begins to rise in his chest, and amidst the fog in his mind, he knows that somewhere some mother is mourning her son, and how is he to explain it to her, when he doesn't even know what her son looked like? He opens his mouth and to his shame realises that what he wants to say is, "It's not my fault!" Jupiter best and greatest, how old was he? Can he not spare a thought for the poor victim first? Or even Cornelius Rufus and the never-seen Rubria? Lucius shakes his head abruptly, but the fog remains.

He looks back quickly towards the dining room and realises that though his family are safe in there, they must be protected from this. Cornelius Rufus has subsided and is looking so miserable that Lucius wants to pat him. Instead, he manages to croak, "Come into my study," and after a few seconds Cornelius Rufus nods and walks a little unsteadily after him. Lucius sits him at the desk and takes Decius' little stool himself, wondering how to open this conversation. Decius enters with a wine jug and two cups. It is good stuff, and unwatered, and Lucius makes a mental note to thank him.

"I shouldn't have been so clever," says Cornelius Rufus suddenly. "So eager to show off, I was, when I shouldn't have got involved. I just collect information and give it out again. Rubria will kill me!"

"Where was he found, this – Look, Cornelius what is his name? Is he a slave?"

It will, of course, be that much easier all round if the man was a slave.

"No such luck," says Cornelius gloomily, and Decius cannot help a slight wince. Lucius notices but has to push it to one side for the moment. "I don't know his full name, but he was a free man, Gaius somebody. He's one of the porters who works for Rubria at the docks, getting the stuff into the warehouse, taking it to wherever she needs it, that sort of thing. He's sort of in charge of a whole gang of them, and he'll have a devoted wife and ten kids and an old granny at home waiting for him. I'll even bet his mother's a widow, the stupid..."

The force with which he speaks intensifies until Lucius

wants to shuffle his stool back a little. There is a silence while Cornelius takes a drink, and Lucius stares at him, not knowing what to do – he puts out a hand towards him but pulls it back before Cornelius Rufus can see it. Cornelius Rufus puts the cup down and covers his eyes for a moment before slowly dragging his hand downwards, mercilessly pulling at his skin. The face that emerges looks old and tired.

"Well, what you did was right," Lucius offers, feeling decidedly young and useless. "I mean it was a good idea to get someone to follow those men, and you can't help it if he... if they... There's no doubt it was deliberate, I suppose?"

"Not unless the stone that bashed his brains out was moved by divine influence," says Cornelius. "Gods, I only just left his body and here I am, cracking lousy jokes about it already."

It occurs to Lucius that he has to make sure that Cornelius Rufus keeps working for the Sestii, and on this case. He will, surely? He is not responsible for the man, Gaius something, the death is not down to him, but... Maybe it is a mugging, or an accident, nothing to do with any of this. Maybe.

"Where is the body?" Lucius asks.

"The last I saw, the two men looked as if they were going to the Forum, but the body was found on the road outside the Capena Gate, like they were going to take the Appian Way. They must have turned south after the Forum."

"Why go through the Forum at all if you're going to end up on the Appian Way?" Lucius asks.

"Oh, come on, lawyer!" Cornelius' tone is gentle. He isn't bitter towards Lucius, who gratefully tries a small smile.

"Yes, I'm being stupid. What can't you find out in the Forum?"

"No point going anywhere else," says Cornelius Rufus the professional. "Now, if they didn't go through the Forum – that might tell us something. But they did. They were meeting someone. And there is no way we'll ever find out who."

Lucius knows Cornelius Rufus is right and imagines asking around the Forum, "Hey, two men came through here earlier. Did you see who they talked to?" Yes, that would work, in Rome's centre, thronged with thousands every day.

"We'll have to concentrate on the Appian Way then," he says.

"Which only goes everywhere south of the city, and if you turn off at the Latina Way, that covers practically everywhere else," says Cornelius, and stands up. "No point in keeping you. If I have any ideas, I'll let you know."

"And I'll do the same," Lucius says. "Where do you live?"

But as usual Cornelius Rufus won't be drawn on this. "You don't want to see where I live," he says. "And you don't want to frighten your slaves. Ask for me at the Forum, at that wine shop on the corner near where we met yesterday, and I'll get the message. Then I'll find you. Get a good night's sleep, and we'll see how things look in the morning, eh?"

With a pat of Decius' shoulder, he is turning to leave when he stops and says, "Oh, and I found out who Sallust's visitor was yesterday morning, if you are interested."

Lucius raises his eyebrows. Cornelius Rufus gives a small grin.

"He's called Titus Fadius Gallus." And he leaves. Lucius, holding his wine, goes into the atrium to see Cornelius Rufus to the door, wondering why the name Titus Fadius Gallus rings a bell.

He feels that he cannot face the family inquest over the dinner table, so he sends in Decius to get his father out. Once he has gone through it all with him, it seems no better and even puzzling. Why is Publius Sittius so suspicious and sensitive? Who is he afraid of? And maybe at that point they should wonder if they are in any danger themselves, but their family is old and senatorial, so it doesn't occur to them. Years of rioting in the city and a civil war have not made them worried enough, it seems.

"We shall untangle this in the morning," says his father, and he gives his son a quick hug. "Go to bed, and I shall tell the girls something. Oh, and I know Titus Fadius Gallus, so leave him to me."

To his surprise, Lucius sleeps well that night.

Chapter Five

The next day it rains, and Rome shrugs her shoulders and stays indoors. The good thing about being both hilly and equipped with a decent sewer system is that the sheets of water pouring down give the streets a free wash. Cicero takes this opportunity to stay on Caesar's estate and enjoy hobnobbing with the Dictator. Sallust sits and broods in his library and wonders what he should have done differently. Cornelius Rufus and his Rubria swathe themselves in sacking and visit Publius Sestius to discuss funeral arrangements for the unfortunate Gaius.

Lucius avoids this meeting but finds work difficult. He keeps wondering what the dead man had looked like, picturing a huddled figure by the roadside but unable to see its face. He might have lived and even fought, a little, through a civil war, but this death is shocking. He sits at the desk feeling wretched and snaps at Decius when he comes in to ask if there is any work for him. Decius' carefully blank face makes Lucius feel worse, and he remembers that twitch at Cornelius Rufus' grief-stricken tactlessness last night. Publius has already tried and given up talking to his son, and so when Decius silently leaves the room, Lucius is left alone.

Just before lunch, as if the family guardian gods have decided that enough sulking is enough, Tia comes in to cheer him up.

"Father says that we have a guest for dinner. He's called Titus Fadius Gallus. We've met him apparently. He was one of the quaestors along with Father during the year of the Catilinarian Conspiracy, and then was tribune with Father when they were trying to get Cicero back from exile."

Lucius is full of admiration – his father has worked quickly. He thinks back, and has the dimmest recollection of a dark, bony man, one of many people who had met at the house during the furore surrounding Cicero's exile. Now, why had he not been round since? Lucius remembers.

"He's only just back from exile. He got a bribery conviction a few years ago but Caesar pardoned him on one of his clemency storms. So he is back in Rome and we know he has been visiting Sallust."

"Do we?" says Tia.

"Cornelius Rufus found out that he'd been with Sallust when Sallust was deciding what to do about the prosecution," says Lucius. Only two days ago, he thinks.

Tia purses her lips. "And where was he in exile? Somewhere in North Africa, by any chance?"

Lucius gives her an ironic round of applause.

"Father says that we have to be kind to him and think of how awful it must be to have to go into exile," says Tia. She knows that her soft-hearted father has not told her something. "So, what else has he done?"

Lucius grins at her. "You're wasted at the loom – how did you guess?"

"Actually," says Tia, pulling a face, "I can make very pretty dishcloths. In about twenty years' time, Mother says, I might be able to try something more ambitious. Rumour has it that a cross-weave, as I believe it is called, may be involved. Anyway, as for Gallus, well – as soon as Father starts pitying someone, you know they're either obnoxious or a genuine sympathy case. I don't think it is the latter. Gallus has been found out and convicted of swindling after all, so he can't be that worthy of sympathy. He must therefore be obnoxious. Has he been rude to someone we know?"

"Not bad," says her brother graciously. "He decided to write to Cicero from exile and a stinker of a letter it was too. I saw Cicero's reply as well, and it was obvious that he was furious with Gallus, but he managed to remain civil. In fact, I was surprised he managed not to let rip – you know how he is."

Tia pulls a face. "I do indeed, and I agree that Uncle Marcus sometimes shows very little judgement, Lucius. Anyway, does this mean that Gallus is going to be beastly about Uncle Marcus all through dinner?"

"Probably. But I doubt if you'll be there to hear it. He won't be rude until the drinking starts, and you'll be long gone."

"Well, you'll have to give me the dirt later," says Tia, just as their father comes in.

"Indeed, there'll be no dirt to give," he says immediately. "What are you two gossiping about anyway?"

Tia slips away grinning, and Lucius asks about Gallus.

"Yes, I thought he would be just the thing," says Publius Sestius. "He's spent some time in Africa, you know, knows all the people out there – he may be able to tell us something about Sittius." He frowns. "There is one thing though, Lucius – I'd rather you didn't tell Marcus Tullius about this. He and Gallus had that unfortunate little disagreement if you remember, and I don't think he would be too pleased with me."

"Who?" Lucius asks. "Cicero or Gallus?"

"Both," says his father with a sigh. "For one who is always preaching class unity in the interests of the country, Cicero can be remarkably good at remembering petty quarrels."

"Has Cicero ever fallen out with you?" Lucius asks.

"Oh, gods above, yes," says his father with feeling. "He really can be – anyway, it doesn't really matter because for some reason, we have always been able to make things up. And he has always been very fond of you children which has helped of course. But I still don't want you to tell him about us having Gallus to dinner if you can possibly help it."

Lucius refrains from pointing out that it is up to them how they investigate cases, even cases that are of interest to Cicero, and promises to be good. His father is reassured but Lucius finds himself puzzling over the strange relationship that mutual obligation imposes on two men. Publius Sestius had helped run the campaign to recall Cicero during the exile crisis and had even got elected tribune of the plebs to try and get Cicero's case repealed. He and Cicero's brother Quintus had put themselves in danger in their efforts – after one riot, both men had been carried back from the Forum with stab wounds, and Publius Sestius was only alive because he had been presumed dead and left, covered in blood, on the steps of the Temple of Apollo. Lucius shivers. It had been a terrible time for the family. He realises that his father is looking at him with concern as he turns back to the desk and gives him the best smile he can muster.

"What about the dead porter?" Lucius asks. "What has been decided? Shall we send some money to his family or something?"

"It's all in hand," his father replies. "Your friend Cornelius Rufus brought his friend Rubria round first thing this morning, and we had a good talk about it. We are paying for the funeral, and Rubria is finding work for his two eldest sons. The family won't starve."

"How many children are there?" Lucius asks.

"Five. And it wasn't your fault. Or Rufus' fault. Somebody made the conscious decision to kill him, and that person bears the guilt. You look terrible, Lucius. Go to the baths – yes, and take Decius, he deserves a break too."

Lucius manages to get away without waiting for lunch (though this disrupts the running of the entire household according to his mother) and on his way out bumps into his upstairs neighbour, just arrived from Capua, and ready to enjoy the delights of the city.

"You look terrible," says Quintus Caecilius immediately. "Where are you going – no, don't tell me, you're off to the baths. Hang on a moment and I'll come with you. I need to wash the dust off. Decius would you be prepared to look after the two of us?"

Gracious as ever, Decius smiles, and Caecilius whisks back upstairs, while Lucius loiters on the stairs and wonders how he can explain to Caecilius that he plans to let Decius have an hour or so relaxing in the baths himself. It would be ridiculous to use as valuable a slave as Decius as a bathhouse attendant anyway. Caecilius bounces down the stairs and more or less fall on top of him, so the matter leaves his mind.

Quintus Caecilius has been a good friend ever since the time of the Catilinarian Conspiracy. It is very strange how that one event, important as it is in the context of state politics, also had the power to affect the Sestius family's life so much. Publius Sestius had been quaestor that year and had been sent down south to Capua at one point to see that things were quiet down there. While in the town, he met various local dignitaries, among them Caecilius' father – they had got on very well immediately. The newly built upper floor of the Sestius house in Rome needed tenants – and in no time the Caecilius family had a new town residence. The Sestii were invited to spend summers on the farm near Capua, and young Caecilius was sent up to the big city to get a proper education with Lucius.

The rain has stopped, and the streets are gently steamy as the two of them walk along the road, with Decius strolling behind them. The civil necessities take up most of the walk to the bathhouse and by the time the young men pay the attendant each is up to date on the financial and social woes faced by the other. Unsurprisingly, they both have unreasonable fathers when it comes to money. They then have to work out an excuse as to why Caecilius has arrived in Rome and immediately gone off to the bathhouse with Lucius rather than flying to pay a call on Tia – his betrothed – and the family.

"I think," says Caecilius, in the tone of one who cannot choose which tunic to buy, "that I felt that it would be rude to barge in at lunchtime while the dust of the road still clung to my person. I could not have sat at table with such an elegant lady as your mother without feeling embarrassed at my barbaric appearance. How does that sound?"

Lucius studies his friend's tall, carefully-draped form and scrutinises his clean, freshly-shaven face. Caecilius has clearly stopped off at a barber's on his way into the city

"Ridiculous," he says.

"Oh well," Quintus Caecilius says cheerfully. "I dare say Father will pop in and do the civil thing. He's come up with me, wants to sort out some contracts with suppliers. Boring. Let's sweat."

The baths they have chosen lie at the foot of the Caelian Hill, in the direction of the Forum, and are small and cheap, with a rather elderly clientele as the exercise area isn't up to much. There are other establishments throughout the city of course, some with huge exercise courts, some with libraries, some very exclusive, while some even put on free days thanks to the generosity of election candidates or rich men with nothing else to do with their millions. Bathing is one of the greatest things Rome offers her citizens. How can a nation call itself civilised unless its people are clean? And only Rome has made the process of getting clean so, well, civilised. It's the only word for it, and it is of course a Latin word. Not even the Greeks can compete there.

But these baths are nearly empty as most people are still doing business or having lunch, and Lucius and Caecilius have an hour or so before everyone else will be along. They take advantage of the quiet and linger through the various warm and hot rooms – bathing is a leisurely affair; you can't just duck and go – and end up wallowing very comfortably in a pool of warm water. No one else has joined them, so they don't even have to make polite conversation with some old bore who would probably turn out to know Lucius' father. Decius, after Lucius has had a quiet word, slipped away as soon as they entered the warm room, so even if he is a bit too gossipy with his friend, Lucius knows that his father won't find out. Caecilius shifts a little and Lucius prepares himself.

"So," he says, "can you tell me what the matter is or is it one of your cases?"

"It is, and I can't," says Lucius. "Sorry – I'd like to tell you about this one, but I really can't. And neither can Tia, so don't bother her."

"I never bother Tia," says Caecilius rather smugly. "Everything I say or do, she loves."

"It won't last," Lucius warns. "My sister has a very definite mind of her own, and you'll have to allow her that if you want your marriage to be a success."

"You've got very serious all of a sudden," observes Caecilius, looking at him curiously. "You know that you don't really believe that I'm going to treat Tia badly. Apart from loving her, I've got too much respect for your mother and father to do otherwise. I know when I'm lucky. Anyway, to shift the subject slightly, what about you?"

"Marriage? I'm waiting to see how you cope. Then if I like the girl, maybe. But there's no one in mind. Mother, of course, has lots of ideas, but she doesn't nag, thank the gods. And before you ask about my love life, I'm fine. Thank you so much for asking."

Caecilius grins. "I see Lydia has moved on then. Never mind, Lucius, she was too good for you, you always knew that. But what about this current business? Do you know how it's going to turn out?"

Lucius looks down at the water swishing gently around his navel and moves just enough to make waves up to his chin. He thinks about the feel of the water against his skin, a soft uncomplicated pleasure.

"I haven't the foggiest where it's going, or how it will turn out. I don't think it will even get to court, there are too many...issues. Apart from that, I really don't know what to think. Someone was killed yesterday – someone working on the case for us."

"By Hercules, that's not your usual style at all!" exclaims Caecilius. He tries to sit up but slips back into the water and needs some assistance to get upright. He snorts inelegantly, and Lucius laughs. Eventually Caecilius can speak again. "What happened to those nice little extortion and bribery cases you used to specialise in?"

"This started out as a favour to a friend," says Lucius gloomily.

"Serves you right then," says Caecilius, and gets up. "Decius! We need drying."

Decius appears with towels which Lucius takes, saying firmly, "We'll dry ourselves. See you in the entrance hall in ten minutes."

"You spoil that slave," says Caecilius as he tenderly dries himself. "Who'll drape my toga? You're useless – no sense of line."

"I like Decius," says Lucius rather feebly. "And why do you have to wear a toga to the baths, anyway? You country bumpkins have no idea – only people trying to prove something feel obliged to dress up to get clean."

Caecilius ignores most of this, merely commenting that Lucius might ruin Decius if he carries on being so soft.

As they leave the baths, a trio of small boys with a young slave in pursuit come running past them up the hill, on their way home from school. The slave is pretending to be a wolf, it appears, and the boys shriek and laugh as he growls after them. Lucius and Caecilius watch them, and stroll up the hill in their wake, with Decius falling five tactful yards behind.

"Hercules, I feel old," says Caecilius, with all the weight of his twenty-five years. "Do you think that Tia will like being a mother?"

"How should I know?" Lucius shrugs, slightly uncomfortable. "Why don't you ask her? Anyway, I don't see you as a paterfamilias – all this stern head of the household stuff isn't you. My father's tried for years and still hasn't got the hang of it."

"Your father doesn't need to with your family. Look at you all – he and Cornelia are still blissful together, you and he work together perfectly well, your sisters are intelligent, educated and loved, and they know it. Albinia manages to be both intellectual and happily married, so Tia happily assumes that she can be the same. You all respect each other and everyone is allowed a say. My father would never tell my mother and sister details of our business. Our dinner table conversations are deadly dull."

"Your sister can weave," Lucius reminds him.

"Yes, and I have to wear the result," says Caecilius, striking a tragic attitude, stretching out one arm to show off the fine, closely woven wool of his toga. Lucius thinks of Cornelius Rufus and his new tunic and wonders if Rubria will ever give him another one.

They arrive just in time to see the family before everybody else goes off to their respective baths. Caecilius is made as welcome as ever, his excuses laughed at, and Lucius looks at his family through his friend's eyes. He is heartened by them. All he has to do now is to endure dinner with Titus Fadius Gallus and everything will be fine. He goes to his father's study where there is a couch and lies down to think.

So far, facts are sketchy. There is no firm evidence that Sallust (it takes an effort to remember that two days ago, Sallust started all this) really is going to be prosecuted. Yet when the Sestii start to investigate, someone is murdered. People do get robbed and even killed on the Appian Way, but usually further away from the city, where the tombs give cover and the opportunity for an ambush. It is unlikely to be coincidence, therefore there must be something in Sallust's story. Lucius sighs and shifts to the other elbow. Is he reading too much into this? His mind moves on. There is the first question everyone asks – why is Sallust being prosecuted? His public career is hardly impressive or threatening, and he hasn't done anything in Africa that many governors haven't already done. Lucius thinks hard about Sallust. What makes him different from the rest? Well, he is sourer than most, and...and... Lucius shuts his eyes and tenses up his whole face, thinking. It is no good. Being bitter and writing history are the only things he can think of – and when did these relatively harmless occupations ever threaten a man's life?

Chapter Six

Titus Fadius Gallus breezes into the atrium that evening, calls Lucius "Dear boy" and compliments his mother and sister effusively. He does it all very well, as if he were the sort of old family friend who is allowed to be familiar and never takes advantage. Tia giggles at being called "a nymph of Diana" and Publius Sestius, who has been a little worried about this dinner, beams happily. He doesn't even think of Cicero.

Over dinner their amiable guest regales them with tales of the strange customs of the people of Africa and the native flora and fauna – entertaining, clean anecdotes. When the time comes for the ladies to retire, everyone is in a very good mood, and Lucius is wondering how this charming man and Cicero could ever have quarrelled. As she leaves, Tia raises one eyebrow at him – she's always been able to do it and try as he might, he can't. Lucius remembers his careless remarks to her earlier and thinks a little sourly of how easy Cicero finds it to direct one's way of thinking. Still, adoring Cicero unquestioningly is a family tradition in this house and who is he to start criticising the Great Man's judgement? His father is looking relaxed, and Lucius looks forward to a good gossip. They all lean forward a little, and while the conversation remains African, it leaves the wildlife for politics. Gallus wastes no time.

"So, is it true that you are supporting Sallust?" he asks with great interest. Publius and Lucius exchange a glance, and Gallus chuckles. "It is! How splendid! Now – who do you think is behind it all?"

"We were rather hoping to ask you about that," says Sestius senior. "And to ask you about Publius Sittius of Nuceria."

"Nuceria!" Gallus gives a contemptuous snort that would have been invaluable to any lawyer when cross-examining a dubious witness. "When," and their guest waggles his wine cup across the table at them, "when did that rogue last see Nuceria, I'd like to know? Call him 'Publius Sittius of Numidia' – that's who he is and where he rules the roost."

53

"You don't think he would ever come back to Rome?" Lucius asks.

Gallus looks at him and takes his time answering.

"I can't see it," he says. "Or at least, he'd have to have a special reason, quite a pressing one. Sestius – how many people do you think would like to have a crack at Publius Sittius, do you think?"

"That depends on Caesar, I would have thought. If the Dictator is clearly not interested one way or the other, then Sittius would be ideal prosecution fodder – you know the sort of young men who like to make an early appearance in public in some showy lawsuit. They could make a set piece out of his Catilinarian connection, maybe get some advice from Cicero. It would make quite a stir, I think. Of course, I never let young Lucius go in for that sort of vulgar business," says his father comfortably.

"Very commendable," says Gallus with a smile. His expression changes as he leans forward. "But I am intrigued as to why you want to know about him in connection with the Sallust case."

Lucius shoots a look at his father and answers quickly.

"We were thinking of who might be supplying information about Sallust's behaviour in Africa, and his name came up. To be honest, he is the only person we could think of who lives anywhere near."

"Ah," and Gallus leans back once more, examining his wine cup. "Well, despite what I just said about Publius Sittius, I wouldn't advise a young lawyer such as you describe to criticise Sittius' present position in Numidia."

The Sestii wait. At last he looks at them and asks, "How old are you, Lucius?"

"Twenty-three, sir," he answers, a little surprised at this turn in the conversation.

"Well, when you want to be considered for office, let me know, and I'll gladly make encouraging noises at as many of the right people as I can. Just make sure that in the meantime you haven't upset Caesar. I owe my return to him, you know. I am one of those many people who absolutely cannot afford to cross his wishes. You are one of the many people who should be thinking about how far you can go before Caesar's wishes become of paramount importance."

This is suddenly heavy stuff.

"Do you have any reason to suppose that I might upset Caesar?" Lucius asks.

Gallus looks carefully at his hands.

"Supposing," he says, "that Caesar were annoyed with someone and wanted them out of the way. Supposing he were to do this by having them prosecuted. How do you suppose he would feel then about any lawyer who defended that person?"

"Mildly annoyed but no more," says Lucius in as calm a tone as he can. "After all it is part of the system – someone has to defend the defendant."

"I don't believe that it would be wise to annoy the Dictator at all, not even in the interests of upholding our precious judicial system," says Gallus. He looks straight at Lucius and sees that the message has been delivered. Lucius stops gritting his teeth and discovers that his jaw is aching. He thinks of something.

"May I ask if you have visited Sallust recently?"

Gallus smiles. "Oh yes. Very recently. I had some news for him, you see."

Both Lucius and his father do see. Gallus is the friend who warned Sallust of the forthcoming prosecution. And on Caesar's orders, no doubt.

"Now," says their guest in lighter tones. "I think I may have some interesting gossip for you about Sittius. Do you know that it is rumoured that he and Caesar met in secret in Africa when our Dictator was fighting there a couple of years ago?"

"Well, of course they met," says Lucius. "Sittius did some useful work for Caesar in the African War – he ran very successful sea operations and tied up Juba's troops in the interior, while the Dictator fought near the coast."

"Ah, yes, but I said a secret meeting," says Gallus. "One they didn't want noised around too much."

"That certainly never reached Rome!" says Sestius senior, his face lighting up. Lucius can see his father's fingers twitching and knows that he is longing to note this down. "And are there any theories as to why this rendezvous occurred? And what the interested parties got out of it?"

"Ah, well now, there is one particular theory floating around, saying that Caesar just wanted to keep Sittius quiet and out of the way. It seems reasonable to me – if anyone is in a position to threaten the new conquests in Africa, then Sittius is the man. He'd cause trouble for the sake of it. He seems to be on good terms with the local aristocracy for some reason. These provincials are easily impressed."

How does he know all this, Lucius wonders? – and resists the temptation to ask. Another thought strikes.

"He isn't actually in exile, is he? I mean, legally in exile, because someone prosecuted him?"

Both Gallus and his father look startled, and a secret part of him rejoices to have caught them out.

"I suppose he isn't," says Gallus doubtfully. "Has anyone actually ever prosecuted him in absentia? Surely one of us would have heard?"

"I suppose we ought to check that, especially if he really is back in Rome..." Sestius senior realises what he has said, too late, and stops. He tries to have a fit of coughing, but Gallus' eyes are gleaming.

"Just a theory we had," says Lucius quickly. "We have absolutely no proof at all. It just fits in with something else."

"What might that be?" says Gallus.

"I'm sorry, that is confidential," says Sestius senior, a bit too late, thinks Lucius, exasperatedly. If he had done something like that, he would never have been allowed to forget it.

By the time Lucius has finished his cross musings on the failings of his elders, the conversation has switched to Caesar's reforms, in particular the new calendar, whose benefits they are all enjoying that year for the first time. Sestius senior considers himself an expert on the topic ever since Decius explained it to him and is covering for his mistake by boring their guest into forgetfulness. Gallus professes himself to be enthralled and to his credit keeps his expression of interest determinedly alive right to the end. Lucius thinks it highly unlikely that he will not pursue that slip on another occasion. He will probably invite his father to dinner by himself and pump him.

"So last year we had another sixty-seven days inserted after November and there we were, all square with the seasons again," concludes Sestius senior triumphantly.

"And what are we to call those extra days?" asks Gallus politely.

"Julius' month?" Lucius suggests.

Gallus laughs. "Wicked boy! Still, I might suggest it to him as a compliment – if the opportunity should arise in conversation, you know."

The Sestii express suitable awe at one who regularly converses with a Dictator and Lucius thinks that achieving this status is pretty good going for a man who has been in exile from Rome for several years. Dinner is coming to an end, and he starts reviewing the conversation – is there anything he hasn't asked? He might double-check that Gallus is the 'friend' who told Sallust of the upcoming prosecution, though after everything Gallus has said, Lucius thinks that it is a certainty. What about Cicero? Not strictly relevant perhaps, but Tia is bound to ask later as he'd laid it on so thick about the hostility between Gallus and the Great Man.

"Have you called on Marcus Tullius Cicero lately?" he asks casually, too late realising that he has crashed through the conversation with all the finesse of one of Hannibal's elephants.

Gallus frowns and sits up. It is clearly time to wind things up.

"I am aware of your family's connections with Marcus Cicero," he says with great formality, spacing the words carefully. "You, I am sure, are aware that despite my efforts on his behalf in times of crisis, he has not seen fit to recognise me as I deserve. Publius Sestius, my thanks for a very enjoyable evening. I shall certainly expect to entertain you in a similar fashion soon. I have no wife as my dear Marcia died when I was in exile, I am afraid. I hope that won't make Cornelia and young Tia feel that they would not be welcome."

"We should be delighted," says Publius Sestius. "May I call on you tomorrow? We haven't even discussed our days in office together and I would enjoy that."

"By all means," says Gallus. "We'll have a good chat without boring all the young people who won't know any of the characters or events we're talking about. Eh, young man?"

Lucius smiles sweetly and, unable to think of a totally innocuous reply, says, "Oh I don't know," hoping that Gallus can't take offence at something so vague. He doesn't. He makes a dignified exit and the two Sestii go to main study for one last cup of wine and a review of the evening.

"Well, I think we can take it as read that Caesar is threatening Sallust and used Gallus to convey the message. However, we're not any the wiser about why Sittius might be back in Rome," says Sestius senior, frowning at his drink.

Lucius grins at him. "I've got an idea. But you won't like it."

"I'm not quite so senile that I didn't understand Gallus' hints quite as well as you," says his father crossly. "But to link Caesar and Sittius in a secret pact of mutual convenience is one thing – to suggest the two are conspiring against one of Caesar's own governors is another. What has Caesar to gain? What has he suddenly got against Sallust? And what could be so important that it would bring Sittius back to Rome?"

"Was it really Sittius?" adds Lucius. "We don't even know that for sure." Suddenly it all seems very confused and he wishes that they were rid of the whole business. "What do we do next?"

As he speaks it occurs to him that he is asking that question a good deal lately. It seems that as he gets older, he needs his father more. Later, when he tells Tia about this strange phenomenon, she says, "No, you're just old enough to realise that Father can be of great help and that you don't need to do everything on your own any more. You are growing up. At last."

"I shall have a good nostalgic chat with Gallus tomorrow," says his father. "I must confess, throughout the course of the evening, I kept remembering why I like him. Perhaps this family is a little too inclined to support Cicero on any and every subject. It's getting to be a habit and Marcus himself expects our approval rather sets out to earn it. But he has done so much for us – it is difficult. Anyway, Lucius, why don't you look into the porter's murder a bit more? Have you thought of asking around at the Capena Gate to see if anyone noticed anything?"

The Capena Gate, being the main way out of the city onto the road to the south, is obviously going to be heaving with witnesses, and they are all going to line up to talk to the famous lawyer Lucius Sestius to help in the investigation of a murder that quite possibly has been sanctioned by Rome's beloved Dictator. Lucius sighs and then thinks of something very obvious.

"You can get to Caesar's estate at Labicum by going out of the Capena Gate and onto the Appian Way. Turn off at..." Lucius stops, feeling very apprehensive. Sallust, Caesar, murder - it is definitely too big for him.

His father looks at him and says, gently, "Go to bed, Lucius."

Chapter Seven

Lucius is now convinced that the Dictator, Gaius Julius Caesar, is involved in whatever is going on. What had Gallus said? "Suppose Caesar were annoyed with someone and wanted them out of the way..." He will work on the assumption that Sallust has annoyed the Dictator. Two years ago, Sallust was given the province of Africa Nova as a reward for supporting Caesar faithfully, so presumably something had happened during Sallust's time in Africa to change all that. There are three possibilities that Lucius can see: firstly, that Sallust has done something during his governorship that displeased Caesar; secondly, that the Dictator has discovered something about Sallust he hadn't previously known; thirdly, that Sallust has discovered something about the Dictator. The first is reasonable enough, if you presume that Caesar is having a fit of conscience about the provinces, but he would not keep his involvement secret in that case. As to the other two possibilities, Lucius needs extra information.

He wants to talk with Cicero and find out how he had got on with the Dictator – if he is back yet. A quick calculation and he reckons that Cicero is either already back or will be back soon, so in the morning, as his father sets off to see Titus Fadius Gallus, Lucius presents himself at Cicero's home, along with about fifty other men, all of whom probably have far more urgent cases than his. Tiro sees him first though.

"Cicero will be back later today and will be expecting to see you," says the faithful secretary (is Tiro related to Decius, Lucius wonders?). "Could you come to dinner?"

Lucius is flattered and swaggers back past all the envious callers, who grip their baskets or writing tablets tighter, and scowl at him. He wanders out, and down the hill to the Forum and looks for Cornelius Rufus. He is on his usual beat, strolling along the portico of the Hall of Aemilius. The Hall is in the process of restoration as always, but the shops keep open. Cornelius also looks in need of restoration. Lucius makes a note: he is thinking about Cornelius Rufus in quips, supposedly witty and somewhat superior asides. That should stop. Cornelius Rufus is proving himself worthy during this case and indeed in many cases before.

"No news," he greets Lucius. "Rubria's still talking to me, the gods alone know why. She wants to know what's happening and I can't blame her. I don't really want to explain it all to her, but I told her about the Sallust case – I thought I owed it to her."

"Fair enough," Lucius agrees. "Let's sit down somewhere."

"I know a place," Cornelius Rufus says immediately. Lucius has never had a drink outside the house with him before, and forgetting his good intentions, immediately resigns himself to some Hades-like pit on the edge of the Subura. Cornelius sees his face.

"Don't worry, lad," he says kindly. "I'll look after you. "And Lucius remembers his new resolution and follows.

It is quite gratifying to find that his forebodings are fully justified: the corner wine shop is dark and unwelcoming. It has a prime position on the corner of the Argiletum and the Forum though, so it is still quite full. Cornelius Rufus is clearly an old and valued customer, for as soon as they find a table an unsmiling old woman puts a small jug of wine and two cups in front of them and disappears immediately. Cornelius lets Lucius pour, and watches – Lucius makes himself take a mouthful of wine and is relieved. At least Cornelius wouldn't get the wine wrong. But he still looks into his cup carefully before every sip.

"You bring Rubria here?" Lucius asks as he fishes a small black speck – a fly or some dust? – out of the wine.

"No," says Cornelius Rufus. "She likes a bit of class, somewhere quiet she can tell her father about without him getting worried. Her sister usually comes along too."

Lucius tries to imagine Cornelius in a bar that has a bit of class and is quiet, the sort girls can tell their parents about. Tia rarely goes outside without their mother and even Albinia, a married woman, will be accompanied by, at the least, a slave escort. Tia has recently been allowed to go out with Lucius and Caecilius, on the strict understanding that a maid is in tow, she is never left alone with Caecilius and that they clear their itinerary with their mother before they go. They walk in public gardens or visit a temple and once went to the theatre. Subura bars are an unknown world to the Sestius womenfolk.

Lucius picks a splinter off the bench before it can pierce any tender parts of his anatomy.

"Anything else happening in Rome apart from our little problem?" he asks.

Cornelius sucks his teeth in sorrow.

"Nothing worth the repeating. The trouble is the Dictator. He's never here and nobody does anything while he's away." Cornelius shakes his head, while Lucius squirms in his seat and hopes the old woman isn't one of Caesar's spies. He steals a careful glance around, but nobody looks their way.

"What else did you think was going to happen?" he asks quietly.

Cornelius shrugs. "Honestly? I thought we'd at least see him. Take this year – we're all dead busy waiting for the Dictator to get back from Spain, celebrate yet another triumph, then hold some elections and we can get on with things. So, he comes back a couple of weeks ago and actually goes around Rome to get to Labicum – not through, around! He spends weeks on his estate, "making preparations". He appoints the magistrates by sending a list to the Senate, says a lot about new building projects, a load of rubbish if you ask me, and the gossip says there'll be a triumph in October to celebrate the campaign in Spain. And what that is going to be like is anybody's guess because we've never had a general actually hold a triumph because he's beaten other Romans. Are we supposed to shout "Hooray!" at that? In the end, the impression we get is that our Dictator doesn't really like us very much. Not enough to actually settle down with us anyway. Ever since he went to Gaul – and that's, what, fifteen years? – he's never been what I'd call a decent time in the city. Every time he comes back, it's to prepare for his next campaign. What's so great about Spain or Egypt or Africa? Especially now he's got that Cleopatra tart over here in his love nest over the Tiber. Oh, Cicero's on his way back by the way."

"Yes," says Lucius, slightly stunned by this tirade.

"Don't bother asking around about the murder," says Cornelius Rufus. "No one knows nothing. Sensible if not very helpful."

"I wouldn't have thought it would have been too much use anyway, asking at the Capena Gate," Lucius says. "Surely it's always too busy for anyone to notice anything?"

"Well, I had a quick nose around first thing this morning, and you're right," says Cornelius, pulling a face. "Nobody was there, and they were too busy as well, so nobody saw the nothing that was happening. Take no notice of me, must be my stomach playing up."

"Hard night last night?" asks Lucius with false sympathy.

"Funeral was yesterday evening," says Cornelius briefly. "Always give me indigestion, funeral dinners. Good food, mind – your father didn't skimp. Everyone appreciated that."

Lucius pays for the drinks and says goodbye. A little awkwardly, he asks Cornelius Rufus to pass on his regards to Rubria. They nod to each other and he leaves Cornelius finishing the wine, flies and dust and all.

At lunch, his father tells him all about the completely innocuous conversation he had with Titus Fadius Gallus. According to Sestius senior, they reminisced about their time as quaestors helping the consuls during the year of the Catilinarian Conspiracy. And nothing more. Lucius finds it hard to believe that Gallus did not want to know about Sittius being in Rome, but his father is not to be shaken – they simply did not discuss Sittius. Lucius reckons that Gallus is just waiting for the right opportunity to get the full story.

To his surprise, his father has also been to see Sallust.

"I thought he needed to be briefed on the recent incidents," says his father, and leaves it at that.

During the afternoon, Lucius takes a very sensible step forward. He tells Decius to send a letter and all the relevant notes round to the Lady Claudia and her concerned husband. The letter explains that a family matter – very private, very delicate – prevents him from taking the case any further. He also advises her that in his opinion she is liable to be prosecuted by her alleged poisoner. He realises that he can't now hope for their support in his future career, but at that moment he knows that he won't need it. And who knows, the persecuted Greek freedman accused by the Lady Claudia, might be worth something. You never know when a rich friend will come in handy.

In the evening, Lucius goes back to the Forum and crosses over to Cicero's house. It is in a prime position for one who loves politics and the law, for, from the lower slopes of the Palatine Hill, Cicero can theoretically look down over the whole Forum – Senate House, law courts, speaking-platforms. Lucius looks up at the house as he crosses over to the steps up the hill and wonders how comfortable it is being so visible, on display, all the time. Cicero used to say that he would give a fortune for a slave who could lip-read at a distance; such a slave would pay for itself in blackmail revenue alone, never mind the information Cicero could use in his speeches. The house itself is by no means the biggest in Rome, but is one of the oldest and most distinguished, and along with its neighbours curving up the hill, has been there almost as long as the Republic itself. It had been sold to Cicero by Marcus Crassus, who was famous for being rich, though that hadn't stopped the old miser charging a huge price for it. "Firstly, he has, believe it or not, reduced the price for me, and secondly, it's worth it just for the location," Cicero told Lucius once. "Anyway, if I can't pay for it, I'll just have to join the next Catilinarian rebellion."

Lucius enters this splendid dwelling and makes up a message of greeting from his family. Cicero accepts it graciously and they go straight into the dining room, where a dark young man is already reclining on a couch. Lucius recognises him from family holidays with the Cicero clan down in Arpinum – this is Cicero's nephew, Quintus Tullius Cicero junior. Unlike the sunny and straightforward Marcus, Cicero's son, Quintus has always been a bit on the edge. He doesn't agree with other people easily, and the fiasco of the civil war split the Cicero brothers and their sons for a time. Lucius thought all that had been mended, hence Quintus' presence in his uncle's house, but there is still just a little bit of an atmosphere, and it takes several cups of wine before Quintus relaxes. The conversation is, by silent agreement, limited to how the new calendar is working, gossip about Cleopatra (whom Cicero has met – he isn't impressed) and Cicero's own writing projects. Quintus doesn't chatter, but his contributions are entertaining, and he has the shrewdness of his uncle. Even the younger members of the Cicero family are intelligent, well-read and witty.

After a small but superb dinner, the Great Man then takes them and the wine jug into his study, which is somewhat larger than Lucius', as well as having more books. The desk, Lucius covets. It is huge, and according to legend is made from a single tree in Cicero's home town of Arpinum. Whenever you enter the study though, Cicero is never actually at the desk – and Tiro has a great story about that. Pompey the Great had once called, says Tiro, and so overpowering is the desk that he had not seen Cicero sitting behind it, so after that, Cicero always made sure that visitors entered to find him standing at the bookcase or sitting in the chair near the door. Lucius does not believe this story of course, but it fits in with Cicero's vanity. And Cicero had from his earliest days clung to Pompey the Great, despite being let down by him more times than anyone cares to remember. Pompey is beyond disappointing his followers now though, and his place in Rome is limited to the theatre complex he built on the Campus Martius. Ironically, he included a temple to Julius Caesar's patron goddess, Venus, and Lucius thinks that it didn't do Pompey any good – Venus did not abandon Caesar. He remembers seeing a nice statue of Pompey in the meeting rooms behind the theatre and wonders what Cicero thinks of it, then brings himself back to the here and now, looking around and longing for the books, as he always does. They are really something – the wall is lined with little niches, all filled with scrolls, whose tags spill out and tangle lovingly with each other. Lucius has spent many afternoons here, helping Tiro to disentangle the tags, and reading in the corner, for many of these works are not widely available, and Cicero won't let him take any of them away.

Despite Pompey the Great, Cicero sits behind the desk and gestures to the chairs in front of it.

"Sit down, you two," he says, and smiles. "Now – the business with Sallust. Quintus knows what is going on, Lucius, and I think the news is good. I feel confident that Caesar will appear on our side." This is so unexpected, Lucius feels his jaw drop. He has just reached the point of being convinced that Caesar was actually behind the prosecution in the first place – what is going on? Cicero continues, "He expressed great concern that his trusted governor is suffering prosecution."

"Oh, that's nice," Lucius murmurs feebly, wondering what that "our side" means. Surely Cicero wasn't...

"So," Cicero continues, "what progress have you made?"

That is a tricky one. It doesn't seem diplomatic to say that in his considered opinion Caesar is lying. Lucius decides to leave that and tell Cicero the news about Sittius and the murder. Sittius with any luck will provoke a tirade, and this might be accompanied by some useful information. If anyone would know about Sittius, Cicero would. So he gives him a brief outline of events but does not mention the fact that Titus Fadius Gallus had come to dinner.

As expected, it takes some time for Cicero to deal with Sittius, but as he uses the opportunity to brush up some insults, it is highly enjoyable. Lucius is storing away some of the richer abuse, when Cicero comes to an end, gives him a stern look and says, "And if I ever hear any of that in a speech of yours, I'll never let you into this library again."

Lucius smiles, promises and asks about Sittius' current official status.

"Now that is quite interesting, if grossly unfair," says Cicero. "He first went to North Africa the year before my consulship and returned to Italy very rarely. In fact, I don't think he has ever come back to Rome. Then, twelve years ago he was charged with treason and found guilty in absentia – Pompey didn't like the connections he was establishing with some of Rome's less lovely sons and 'discovered' that Sittius had been involved with Catilina." He sighs. "It was a difficult time for me, or I would have enjoyed prosecuting him myself."

Lucius nods sympathetically, for Cicero had indeed had a difficult time, spending half that year in exile. Publius Sestius had had an exciting year as tribune of the people, working hard for Cicero's return – that would explain why he had not remembered about Sittius, thinks Lucius.

"Be that as it may," continues the Great Man, after a suitable pause to look noble, "when Caesar was in Africa a couple of years ago, it would appear that Sittius was of some small help. In return, though the sentence of exile is not quashed, the Dictator granted to Sittius the right to carry on living in Numidia, thus merely approving the status quo. If Sittius has indeed come back to Rome, he is taking a risk and can be prosecuted for breaking his exile. What Caesar will do about such an eventuality is interesting. However, I wouldn't let that deter you."

Lucius stops nodding and looks properly at him. "Deter me from what?"

Quintus stirs. "From a full investigation. What else were you going to do?"

"Considering that the man murdered some poor ignorant porter on the way to what was certainly an arranged meeting with Caesar – nothing, I rather thought!"

Lucius is indignant. Of all people, this family should know of the dangers of crossing powerful individuals. What world are Cicero and his nephew living in?

"All the more reason to investigate then," says Quintus. "Or do you think that he has acted reasonably?"

Lucius decides to come clean. "It's Caesar," he says bluntly. "I don't think he is on our side at all. I think he and Publius Sittius are working together to destroy Sallust. If I go after Sittius, then I go after Caesar and I risk everything. I honestly don't know whether I really want a career in the Senate, but I'd like to have that choice."

"I can't see the point of the Senate at the moment," says Quintus.

Cicero sits for a while, looking at the scrolls in front of him; then he says, "Come with me," and he walks out of the study and through the atrium to the door. Lucius and Quintus follow and the three of them walk down the street until they are at the top of the short flight of stairs leading directly into the Forum, and there they stop and look down on the darkening scene. The temples are huge blocks of shadow, in between which people cross the floor of the Forum, wrapped up in their cloaks, in groups, noisy and lit by torches, or singly, silent and furtive.

"I wake up very early in the mornings now – I'm getting old, I suppose. I come out here and look at it all nearly every day," says Cicero. "There's none of this bustle, no people apart from the odd temple slave. On a spring morning, the air is cool and clean, and the light is golden – and I can see Rome clearly. Those buildings come to life then. You see their edges so sharply in the sunlight, and their roofs stretch up to the sky, and they each perform a sacred duty for Rome. The temples glorify our gods, the law courts uphold our dignity as free men, even the boring old government buildings, Senate House and Record Office, do you know what they do? They proclaim the greatest heritage a man can have on this earth – to be a Roman citizen. The poorest man in the Subura can walk down here every day and gaze upon this splendour, knowing that he has a share in it. And the richest man on the Palatine has no more and can be equally proud of it."

And Cicero turns and starts walking back to the house. Quintus and Lucius look at each and Quintus says, "It's all bollocks, isn't it? There never was a Rome like that, and there isn't one now. Caesar is transforming it."

"Into something better?" asks Lucius.

Quintus shrugs. "I'm not sure if that matters any more. He is changing it into something he can manage on his own. He likes being Dictator and he is getting more and more dictatorial. I'm one of his fans, and even I can see it."

They follow Cicero back to the study and he sits the two of them down once more.

"You know," he says, "the Republic will be destroyed soon, by Caesar or men like him, and when that happens I don't want to be a part of Rome any more. I couldn't if I did want to, because this Rome that I see every morning will not exist. That's why someone has to remind Caesar, just occasionally, of who he is – a Roman, no less and certainly no more."

Lucius has to admit that it has been a great performance.

Despite Quintus, there are tears in his eyes and in his mind, as he looks at the dirty, noisy, smelly old Forum and sees it as it should be. For a moment, what Cicero says is true and Lucius can't think of any greater compliment to give an orator.

Lucius clears his throat – it takes rather a long time. Then the cautious young politician-in-waiting takes over and he says that he had better be going. As an answer to what Cicero said, it is a bit lacking.

"I'll come with you, part of the way, at least," says Quintus. "I could do with the exercise before bed. I'll see you tomorrow, Uncle Marcus."

Once out of Cicero's house, Lucius goes back down the steps and through the Forum and looks in every corner for Rome. What he sees is Cornelius Rufus, and so he stops and watches as the informer trudges up the Argiletum to the Subura. Lucius wonders if Cornelius Rufus would join in his search or even understand what he is looking for. Quintus is a silent shadow beside him, not asking why they are standing still, and Lucius has no idea what to make of him. They carry on and Quintus says nothing until at the edge of the Forum he stops Lucius abruptly and asks, "So – are you going to give up the case? Or has Uncle Marcus' bollocks given you some balls?"

Lucius has to laugh, but to his surprise his feelings have changed.

"Maybe I will carry on," he says. "Maybe Sittius needs to be stopped, and if he is connected to Caesar so closely, maybe people should know that."

Quintus nods and wishes Lucius a good night and turns off back towards the Palatine. Perhaps he really did just want a bit of exercise.

Chapter Eight

"Perhaps," says Tia, "Uncle Marcus wasn't just being an orator."

"I don't think he's capable of saying anything without it being oratorical in some way," Lucius answers. "You don't get to be that good for so long without it taking over."

Tia frowns. "Yes," she says, "but what I mean is, even for Uncle Marcus, even with him having to be oratorical all the time, maybe he still really meant it."

"I knew what he was talking about." Lucius pauses and feels decidedly awkward. "I feel something like that about Rome sometimes – I think. I mean, I really do believe that our law courts matter, and that people should trust that they can get justice."

"Did you feel like that when you were in Africa?" asks Tia, who out of all his family has been very tactful in her questions about his time as a less than glorious warrior.

Lucius thinks back to that brief time – a few months at the beginning of the previous year, when he seemed to be constantly on the move. He had arrived in Africa along with a consignment of troops at the beginning of January after they had rather embarrassingly lost their commander; he could still remember the relief they all felt on crawling into Hadrumentum harbour and finding Caesar waiting. Caesar had already scouted the surrounding area of course and decided his strategy – all the late-comers had shuffled their feet and agreed. It had not been particularly patriotic – Lucius feels that they had not been acting for Rome, but for Caesar.

He answers his sister. "No – I was too busy being scared," and grins at her, the sentiment expressed, however poorly, and the moment over.

"Did Cicero say anything else about Caesar apart from that bit about him supporting Sallust?" asks Tia.

Lucius thinks back. "No. They must have had a lot to talk about, but I suppose Cicero decided that most of it just wasn't important as far as I am concerned. They get on quite well, or so Cicero seems to think. It seems strange with Cicero being such a staunch Republican."

"There is nothing unconstitutional about a Dictator," says Tia in a mock-pompous voice. "A Dictator is a man who stands between our beloved country and total mayhem in a time of great crisis, when the consuls fail, when the Senate is tottering, yes, when the very foundations of the Republic are crumbling beneath us. A more noble office does not – cannot – will not exist."

"Ascending tricolon!" Lucius applauds, and Tia laughs and carries on, her voice returning to normal. "I love the way Uncle Marcus conveniently forgets the fact that Caesar was appointed Dictator for ten years last time, and even Father says that that is not what the office is for."

Perhaps everyone realised that we would be having crises for ten years – especially if Caesar wasn't given what he wanted," suggests Lucius. "Anyway, it's not all bad. At least we don't have any more fighting to do, apart from the usual foreign wars."

"I thought Caesar started all the civil wars?" says Tia sweetly.

"Well, yes, but it was heading that way anyway – it is just that he actually started it – oh come on, Tia, you know all this as well as I do. Anyway," his voice drops to a reverential whisper, "there is the Calendar."

"I shall never understand why everyone makes such a fuss about that wretched calendar. It's not as if it proves Caesar's brilliance," says Tia. "It's just a very sensible thing to do – any farmer would have thought of it as the first reform needed. What's so special about Caesar getting some Greek mathematician to do it?"

"I think it's more that now someone has the time to do things like that," says Lucius. "Now it looks as though we're over the civil war, maybe reorganising the calendar is the signal we all need that things are getting back to normal. The seasons will all happen when they're supposed to, the farmers will be in the same month as the rest of us, we'll be – well, normal. Like we were in the good old days."

"You sound like a speech for the defence," says Tia scornfully. "Thanks for the end of war, an appeal to agriculture, and nostalgia – stock blather. And it's all nonsense because you and I can't even remember the good old days. Ever since I can remember, Rome has been on the road to ruin. What's normal? What Father and Uncle Marcus are always on about? Because I don't believe Rome was ever like that. Look at the story of Cincinnatus: no one ever really left their ploughing to become Dictator – a proper Dictator, there to deal with a real crisis – then went back to the plough once he'd cleared up the problem. No one really returned to his enemies to be killed because he would be keeping his word like that general in the Carthaginian War. What's the use of telling children these tales when we weren't ever like that and aren't ever going to be like that?"

This seems most unlike his pious and dutiful sister. In the Sestius family, Lucius is the cynical one – he prides himself on it.

"What's up with you?" he asks, stung at the thought that his sardonic throne is about to be usurped.

Tia looks surprised. "Nothing. Why?"

"Seems a bit grim for you."

"You've been listening to too many speeches of Ciceronian patriotism – all blather," says Tia. "Just because I've got a bit of sense doesn't mean I'm becoming a radical pleb-rouser."

"I'd like to see you survive a meeting as a Tribune of the People, up there on the platforms in the middle of the Forum, dodging the rotten vegetables and eggs."

"The people don't need their tribunes much if they can afford to waste eggs." And with that, Tia is off to the kitchen to organise the dinner to welcome her fiancé, Caecilius. The family has been entertaining a lot recently – Lucius decides that it must be the new case. Obviously, being in the middle of a political scandal is good for their popularity.

He calls on Quintus Caecilius and the two of them walk through glorious September sunshine to the baths again, leaving behind their lunches and two irritated households. Preparations for Caecilius' dinner at the Sestius house are so consuming that lunch is reduced to the grab-your-own-and-hop-it variety, and yet Cornelia is still annoyed when Lucius says that he will give lunch a miss. She smiles graciously at Quintus Caecilius, however, when he offers his father's apologies. Caecilius senior, it turns out, has a prior engagement, dinner with a colleague over on the Aventine Hill.

At the baths, to Lucius' slight dismay, they meet Sallust. But when he comes over, introduces himself and chats pleasantly, Lucius is astonished. He watches while Sallust and Caecilius discuss literature as they move from warm room to hot room and then to the favourite wallowing pool. Caecilius is a charming young man – his elders have always approved of him, and when he says that he is betrothed to Lucius' sister, Sallust nods approvingly. Lucius is not surprised when, with an enquiring look, Sallust asks, "Lucius Sestius, would you have any objection to allowing your neighbour to be admitted into our confidence?"

Naturally, Lucius is delighted. To be able to talk to Quintus Caecilius about this horrible business would be extremely useful. So, Sallust begins the account and Lucius finishes it off with what Cicero told him the day before – that Caesar had said that he would support Sallust. He does not mention that he does not believe this himself, but when he sees the cynicism on Sallust's face, he knows that he is not the only non-believer. Caecilius, he is rather pleased to see, is astounded. In fact, there is a little silence at the end of the story. Sallust then clears his throat.

"Your father visited me yesterday morning. This business about the murder is distressing to say the least. Sittius' presence is also alarming – he is definitely not to be trusted. Now, what I have to say is to be mentioned to no one – I hope you understand."

They nod, Caecilius' expression suitably agog; Lucius wonders if his own is too.

"Despite the assurances given to Marcus Cicero, we must conclude that Caesar is not going to be on my side," says Sallust in the driest tone he has so far used in this conversation. "He must have welcomed Publius Sittius of Mauretania while the rogue still had a citizen's blood on his hands. Sittius arrived in Rome as I was being threatened – the two are almost certainly connected. In fact, we can stop tiptoeing around the issue and acknowledge that Caesar is probably trying to get rid of me. Why he should do this, I have no idea."

Silence descends once more on the little pool. Lucius can't think of anything to say to a man who has just confessed that his patron no longer requires him and is in the process of breaking the ties. Caecilius nudges him and starts pushing at him to get out of the bath. It takes a few moments before he realises, but when he looks at Sallust, tears are running down the man's cheeks. Lucius and Caecilius return to the changing room and silently get dressed.

Outside in the sunshine, the relief of being out of the situation creeps over them, Caecilius stretching and yawning, Lucius being seized by a desire to get drunk enough to give him an excuse to do silly things.

"Gods above!" says Quintus Caecilius. "Never let me depend on another man so much!"

"Don't be ambitious then," Lucius advises.

"Ambitious? Hah!" he says derisively. "Let me tend my estates and risk the odd fortune in a ship's cargo, and I'll not moan about not being a consul. No good having the supposedly highest office in the land if someone has got ahead of you by chiselling out all the real power."

It occurs to Lucius that they still haven't worked out why Sallust is being treated like this by the leader he served loyally, who offered him his second chance in public life. That question will not go away – what has Sallust done? Why is Caesar so suddenly determined to get rid of him? The two of them muse on it unfruitfully until they get home.

"We're going to have to get back to Sallust and ask again," says Caecilius. "I know he says he doesn't know, but he must have an idea or maybe if we go through his career since he was restored to the Senate, we'll find something. How do we approach him?"

"It'll have to be an official morning call," decides Lucius. "I'll go tomorrow – do you want to come too?"

Caecilius thinks about it. "It is interesting," he says slowly, "and I don't think he will break down again. So – yes. Better not drink too much tonight then."

"I won't," Lucius assures him. "There's some old fart coming around to dinner tonight – no chance of anyone getting drunk with him around. It'll be as boring as military service in a Gaulish swamp..."

They shout a few more insults as Caecilius goes up the outside staircase to his family's apartment.

Midway through the afternoon as Lucius is having a nap, Decius comes in to tell him that Sallust is waiting in his father's study. Lucius shoots out into the atrium, stops and hurriedly smoothes his hair, tugs down the rumpled tunic, avoids his mother's reproachful look, and walks into the study.

Sallust is sitting in the visitor's chair, just as he had been that first morning when he had asked the Sestii to help. Now, as he looks up, the face that had been so ready to express criticism then, welcomes Lucius with what looks like relief, and for a moment Lucius sees again the face of the man he left in the bathhouse just a couple of hours before. Publius Sestius is pouring some wine; Sallust nods to Lucius, but says nothing, occupying himself with his wine cup. Lucius waits until Sallust has taken a good long drink.

"What's wrong?" he asks.

"I've been robbed," says Sallust. His eyes look off into the distance. "My books... They've taken my books. My study is – it's terrible, papers everywhere, torn... I..." He stops and looks at Lucius. "I thought it might have something to do with what's happening, but I don't know – I thought I should tell you..."

"Now you just sit quietly, Gaius Sallustius Crispus," says Publius Sestius firmly. He pours out more wine to distract Sallust, who is on the brink of tears. "When you're feeling a bit calmer, you can talk."

Patiently, they sit and sip wine, and Lucius and his father have a gentle conversation about the forthcoming dinner with Caecilius. Presently Sallust sits up straight and takes a deep breath and says simply, "Thank you. I feel better now."

There is no likeness between this man and the man they first met a few days before. Lucius wonders if he likes him better now simply because he is more vulnerable. Certainly, the fact that he has turned first to the Sestii in this fresh crisis makes Lucius feel more able to help him.

The story doesn't take long to tell. Towards the end of the morning, when Sallust was already on his way to the baths, his doorkeeper had been bribed to let in a man "to wait for Sallust's return". This man had sat patiently in the atrium and the slaves had forgotten about him until Sallust returned at which point they had realised that the mysterious visitor had not been that anxious to wait after all. The household then also realised that none of them could remember the man leaving. When the robbery was discovered, they finally realised that they had been very silly. The doorkeeper is now feeling particularly sorry for himself and will be sold on when he has recovered. As no one will trust him as a household slave again, he will probably end up in a job with a short life expectancy.

"It is when I realised that my copy of my history of the Catilinarian Conspiracy is missing that I thought that I must see you," says Sallust.

Lucius and his father look at each other.

"What do you mean, you thought of us? Don't you have other copies?" asks Sestius senior.

Sallust looks surprised, then thinks about it.

"Well, yes, there are a couple of other copies, one with Cicero, who said he was going to show it to you two, and one with my secretary," he says. "I immediately thought that the robbery might be the work of Caesar, or whoever it is who is prosecuting me, and it occurred to me that I must tell you. So, I came round."

"It is connected, isn't it?" Lucius asks. He looks at the two faces, suddenly noticing the lines and grey hair, the tired expressions and bowed shoulders, and a feeling of panic arises within him. Sallust is vulnerable even in broad daylight. Lucius had not thought of that.

"We can't afford to take the chance that it isn't," says his father. "I must have a word with Decius – he can tell the slaves to be extra careful. Excuse me, Gaius Sallustius – I shall be back

76

soon."

He bustles off, and Lucius turns to Sallust, for something else has to be asked. Something is wrong.

"This history that you're writing, sir – when do you think it might be published?"

"Oh, I don't know," says Sallust. "It is more or less written, just needs checking over. I thought after the trial. It won't be anything more than a short roll's worth. No longer than a law-court speech, really."

"How long have you been working on it?" Lucius asks and holds his breath.

"Well, off and on, ever since I went to Africa – actually, a little while before that. But the idea's been there for many years. I was a young man when it all happened, and it made a great impression. I suppose you're almost blasé about it what with hearing about it from your father and Cicero, but it really was a remarkable time. I was actually in Rome, putting in some work on my Forum education, following the day-to-day business of the Senate. I can remember the city waking up to tension for days on end, crowds around the Senate House every time Cicero spoke, then the relief when the conspirators were executed and the Battle of Pistoria won. Marcus Tullius may be a dreadful old wind-bag, but I respect him for what he did then." Sallust suddenly smiles. "He hasn't said anything, but he won't be too pleased at my history of the events – I've given him too small a role!"

Lucius barely hears most of this.

"Sir," he says, trying not to sound excited, "what have you said about Caesar in this work?"

Sallust shakes his head. "I have hardly mentioned the Dictator. I used his contribution in the Senate during the debate on the punishment of the conspirators – Caesar made a remarkable speech, you know, and very much in line with his current policy, he recommended clemency. I was not such a fool as to include anything that the Dictator does not wish to be included. I owe a lot to..." His voice trails away as he remembers. For a moment there, as he talks about Caesar's "remarkable speech", he draws himself up, but now he is defeated again by Caesar's infidelity. They wait in silence for Publius Sestius' return. When he comes hurrying back with offers of a couple of slaves to escort Sallust home, Lucius slips out of the study and goes to his own room to think out this new possibility. He remembers his musings of – is it yesterday, or the day before? – it seems a long time ago. "The only things that set Sallust apart were his bitterness and his history of the Catilinarian Conspiracy..." So until he was given proof that Caesar is persecuting Sallust for his temperament, Lucius Sestius is going to try to find out what is so special about a failed conspiracy of twenty years ago.

Chapter Nine

A lot has happened that day, and there is still the dinner to come. Thankfully, that will be no strain – just a family dinner with Caecilius as welcome guest, and Albinia and Marcus Apuleius expected as well. If he knows his sister, she will have read Sallust's manuscript already and have something to add to the mix. There is also every chance that he can get Caecilius on his own for a talk at the end, and he can try out his ideas on him. He rather looks forward to a civilised conversation, tackling the problem as though it were an after-dinner entertainment, and drinking a lot as he does so. He feels almost relieved as he gets ready. Tomorrow, there are lots of things to do, an aim in sight. He makes plans and whistles.

As Lucius crosses the atrium, he sees Mico sitting on a little stool just inside the main door, with a cudgel on the floor beside him, a reminder of reality. Decius is certainly treating his father's warnings seriously. He wonders how the other slaves are taking the idea of this possible threat, and whether they have heard about the fate of Sallust's doorkeeper. There is nothing like the hint of the mines to keep a slave worried. With this tasteless and uncompassionate thought, Lucius waves cheerfully at Mico and goes in to dinner.

As a special treat, Tia is allowed to share a couch with Quintus Caecilius, but her mother Cornelia keeps an eye on them both throughout the meal. Lucius joins Albinia and Apuleius, and they all cheer on Paulus, the youngest of the house-slaves, who is serving at table for the first time. He looks a little nervous, and his plate of eggs only just makes it onto the table. They start with the eggs, as usual, served with fish sauce, and mushrooms and leeks in oil. There is a rather good hare stew to follow, but the real show-stopper is a selection of shellfish in white wine. Tia is complimented on her cooking by Caecilius and has the grace to blush, while her siblings scoff and embarrass her with descriptions of the flap she had got into when she couldn't prise open the mussels. Cornelia reveals that the cook, Melissa, had at last taken pity on Tia and done the shellfish herself. Pomegranates and peaches from Caecilius' estate in Campania round off the meal, and Lucius and his sisters resist the temptation to play the old game of seeing how much pomegranate juice you can surreptitiously flick on your neighbour, while trying to extract the seeds.

Publius Sestius begins telling jokes, which he does very well, despite Cornelia's protestations and supposed embarrassment. When the ladies say goodnight, Tia and Quintus Caecilius exchanging outrageously big-eyed looks, they all know that the dinner has been a success – as indeed, dinners with Caecilius usually are. Albinia and Apuleius announce that they are leaving just as Lucius realises that he has not had a chance to ask Albinia about Sallust's work. But as she hugs him goodnight, Albinia asks him to drop in the next day, adding, "I've read the work, and it is interesting, but I want to talk to you without distractions."

Lucius, aware that he and Quintus Caecilius will be drinking late, and visiting Sallust in the morning, promises to do his best to get to her house before noon.

Back in the dining room, Publius Sestius and Caecilius and Lucius take their places once more, and over some unmixed wine, as he fills up with nuts and figs, Lucius puts forward his new theory.

"I can't think of anything that would spark off these reactions except this history of the Conspiracy that Sallust is writing. We all assumed that Sallust had been writing it just to get Cicero on his side, but I think that we're falling into the family trap again. Do you remember what he said to us when he was here?"

"Who, Sallust?" Sometimes, thinks Lucius, his father is very slow!

"No – Cicero!" Lucius is getting carried away. "He said that he is a has-been and that there is no reason that Sallust should need his help. We said, no, no, you're still important – we couldn't bear to think that he might just be right. And we forgot to check up on the story about Sallust writing this account. Well, he's been thinking about it for years, and started writing it in

Africa. He's been surrounded by people connected with the affair – Sittius was probably on the fringes of the plot, Fadius Gallus was quaestor at the time of the Conspiracy, Caesar got involved in the debate over the fate of the conspirators. Father, you remember that Cicero left a copy of the manuscript here the other night, don't you? Well, Albinia is reading it for me – has read it already and is going to give me her ideas tomorrow."

"You must make sure to get the manuscript back," says Quintus Caecilius. "And maybe put it somewhere very safe. Don't give it back to Sallust."

"No, I'll hang on to it," Lucius says. "But I do wonder how many people know we have that copy... Just Cicero and us."

"And Sallust can probably work out that we have it," points out his father.

"And Sallust. Oh, Father, I have been meaning to ask you this – how important was Caesar at the time of the Conspiracy?"

"He got himself elected Pontifex Maximus round about then, if that's the sort of thing you mean," says his father brightly.

"Right!" says Caecilius enthusiastically. "Even now, if my father hears Caesar officially addressed as High Priest of State Religion, he gets absolutely furious and says it is a disgrace that a nobody who hadn't even held the praetorship should be elected. Especially as there was some aged worthy hanging around who everyone thought should have won."

"Well," says Lucius firmly, trying to get the conversation back on track, "suppose that Sallust is likely to come across something in his researches – something Caesar doesn't want known. That would give us the motive we've been looking for. All that's happened could be a diversion."

"Or a threat," says his father.

Quintus Caecilius isn't convinced. "What could Sallust know that no one else knows about the Conspiracy? Look at everything that's been written and said about it – surely it's safe to assume that everything that could be found out has been found out and broadcast. It's not as if every schoolboy in Rome hasn't read all Cicero's speeches about it."

Catching his eye, Lucius grins at him, and they forget political intrigue for a moment as they strike serious poses and declaim at one another, "How long, O Catilina, how long?"

As he laughs, Lucius suddenly feels very tired. The day has been too long, with too much thinking, and the wine suddenly catches up with him. He decides to just sit and listen for a while.

Publius Sestius and Quintus Caecilius take up the search for What Sallust Knew (But Didn't Know He Knew).

"I think that it's a good point that Sallust might have talked to people like Gallus in Africa," says Caecilius. "But it seems strange if he met Sittius and didn't mention it."

"He didn't say anything about meeting Gallus, and Gallus didn't mention him," says Sestius senior, frowning. "I can ask one of them to confirm, but I think their paths didn't cross. Sittius is different – if I had met up with Publius Sittius, I wouldn't want people to know. But if he had, surely, he would have told us, Lucius, don't you think? Especially after the murder of that poor chap of Rubria's."

"Have you asked Sallust, straight out, to his face?" asks Caecilius. "Try it – it might be interesting. Anyway, we had planned to go around tomorrow morning, remember, Lucius? We could ask then – 'Did you ever actually meet Publius Sittius?' Nice easy question, yes or no answer."

"You two should certainly do that," says Sestius senior. "But it is intriguing to speculate on what it might be that Caesar doesn't want known."

Lucius smiles at the note of glee in his voice.

"So, you do agree that Lucius' theory is the likely explanation for everything that's happened?" asks Caecilius respectfully.

"I think that it is certainly worth investigating. But I can't imagine what could be so disgraceful that our Dictator could not survive it," says Sestius senior with a surprising trace of irony in his voice.

Lucius stares at him, as Caecilius comments, "Yes, it can hardly be sexual. He manages to keep Cleopatra and that infant in Rome without worrying about the gossip, and his past life has certainly been intriguing. Even if he had slept with Catilina himself, that's not going to do anything more than raise a few eyebrows. Cicero might make a speech about it if he felt very brave, but it won't set the Tiber on fire. Caesar's rich, fabulously, and has been since he governed Gaul, but he is also famous for surviving even when he is down to his last few overdrafts. So, it's not sex, and it's not money. What else is there?"

Lucius says slowly, "Whatever still has the power to turn Rome against him."

His father says kindly, "Yes, Lucius, but we can't think of anything that would do that. He is Dictator for the next ten years, and I expect he'll be made Dictator for life soon. He's untouchable."

Lucius thinks of Cicero's beloved Republic. When Gaius Julius Caesar becomes Dictator for life, that Republic will cease to exist, just as Cicero said. Will anyone care?

"I need a walk," he says, and makes an unsuccessful attempt to get up.

"Not now, you don't," says his father, coming around the couch to give him a hand. Walking needs so much concentration that Lucius decides that, for once, his father is right.

They go out into the atrium, and Quintus Caecilius makes his farewells with just a trace of slurred words. He even remembers to say thank you nicely, and Lucius looks after him enviously as he wobbles his way to the door. The stairs to the Caecilius family flat are on the outside of the building and they see him turn outside the door. As they make their way towards Lucius' room, Lucius listens for the scrape of his friend's sandals on the stairs, and when, almost immediately, they hear him yell, it is completely unexpected. His father lets go of Lucius, who loses his balance and falls over ignominiously. Mico, who is still sitting beside the door, leaps up and disappears around the corner, with Sestius senior behind him. Decius comes running from the back of the house, and after a moment of sitting on the floor and gaping, Lucius follows.

The light from the door picks out a confused scene, and he cannot see anyone he recognises. Almost immediately outside the door, three figures sway over a body on the ground, and another group of men struggle a little way distant, exchanging blows and curses. Lucius makes for the first group, and the men separate out into individuals. Mico, with his arms around an unknown man, is trying to drag him away, while the other assailant lifts a club and brings it down on the shape on the ground – Quintus Caecilius? Lucius runs at them, and surprise makes him partially successful; the man with the club gets Lucius' elbow in the face with a horrible crack that makes Lucius' own nose ache in sympathy. He staggers away, and Lucius does not see him again. The other man struggles out of Mico's grasp, stands back for only a moment, then drives a fist into Mico's stomach. Mico goes down on his knees, and the man launches at Lucius. He is holding something – Lucius prays it isn't a sword, but he cannot be sure as he is half-bent over the body, convinced that it is Quintus, crouching over him to protect him, and lashing out at whatever dark shape comes into vision. Shouts come at him from the second group of struggling figures, and part of him notes that Decius and his father are still occupied, but his fight over the body is silent except for the sharp breaths and the thud of blows connecting. One of these catches him on the bone as he raises his arm over his head to protect himself – at least his prayer is answered, and it is only a stick and not a sword. As his wrist explodes with a pain that takes him quite by surprise, he hears himself yell, and his arm whips back, pressing into his body for shelter. Where is Decius? Where is his father? The attacker hesitates, his eyes flicking over him, so Lucius gratefully punches him in the groin with his good hand, and stumbles back. There is a whoosh of air as the attacker gasps and the air suddenly stinks of wine and garlic. Lucius stumbles back a little to keep out of the way - just in case. He looks round and sees his father running towards him while several shapes flit down the street and then disappear.

At this point, Lucius unheroically trips over someone – he doesn't know who, probably Quintus – and the force of hitting the ground goes down his injured arm to the broken wrist. He doesn't quite lose consciousness, but all he is aware of for a few moments is the need to cradle his hand and beg it to stop hurting. When he lifts his head, he finds that he is moving; someone is supporting him, sitting him down in the doorway, back to the wall. Lucius turns his head and seeing the light streaming out from the atrium, he is tempted to drag himself indoors and leave everything else. But the noise of people talking comes from the darkness outside. He turns his head towards the shadows and sees the flickering lights of a couple of lamps moving towards the dark.

Half-lit figures – his father, Mico, and Decius – come into focus, gathered around the heap that is Quintus Caecilius, still on the ground. Lucius knows that it is Quintus, even though he can't remember actually seeing his face during the fight – would he have guarded him so fiercely otherwise? And the people around Quintus would not be so careful in their movements if they were examining one of the attackers. Someone brushes against his arm, and he yelps.

"Sorry, sir!" It is young Paulus who is facing him, squatting down to look at him, his face scared.

"Shall I fetch your mother, sir?" he asks.

"No." It is an effort to speak. He hasn't realised that his mouth is so dry. "Go to my father and do whatever he tells you."

The boy scuttles over, and Sestius senior, seeing him, takes him by the shoulder and says something short and urgent. Paulus nods and scoots off into the darkness. The tableau is only a few yards away; it seems to Lucius as if he were watching a scene from the top seat of the theatre, but it is so hard to follow. He stops trying to listen to what they are saying and closes his eyes. When he opens them, Decius is kneeling at his side, careful not to touch him, but looking closely at him.

"Where does it hurt?" Decius asks, his voice calm, and the bliss of Decius being there means that Lucius can sit back in relief. When he explains about the pain, Decius makes no attempt to look at his wrist, but says, "What about your head?" Lucius doesn't know, so Decius puts one finger to Lucius' chin and turns his head gently, saying, "You have a cut here – how does that feel?" Lucius thinks it might feel sore. Decius helps him to get up and steers him towards the light and warmth of the house's interior. But he cannot walk inside. He turns around and slowly walks over to his father and Mico. Mico looks as dazed as Lucius feels, and there are trails of dark blood running down his face and arms. At a word from Publius Sestius, he limps back to the house. Lucius realises that there is no sign of any of the attackers. He and his father and Decius keep vigil over Quintus' body until the doctor arrives to tell them what they have never doubted. Albinia and Apuleius appear – how did they know? – and their slaves start to move Quintus Caecilius' body into the upstairs flat. The question of Lucius' injuries is raised, and Lucius lets Albinia steer him back to the house. It is only when he is inside that he sees his mother and Tia standing with Cornelia's maid, Phoebe, in a little group on the opposite side of the atrium. They start at the sight of him and Tia says sharply, "What's happened?"

Lucius realises that he is crying and can make no answer. She takes a step forward and says in a stronger voice, "Where's Daddy?"

Cornelia's face goes a terrible, sweaty grey, and Phoebe takes firm hold of her, but Tia comes right up to him and looks straight into his face. He manages to croak, "It's not Father," and holds out his good hand to her. She keeps eyes fixed on him, and takes his hand, holding it very carefully and shaking her head slightly. She says nothing.

While the terrible explanations unfold, she holds on to his good hand, and then through the agonising attentions of the doctor, until he is given a sleeping draught and allowed to go to bed. His father and the slaves look after the body of Quintus Caecilius.

Chapter Ten

The morning after that dinner is not worth remembering.

Lucius awakes (once more a mere crisis has not deprived him of sleep) to find Tia sitting on a stool at his bedside and staring at the wall opposite. The memory of the night before does not come flooding back, jolted maybe by the look on Tia's face, the ache in his head or the pain in his wrist; rather, he awakes with it in his mind and feels that he has dreamt of it all night. He can see Quintus' body in front of him, eyes closed and face calm, but the head is lying awkwardly in a dark pool. The rest of his body, as he remembers the scene, looks all twisted and wrong, his clothes bunched up and his arms and legs sprawled with a gracelessness that he would have deplored. His clothes have got all dirty from the street, Lucius thinks, and he chokes at the thought of the dry comments Quintus would have made. "Did you have to plant your ugly great feet all over me? Look at this – a perfect sandal mark on the front of my tunic – really, Lucius, I shall have to spend ages chatting up our laundress to get this out!"

As Lucius tries to move, he discovers that he is stiff with bruising up and down his arms, and his head swims – whether the result of his injury or the aftermath of whatever it is the doctor gave him, he does not know. But his slight movement has alerted his sister and Tia turns her head towards him; she is very pale and has ugly dark marks in the skin under her eyes, but she manages a smile as she sees that he is awake. He smiles back weakly, feeling awkward and guilty, needing her reassurance and yet embarrassed to be so concerned for himself.

"It's all right," she says at once. "I've been thinking about it all night. I feel so proud of you all – and Mico and Decius were so brave! I shall have to ask Father about what we can do for them. My family really are a great help." This comes out in a rush, and she has to stop to swallow. "But I still am going to need you all so much."

"Of course," Lucius says, unable to think of anything more

profound.

"I must say," says Tia in a very wobbly voice, "having said all that, I don't know what I'm going to do."

They sit in silence together until their mother creeps in and checks that Lucius still has all his wits. She then puts her arms around Tia.

"Darling, will you rest now? Lucius is fine, I promise, and you need to lie down."

"Yes, you must rest," he adds.

"Lucius, Albinia is waiting to see you, so she can sit with you while I see to Tia," says Cornelia.

"All right," Tia and he echo each other dutifully, and Tia allows her mother to lead her away. Lucius lies and looks at the ceiling and thinks back to the day Sallust walked into their home so disdainfully. He shudders to remember his own attitude – impatient, arrogant and uninterested. Now, he feels sick with guilt, for he knows the real target of last night's attack – himself. Whoever their attackers were, they had been told to kill the young man of the household, and Caecilius had been unlucky.

He can hear low voices in the atrium, and Albinia comes in, taking her place on the small stool.

"You are going to need to sleep a lot, I should think," she says after a long careful look at him. She takes his good hand. "Just say if you need me to be quiet, but I'm not leaving."

"All right," he says and manages a smile. "Tell me what is going on, please, Albinia."

His sister goes through everything for him, nice and slowly and with pauses to give him water. There had been four attackers and they had melted away into the darkness once Quintus Caecilius was dead. At least two of the assailants were injured, but not enough to stop them from running. Caecilius' body is in the main room of the upstairs apartment: Caecilius senior had arrived back from his dinner on the Aventine to find that Cornelia and the female slaves of both households had already laid out the body. Visitors have started calling to pay their respects. Tia has stayed up all night watching over him, and their father and mother have watched her. Nobody but Lucius has slept last night.

"Lucius, I don't know what is going on, but I am so worried about you. Is Caecilius a mistake? Was it meant to be you?"

"I think so," he whispers. "But I don't know why! What is going on, Albinia?"

"I don't know," she says miserably. "The street was empty as Apuleius and I left. We've asked our slaves if they saw anyone, but they stayed just outside the door all evening and saw nothing. Either those people must have arrived after we left...." Her voice trails away. She cannot think of a sensible explanation.

"Who sent them though? All we did, all we did is to take on the defence of Sallust. What's so wrong with that? You said last night you had read the manuscript – did you find anything, anything at all?"

Albinia shakes her head. "I can't see anything. Do you want me to tell you about it now, Lucius? Do you need to sleep?"

"No, I can't sleep. I need to talk – or listen, anyway. Just tell me what you think of Sallust's work. Give me an outline. I'm not bothered about its literary value."

His sister pulls a face. "I'm glad about that at least. It isn't my sort of thing at all. Very terse. And some words, I had to look up. Talk about archaic! The account itself, when he gets around to it is pretty good, well-paced, hangs together more or less. Catilina comes over as a monster, though he dies well, almost traditionally Roman at the end. Cicero has a decent role, but during the debate on the Nones of December, when the five conspirators were condemned, the key speeches are given to Caesar and Cato. Father barely gets a mention." She smiles. "Quaestors don't get any glory, do they?"

He tries a smile back. "Cicero gave Father quite a lot of the credit in the speech he made in the trial ten years ago. I have to say, Albinia, it all sounds terribly worthy and not at all dangerous."

"Exactly," his sister agrees. "There are of course some bits which are not yet complete, and Sallust has left some gaps where he is clearly going to check facts, that sort of thing."

"Tell me about the gaps," says Lucius, sleepily. "Where do they appear?"

"Well, there is one just after the beginning, where I think he needs to give a bit of background to Catilina's early career. Let me see – there is one in the middle of a long description of Catilina's followers. And the Battle of Pistoria is only sketched in really. It needs a full description. That's all I can remember now. How's the arm feeling?"

"Painful," he says truthfully, and can't stop a yawn.

Albinia strokes the hair back off his face and says gently, "Sleep. I'll sit here and wait."

When Lucius wakes again, Albinia says a couple of hours have passed, but he has in his sleep formed a plan. He has to leave Rome and the family – it is the only sensible thing to do. He doesn't want to; it seems a form of cowardice. Running away, just when his family need him – except of course, he is the last thing they need. If he leaves, disappears, he will be giving a clear message to their enemies and they might be content to let things lie. His father will very publicly break with Sallust and use Cicero to ensure that the men in power know that the Sestii are neutralised. Lucius knows that he will not be able to help Tia though, and that hurts.

The next part of the plan is to work out where he should go and how he can get there. The obvious person to ask here is Cicero, for though the Great Man loves Rome passionately and has endured much teasing about his attachment to the city, he also owns several villa estates and stop-over houses throughout Italy. One of these will be a good start, though rather obvious: he will then have to move on to somewhere far away, perhaps even outside the Empire? Perhaps, he thinks hastily, that is a bit extreme. He can go to Africa or maybe Greece, where he can take some lessons in fancy oratory from one of those famous teachers of rhetoric. But rhetoric, he discovers, seems unimportant, and he finds himself considering Africa. This whole affair had started there. Perhaps there, if he were very careful, he can go on making enquiries. He marvels at his own persistence and shelves all such thoughts for the time being.

He looks at Albinia to find she is frowning at him. "What were you thinking of just now?" she asks. "You looked pretty grim. What have you decided on? Exile?"

"You're good," he says. There is a silence.

Albinia sighs. "This is going to sound heartless, and it isn't meant to be, but I think you are right. By now, whoever attacked Caecilius is going to know that they didn't get the man intended. They are going to be asking for fresh orders – do they now go after you? If you disappear, it will probably protect the rest of the family as well as yourself. I shall certainly feel a lot happier if I know you are miles away, though I wish..."

She stops. He holds her hand. Nothing is left to be said. He changes the subject.

"How is Mico? What happened to his head?"

Albinia smiles a little. "He is going to be all right, the doctor thinks, but he took a nasty clip to the head from behind, while he was trying to keep one of them off Caecilius. He's been in bed all day and suffering Melissa's ministrations. Father is considering rewarding him and Decius, but we are going to think about it properly when – well, you know..."

"I can't think why we haven't freed Decius before now," says Lucius.

"Father cannot bear the thought of Decius wanting a life outside the family," says Albinia. "I think there's very little risk of that. I'm pretty sure that if we did free them, Decius and Mico would stay on."

"Maybe someone had better ask them," says Lucius, with a huge yawn. Gods! When is he going to stop yawning? Albinia goes off in search of soup, and Lucius' feelings of revulsion at the thought of ever eating again are transformed as she comes in bearing a steaming bowl and he smells onions and lentils.

Later that day, Lucius makes an official recovery to the heart of his family, and despite the misgivings of his mother, gets up. He joins in the task of helping with visitors; Quintus' family have made their formal visit in the shape of his father, Quintus Caecilius senior, who has invited them all to the funeral. Quintus' mother and sister are on the estate near Capua and will be travelling up as quickly as possible, though it is unlikely that the funeral can be put off until they have arrived. At that point, Caecilius senior has to go back to the flat upstairs with his slave supporting him.

Lucius knows that he cannot wait until after the funeral; he has to leave as soon as possible, that night. A broken wrist won't stop him walking.

His father, it appears, has also been thinking, and without talking with him first, has called a family conference. This is a very serious business in their household – the last occasion was when Quintus Caecilius asked to marry Tia, and Publius Sestius and Cornelia had decided to let them all in on their discussion. Easy to be so democratic, when they were all in favour of Quintus. Now as the hour for dinner approaches, Sestius senior stations Decius at the front door and puts Paulus on watch in the alleys at the side and back of the house and takes his family into his study. The single high window is narrow and shuttered in mourning. The slaves will make sure that no one loiters underneath in the alley. The Sestius family, very scared and quiet, gather together, all squashed onto the couch except for their paterfamilias who sits at his desk.

"My dears," says Publius Sestius, and he takes control. Lucius and Albinia watch appreciatively. They are, their father explains, under a form of siege. It is true that for a long time Rome had suffered from a casual brutality on the part of some of her citizens, and these men seemed to unleash their violence all too easily; the worst may not be over. The people who killed Quintus Caecilius were almost certainly not chance muggers, and the Sestii have to face the probability that the intended target had not been attacked. As Lucius listens to his own reasoning explained in Publius' careful way, he seems to see himself, thirty years older, a little fussy, too fond of chatter sometimes; he wonders if people will love him too.

"The case that Lucius and I are tackling is at a delicate stage," his father is saying. "We have just reached the unfortunate conclusion that our client has displeased the Dictator and is suffering the consequences. I don't think it is any coincidence that on two occasions over the past four days extreme violence has caught up with those involved in the case. We must now decide how we may defend ourselves."

Tia wipes away a tear and presses closer to Cornelia, her eyes staring. Lucius feels that he can't bear the thought of her fear. As he watches, Cornelia strokes Tia's hair and looks up at him. She knows all too well that to the faceless men behind Caecilius' murder, she and Tia seem a weakness in the Sestius family defences. Lucius feels himself drawing apart from his family, in preparation, but Albinia's arm goes around him and keeps him close.

"Now, as Lucius and I are the ones involved with this case, and the case is what is attracting the attention, we must distance ourselves from it," continues his father. "Then we will be no threat to these people, whoever they may be. We shall show clearly that we have no wish to be further associated with Sallust's case and they will leave us alone – to mourn."

"Is Sallust in danger?" asks Albania. "Or rather, why isn't Sallust in danger? Father, you have just said that Sallust has upset Caesar and we are suffering the consequences. And I don't see why. What is it about us that makes us a target, while he is left alone?"

"Maybe he hasn't upset the Dictator that much," says Lucius. His father sighs.

"I think that it may come down to the fact that we are not Caesarian supporters as Sallust is. Maybe we are expendable and Sallust is not. And, yes, I know that is not a very satisfactory explanation, but we clearly don't know the whole story. So, we back out of the whole thing, and quickly."

"Albinia and I have had an idea," Lucius says. The effect of all those eyes turning towards him make him feel even more lonely.

"While Father stays here and publicly drops the case, I shall draw their attention away from Rome. If I leave and go somewhere far away, it will reassure them – they will know that we are taking them seriously and not fighting back. And... anyway it will be better for all of us."

The opposition is unexpected.

"You mean," Tia says angrily, "that if they are still suspicious of us, they'll presume that you are the one with any dangerous knowledge – whatever it may be. I wish we could work that out, Lucius! Anyway, then they'll pursue you! Very noble, dear brother, but losing you won't help."

There is a short silence, then Albinia speaks. "I don't want you to go either, Lucius, but I think you are right. He is, Tia. He is the focus at the moment and he has to deflect attention."

"He mustn't go," says Tia. Her voice is calmer. She is trying a different tactic. "He wants to get himself killed in some idiotic belief that it will make up for Quintus Caecilius. Lucius – you should know that you don't have to feel guilty about him. You tried to save him – if that didn't work, it isn't your fault."

He tries to explain. "If I stay, all their concentration will be on us, on this house, no matter how much we try to convince them that we're harmless. Please, Tia, I know it looks like I'm running away..."

She explodes. She jumps up, ignoring the hands stretched out towards her, and shouts at him.

"Don't you listen to anyone? I said that you don't have to feel guilty – so don't call it running away! And try listening to yourself sometime – you don't know what is happening or why and yet you still want to leave us! You talk about running away – but you don't know who is chasing you, so how will you succeed? And how will we ever find out if they do get you, and you are killed in the middle of nowhere, in a place you haven't told us because you are so busy trying to protect us? We won't even be able to bury you!"

As she screams at him, she begins to cry, and the sobs and anger between them shake her so much that she can hardly stand. Cornelia catches her and wraps her arms around her as Tia cries and cries into her shoulder and the rest of the family sit in miserable silence. For a long time, the only sounds are the strange staccato crying and the whispered hushing as Cornelia rocks Tia like a baby. At last, she seems drained and quiet and Cornelia, without a word, half-carries her from the room. Albinia watches them go, then gives Lucius a hug.

"I don't think they'll catch you, Lucius," she says. "There will be no need if they understand the message we are sending. Father, you do agree, don't you?"

Before Publius Sestius can speak, an apologetic Decius enters to whisper the presence of Sextus Cornelius Rufus. For some reason, it does not occur to any of them to wonder what

94

he is doing here, he seems so tied up with the past few days and their horrors.

"Oh yes, we shall receive Rufus," says his father. "He has been of great help to us, and we must let him know what we decide and why."

Cornelius Rufus enters wearing a plain tunic and freshly laundered toga – the uniform of a Roman citizen on parade. As he and Publius Sestius exchange dignified and sincere greetings, Lucius suddenly feels very touched. Even old Cornelius, dismissed by him as a Subura rat with whiskers twitching as he senses morsels of gossip, is, in a time of crisis, a more noble creature. Albinia takes over as hostess in the absence of Cornelia, asks Decius to bring some fruit and wine and graciously serves them to their guest.

"Now, gentlemen, Albinia," begins Publius Sestius, "Let's review the situation. Sallust is supported by Caesar and gets the governorship of the New Africa province. When he returns, there are rumours of a prosecution, so he tries to find out the source of these rumours. Cornelius Rufus, recognising the notorious Publius Sittius, and connecting him with the sudden hostility towards Sallust, finds that his colleague is killed. Sallust himself is burgled, and books and papers are stolen from his study. Meanwhile, the lawyers on Sallust's side continue their work and suffer an attack outside their home. Normally misbehaviour by a governor in his province does not lead to such violence in Rome so the matter must be of far more importance than might be supposed. Sittius' presence leads us to suppose that there is a link with Africa and Sallust's governorship. When we realised that Sittius was taking the road which leads to Caesar's estate, this, combined with evidence of a link forged between him and Caesar in Africa, indicate that our Dictator is involved." He sighs. "And since Caesar is rarely merely 'involved', let us go one step further and admit that we think he is the figure behind all this. Cornelius Rufus, I am sure that you can see why we are withdrawing from the case. Sallust, I am afraid, is lost."

"Maybe," says Cornelius Rufus, frowning. "But I still need to tell Rubria why that poor sod..." he suddenly coughs,

"...pardon me, Gaius died – and you'll want to know about your friend as well. What is it about this Sallust that makes it so dangerous to be his friend?"

"He is writing a history of the Catilinarian Conspiracy," says Albinia. "He started it in Africa and Lucius and I think that he showed it to Sittius or told him about it or something. Sittius has always been suspected of being involved in the planning of the Conspiracy – perhaps Sallust thought that he could be a useful source. And we think that Sittius got alarmed and told Caesar, who also got alarmed."

They all look at Lucius.

"I have no proof," he says. "But I'm going to Africa Nova, so I might find out something. Albinia, you have to hide that manuscript of Sallust's account of the conspiracy – where?"

She looks at their father. "Don't worry. We've hidden it already. Just in case."

"Now – practicalities," says Publius Sestius. He will arrange to go down to his banker near the Forum with Decius in the morning and they will withdraw money for the journey.

"So you can't leave immediately," says Albinia. "You can stay at my house for a few days, while we make some arrangements. Father and Apuleius will get you the money you need immediately, and we shall use the governor's house in Old Africa for sending and picking up mail and luggage, if you have to leave anything we think might be useful."

"Isn't this all going to be pretty obvious to everyone?" asks Lucius, feeling a little uncomfortable at the thought that someone out there wants to know his plans as much as he does himself.

Albinia smiles. "I hope so. We don't have the resources to get you out of reach of Caesar, so what we are doing is signalling defeat and retreat – loud and clear. I have no doubt they will realise that you are still in Rome but they will also watch us all and figure out that you are leaving and going a long way away."

His father and Albinia are the only people who know of his final destination; Cornelia does not argue. As darkness falls, Lucius slips into Tia's room, and says goodbye, and promises to be back. She smiles and says that of course he will. He can't see her face clearly.

When he leaves her room, Cornelius Rufus is waiting for him in the atrium. It seems that Africa is an unmissable business opportunity, and so Lucius will have a companion on the journey.

Chapter Eleven

As soon as Lucius gives the signal, Albinia leaves in a litter for her home, accompanied by her maid, four litter-carriers and a couple of torch-bearers. They make quite a procession, so Lucius, Decius and Cornelius Rufus hope that they will not be seen as they themselves leave by the back door and make their way to Albinia's house by narrow streets and alleys. They arrive undramatically safely and Cornelius Rufus and Decius stroll away with careful carelessness, leaving Lucius to vanish into his sister's house. There he spends a couple of days very quietly, keeping his injured wrist still, lying down whenever his head aches, and exchanging notes with his father. He sees copies of the letters his father sends to Sallust and Cicero explaining the Sestius family's decision to withdraw from the case. Officially, Caecilius was murdered in a street brawl, and with no culprits taken or witnesses who can identify them, the matter will be left at that. The letters also mention that he, Lucius, is "going away", and his father manages to imply that he is seeking an extension of his education. Along with these copies, comes a letter of condolence on the death of Quintus Caecilius. It is from Cicero and is a small masterpiece, of course. Albinia reads parts of Sallust's work to Lucius, and he tries to listen to it as an entertainment, rather than worry at it to work out a hidden message. It has some merit, he has to admit – he enjoys the description of the capture of incriminating letters at the Mulvian Bridge, and the pitifully botched attempt on Cicero's life. He has to keep reminding himself that this was all real, but the few mentions of their father, rather than inspiring awe or pride, make both of them giggle. They still cannot believe that their father could possibly be involved in something as important as suppressing a rebellion.

Lucius has one person left to see, and on his last evening in Rome he is collected by young Quintus Cicero and the two make their way to the Palatine Hill once again. From Albinia's house, it is a straightforward journey, though they have to cut right across the Forum, and Lucius makes sure that he keeps his head down. Quintus, thank all the gods, keeps his counsel and a quick pace, and Lucius strides along, resisting the temptation to look behind him. He knows that all he will see are Albinia's two biggest litter-slaves, ten paces behind, watching his back.

At the door of the house on the Palatine, Lucius leaves the slaves watching the street and steps into the little atrium to find Tiro ready to take them to the study. Once more Lucius wanders along the bookshelves, automatically pushing scrolls in to their cubbyholes and making sure that the seals are outside and hanging straight, while Tiro vanishes to lever Cicero out of his dinner party. Quintus takes a seat and watches Lucius with no expression on his face. At the sound of footsteps Lucius looks up to see not only Cicero but Sallust as well. That is useful.

"My dear Lucius," exclaims Cicero as soon as he sees him, "I've heard the news, as you know. I really am very sorry, especially for your sister. Cornelia told me that there was real affection between her and young Caecilius. And you were injured as well! How are you?"

Lucius can confirm that his head seems to have suffered no lasting damage and the wrist, while painful, is fine as long as he keeps it tightly bandaged and still. He cannot talk about Caecilius, but it is good that Cicero and Sallust seem to understand the loss.

"An outstandingly good-natured young man, he struck me," adds Sallust, sounding very awkward. "He was a special friend to you as well – your whole family, and his of course, have suffered greatly." He obviously finds all this very difficult to say. Normally, Romans are rather good at expressing grief – the condolence letter is a set-piece in school, but Sallust is, touchingly, struggling to say the right things. The two men look really worried, and the lines on their faces seem dark and deep, but that of course is the effect of the lamp-light. So many people affected by Caecilius' death! And yet, if Lucius and his father and Albinia are right, it is just a horrible mistake. It is no good trying to tell these two that the murder is merely one of the many squalid acts of violence that are a daily feature of city life – he knows that Cicero is a highly-trained connoisseur of intrigue and deceit and from what Albinia has read to him, so is Sallust.

"It was supposed to be me, I'm sure of it." He had meant to

lead up to this, but, all finesse gone, the words tumble out and he sounds whiny. Cursing, he takes a deep breath and starts again, outlining the circumstances of Caecilius' death and telling them of his decision, without revealing his final destination. He does hesitate over whether to reveal their theory about Sallust's book, but decides that he has to warn him.

"My advice as your ex-lawyer," now his tone is ironic – and completely inappropriate; he sees their eyes widen, "is to stop writing that book and to make sure that people know that you are not intending to publish it anymore. I don't know what you can have said, or what they think you can have said, but I'm sure it has sparked this whole thing into life." And Caecilius into death? The metaphor is all wrong.

Sallust does not exclaim or protest, to Lucius' relief; instead he nods at him, and says, "That seems reasonable. "It is only much later that Lucius wonders about this unquestioning capitulation.

Cicero then launches into an enquiry about the practicalities of flight. As Lucius had hoped, Cicero offers him the hospitality of his villas – the ones at Antium and around the Bay of Naples would be the best – and gives him letters of introduction. One is to an old friend of Cicero, who has lived on the island of Rhodes ever since the two of them studied there, way back when Sulla was Dictator. Lucius notes the assumption that he is going to Rhodes but decides to say nothing of his intended destination as it is a decision too new for comfort, and he does not feel able to defend it yet. Another letter is more general: "To whom it may concern..." Lucius thinks this one will be of more use. A letter signed by Cicero will impress the staff and governors of most provinces, and this helps keep his options open. He thanks him and makes his farewells. Outside the front door, he finds that Quintus Cicero has once more fallen into step with him, and he is glad of the undemanding company.

They walk out of the Forum together then turn left towards Albinia's house, and her slaves unobtrusively fall in behind them. Just where he would have carried straight on for the Caelian Hill and home, Lucius stops. Suddenly, it is all too much. He can't go home, and a weight suddenly descends onto his shoulders and the tears well up. The idea of crying in front of Quintus Cicero is shameful, but fortunately Quintus seems to think so too, for he takes Lucius' arm and drags him into the nearest wine shop. Lucius is sat down, rather roughly, he thinks resentfully, in a dark corner, and a jug of wine with two cups materialises. Determined to wallow, he lets Quintus Cicero pour the wine and only moves to take the cup thrust in his face. With an effort, he tries to think ahead. In his mind, he has kept the panic at bay up until now by thinking of the details of the journey ahead of them, and he begins to go through this again. Thanks to Caesar and his campaigns, Lucius knows how to get an army, with cavalry, to Africa, but the journey seems much more difficult for private individuals. Still, at least he knows some landmarks, and the first stages are relatively straightforward. Talking it over with Albinia and Apuleius, he has decided that he and Cornelius Rufus are going to make first for Cicero's house at Antium. This will be just a day's journey from Rome, and he can use it to see how his wrist copes with riding. Then they can follow the coast down to the Bay of Naples, maybe even sail part of the way if they find a boat. Cicero has properties in the area where he can stay, and there they can find out about crossing to Africa from Puteoli. He goes over all this in his head and the tears retire. Quintus Cicero echoes his thoughts.

"The hard bit's over now," he says. "Because you've made a decision. All we have to do is make sure that decision is carried out. Now – where are you going?"

"We've got to leave by the Appian Way," Lucius likes the way his voice sounds so confident. "Then we turn off to Antium. I did think about heading off towards Ostia, getting a ship there, but it seems too obvious. I don't want to be too predictable, and we have to take some time, so that Cicero and Father get a chance to spread the news. So, I thought Antium first, then down to Pompeii, and after a few days there double back up the coast to Puteoli. We can use a couple of houses your uncle owns."

Quintus stares at the table, and draws a little map in spilt wine, then nods. Lucius feels comforted at his support. But he still does not mention that he is going to Africa, not Rhodes. Quintus looks around and says, "Got to drink that wine up – I'm not going to let you get away with just swirling it round and pulling faces at it."

"What about horses?" Lucius asks, suddenly flustered again. "I haven't arranged for horses, and I don't think we should use the place we usually go to. Do we have to walk?"

Quintus laughs. "Walk? Not likely! Don't worry, your father and that informer you use, Cornelius – they've got it all organised. I've agreed to take you to the meeting place and you'll pick up the horses there. Come on, we'll go back to your sister's. You need to get your stuff."

"My father and Cornelius Rufus?"

"Yes, while you were at your sister's, they sorted out some details together, and my uncle asked me to do the ferrying around. So – how many times do I have to tell you? Drink up!"

Quintus Cicero watches Lucius as he obediently drains the cup and thinks that he will probably do fine in the end. Then he asks if he is better now and, without waiting for an answer, whisks him out of the wine shop and along the street. Albinia's two bodyguards fall in behind them and the short journey is uneventful. Quintus Cicero melts back into the night as Albinia's door opens, with a quiet, "As quick as you can. I'll wait here."

There is only time for the briefest of goodbyes with Albinia, then he slips back out the door and he and his escort strike out for the Sacred Way. They turn left and pass the road going up towards the Caelian Hill and home, and Lucius stops for just a few seconds, gazing at the street sloping up the hill, past the little suite of baths that Caecilius and he had used. But he doesn't linger, and he and Quintus Cicero turn for the Capena Gate. Like the unfortunate, anonymous dock-worker, who was killed, they are heading south down the Appian Way. As they leave the city walls behind, carts coming towards the city fill the road, and the tombs on either side fade into the darkness. He thinks of faceless men lying in wait in the shadows and walks closer to his companion.

After a mile or so, Quintus dives off the road and into

darkness. Thinking that the wine has caught up with his bladder, Lucius politely turns away and scans the road both ways, but a shout calls him over. Off the road is a group of unremarkable buildings and an open door pours out friendly yellow light. He walks over and sees inside a stable which contains two horses and a cheerful boy of about thirteen, and to his unexpected relief, Cornelius Rufus. Lucius suddenly feels very tired and stumbles as he walks over the threshold. A bad omen, he thinks.

"Are you feeling all right, sir?" asks the boy.

Without waiting for an answer, Quintus turns to Cornelius Rufus. "He's dead on his feet – do you have to set off now? Why don't you have a sleep here? Go at dawn and you'll be able to travel faster as well, in the light."

"I know what happens at dawn," Lucius says crossly. Cornelius and Quintus look at him, and as though they have had a detailed conversation, take him over to a heap of straw. One cloak under and one on top, and he is in bed and so ready to sleep his eyes ache. But Quintus hasn't finished.

"I have to go now," he says and hunkers down next to Lucius, who wonders if Quintus is going to tuck him in. Quintus checks that Cornelius Rufus and the boy are a few feet away and haggling over the price of a night's lodgings and some food in this sumptuous setting. Quintus turns back to Lucius and speaks very softly.

"If you come back to Italy, let me or my cousin Marcus know. Remember that my uncle is not that dependable – I know he has given you help, but he gets scared and he can't take threats. He will let you down in a crisis. He's done that to his family before now. Anyway – I hope it goes well. Travel safely."

And he is off, clapping Cornelius Rufus on the back as he goes, filling the door for a moment, then gone. Lucius does not even have time to go over what Quintus has just said. He is asleep before Cornelius Rufus and the stable lad have a chance to finish the bargain and get onto gossiping about him.

It is raining hard when he wakes, and Cornelius Rufus is in a good mood.

"We're safe in this, lad," he says, adding hurriedly, "Not that

I think we're going to be pursued hotfoot or anything, but if anyone is worried enough to, say, send someone after us, they'd find it hard going. Enough to put them off for a bit."

None of this makes sense to Lucius as he struggles to get out of his nest of straw, and Cornelius Rufus has to pull him up. He remembers his sense of helplessness the night before, and blushes at the thought of Cornelius Rufus and Quintus having to put him to bed. At least he didn't get a bedtime story, he thinks, then remembers Quintus' words. He shivers. He hadn't realised how deeply the rift in the Cicero family had gone.

The two horses and their young guardian are still cheerful, despite the rain. The boy provides bread and water for a quick breakfast and passes to Cornelius a package containing a rabbit pie. Lucius is surprised at such service and grabs Cornelius as he merrily loads bundles onto the horses.

"No, you don't have worry about a thing," he says easily. As Lucius opens his mouth to object, he says more seriously, "We've paid them well, and if they still think we owe them a favour, they'll ask for it later, don't you worry. My cousin owns the stables, and he knows that I sometimes need a quick and quiet exit."

It occurs to Lucius that a Subura rat does not usually have the means or the time to take up horse-riding. Cornelius' relatives are coming in useful.

The ride to Antium is ghastly. They have to turn off the Appian Way, and the road is not nearly as good. They can't go very fast in the rain and mud in the morning, and although it clears up later in the day, Lucius begins to worry that they will never make it to Antium before the darkness falls. While his head is fine, his wrist has started aching. He uses it as little as he can, but jolting is unavoidable. After a while, he tucks his lower arm through his belt to help keep it steady. Cornelius Rufus starts to worry about him and comes up with a distraction by asking about the journeys made by the Sestius family to the coast or Capua, when Lucius was a child.

"Your father told me it took days to get you all down the coast when your family went on holiday. How many carts did you have to take?"

This is a good distraction, for Lucius remembers those journeys well, and starts to tell Cornelius Rufus about them. He particularly remembers one summer visit to the Bay of Naples with Cicero and his family, a year or two after Cicero's return from exile, both families travelling in one untidy procession down the leg of Italy. The fuss and packing were incredible, the number of people and carts seemed vast and the journey to Bovillae alone took two days because of all the stops necessary to allow overexcited Romans to water the vegetation. Someone, he remembered, had been sick all the time – now, who was it? He rather thinks it had been Cicero's son Marcus. But the present journey can hardly compare with those holiday outings, when it was summer and dry and hot. Cornelius Rufus keeps prompting the anecdotes as long as he can, but the road stretches out ahead of them in the rain, and it seems very unfair that it should take so long. Lucius sinks into a worse and worse mood as he tramps the poor horse through the mud; it turns out that he is riding an equestrian comic, but playful attempts by the animal to bite Cornelius' horse or snap at raindrops fail to amuse. After a while, Cornelius Rufus wisely keeps ahead and leaves him alone.

And so, the countryside south of the city rolls past, grey and brown in the rain, while Lucius hates everything, and even the horse gives up. As evening falls, Cornelius' patience runs out. He has just drawn level with Lucius to consult over whether they should find somewhere to stay or plod on through the night, and Lucius has helped the decision-making process by grunting.

"Right," says Cornelius Rufus. "You've had a day to moan to yourself and that's enough for anyone. Now you're going to start thinking again, lawyer. I know that you can't do anything, but I would still like to know just what exactly is going on to force us out of Rome – don't you care anymore? Your sister's got to get through her man's funeral – are you going to sit there and let everyone know that you're miserable, or are you going to work out who killed him and why? "Lucius scowls at him and he laughs. "Think about it, lad! Now what are we going to do tonight?"

Lucius makes himself respond. "I don't want to go to an inn.

I don't know if we can really expect to be followed – perhaps I'm a bit too worried there. But I'd rather not make it too easy if they are checking up on me."

"Just what I said last night," says Cornelius approvingly. "Nice to know you listen to me, lad."

"Yes, well," he mumbles, not knowing how to cope with this avuncular, familiar Cornelius. When had he become a "lad"? "Er – well, presuming that you're as eager to carry on riding as me, where shall we sleep then?"

"Too wet for outdoors," says Cornelius. It had not occurred to Lucius that staying outdoors was an option. "We'll find a barn – there's a few villas out this way."

"We can't just walk up to someone's country estate and ask for their barn for the night," Lucius objects, wondering if anyone he knows has a villa in these parts. Maybe if you went to school with the owner it is all right to doss down in their barn.

"Course we can," says Cornelius. "We find the manager and ask him. No problem."

Lucius can't believe that any responsible farm manager is going to give barn room to a couple of strangers like him and Cornelius, but he is mistaken. They don't even have to think up a story to account for themselves. The overseer of the first small farm at which they present themselves recognises the horses, asks after Cornelius' cousin, and happily pockets the modest bribe – sorry, payment! – offered. A barn is there just as Cornelius has said, and they even join the overseer and his family for dinner. Lucius is introduced with no ceremony as "my young friend", and no further explanation seems necessary or is expected. Large-eyed children gaze speechlessly at them through the meal, then all fall asleep immediately they have finished. Lucius is impressed at this example of how to rule your household and tries to see how the man does it, but apart from giving his wife's bottom a fond squeeze as she leaves to put the children to bed, there doesn't seem to be any special trick. As Cornelius Rufus and he walk to their barn, he acknowledges that his fellow traveller has been absolutely right, and Cornelius Rufus graciously winks and says that if Lucius is good he'll give him a few tips. Lucius' mind boggles and he says goodnight very quickly.

As he lies there waiting to sleep, he thinks of what Cornelius said to him towards the end of the day's journey – Lucius has barely thought of Caecilius or his family all day, so busy was he enjoying a destructive misery. And it is interesting that Cornelius wants to find out more. Lucius still has to work out what he is going to do about that. He risks so much – his family are hostages to good behaviour in Rome, while he has deliberately chosen to go to Africa for his self-imposed exile. And yet, he knows that, despite everything, he has decided on Africa because he is hoping to find some answers. Just how much of a risk is he taking? And with that, he falls asleep.

He dreams that night of Caecilius, who is running up the Caelian Hill, shouting out Lucius' name and grinning at him when Lucius turns to meet him. He says that they have to go to the baths to look for Tia. "We can't," Lucius says. "You're dead." Caecilius laughs and slaps his shoulder. "No, I'm not – didn't they tell you?" he asks. "They made a mistake – you're the one who's dead, so we must get to the baths." And he takes Lucius' hand and turns him around to face a man who has a stone in his hand and is about to bring it down on Lucius' head. As he ducks and cries out, he wakes up, to find that Cornelius Rufus has one arm around him, and is saying, "Come on now, lad – that's right. That's right." He fetches some wine, and Lucius drinks it neat, concentrating on the quiet shapes of the horses in front of him. He finds that even in the dark, he can work out which horse is which, though he can't tell how he knows. Puzzling over this strange ability, he falls asleep again.

On the next day, they reach Cicero's house at Antium and the first leg of the journey is over. Relieved at having come this far, and without wanting to spoil things by thinking of the many miles to Africa, Lucius sleeps and sleeps, waking only to eat and have a bath. There are only a few slaves, but as he would expect from Cicero's household, they are efficient and discreet. Every time he wakes there is someone sitting in the room, and he is grateful to Cornelius for making sure that he is never on his own. He does not think about the Sallust affair again, having no taste for the nightmares it inspires.

Chapter Twelve

Needless to say, no one follows them to Antium or later as they travel to Pompeii – or no one seems to anyway. Cornelius Rufus says that it just shows how closely the Sestii have predicted the situation, and that he for one is quite relieved at the thought that he might get to Africa in one piece.

"You see," he explains, "we've done all the right things – got the wind up good and proper, gone into hiding, scuttled off in a panic. Sure, they'll have tracked you to your sister's easy, and probably made sure we left Rome, but the point is, we look scared and sorry. It's good for their ego; now they're feeling all big and bad and effective. They probably quite like us."

Lucius looks at him and risks the awkward question. "They?"

Cornelius Rufus does not look at him as he answers, "Publius Sittius and the Dictator. I don't think we need to be shy of saying that anymore. I just hope your friend Sallust has done his part and convinced them."

The weather is beautiful as they travel down coast roads to the Bay of Naples, and after a day or so of looking fearfully at every traveller they meet, no matter the direction of travel, Lucius gradually lets the rhythm of the horses' pace soothe him. He finds that large chunks of time can go by without remembering Caecilius or Sallust: the trick is to get his mind engrossed in something else and then let it wander. Here Cornelius Rufus helps, as he begins working on educating Lucius, starting with Subura slang; Lucius thinks that he will never again be able to look at a certain type of small pot without thinking of Cornelius Rufus. It is all very interesting, though of no use whatsoever as he can never repeat it to anyone.

They stay at Cicero's villa at Pompeii for some days, enjoying the sunshine of an early autumn, as the month changes to October and the countryside is still green with vines and olive trees. On the eighth day after their departure from Rome, letters from home arrive, carried by Mico and a slave of Cicero, a man who knows the journey to the villa well. They have taken care not to set off together and have had no trouble on the road. Publius Sestius' letter seems to explain that:

My dear Lucius,

Your mother and sisters and I are well and send our love. Please don't worry about us. As you will read in this letter, we think we are safe.

The situation regarding your departure is as follows: on the morning after you left, Cicero sent a letter to Caesar, thanking him for the visit to Latinum, and giving him all the Forum news. He mentioned the dreadful business of Caecilius' death, and your abrupt flight, among all the other items of interest. A very prompt reply came from the Dictator, mainly discussing his plans for yet another triumphal celebration coming up, but he also casually remarked on the news about us. He said that young men were forever getting into trouble and hinted that you had something to do with Caecilius' murder yourself. He added that you had no doubt done the sensible thing in leaving, though he is sorry to think that a promising career had been wrecked.

Naturally, we were all very annoyed at the tone of this, and there is more than a hint that you had better keep well away from Rome, but Cicero believes that it means that our attempts to distance ourselves from this Sallust business have succeeded. He says that the Dictator would not have bothered to mention you at all if he did not have this personal message: as long as you stay away for some time, all will be well. Interestingly, Caesar has also invited Sallust to dinner since you left but has made it clear that he will not be assisting in the court case – which is just as well considering our current theory that he instigated the whole sorry affair! Sallust in turn made it clear that he is no longer writing his history of the Catilina Conspiracy, and that, we are sure, has got Caesar's attention. We are not fully clear of the woods though, because Sallust has made discreet enquiries with the praetor, and discovered that the case has now been formally lodged with the authorities. What we both find very interesting is that no one has declared that they will be conducting the prosecution, and normally I would be amazed that the praetor allowed the case forward at all.

Sallust and a young relative (a very obscure connection of his mother) will take on the defence, but it is generally agreed that he hasn't much of a chance, and some are advising that he quietly slip away into exile now, while he is able to save his wealth. So, it appears that Caesar is not going to let Sallust off the hook, not yet, and maybe not at all.

Decius has asked me, in the most proper and unassuming manner to convey his regards. The slaves have been very good, I must say. I have rewarded them all, and I still fully intend to free Decius formally, but not at the moment. I haven't said anything to him, but I'm sure he understands.

Take care of yourself.

Lucius does not fail to notice the Dictator's threat – prosecution for Caecilius' murder if he returns. For the first time since leaving Rome, he feels angry. What sort of man kills your best friend, then coolly announces his intention of making sure that you get the blame? What sort of friends does the beloved Dictator have, that his own views on friendship are so cynical? But he makes himself calm down; it gives him a small measure of satisfaction that he has not allowed himself to be provoked into cursing and shouting and stamping. Also enclosed are notes from his mother and sisters, all determinedly cheerful, and with instructions to look after himself. Albinia says that he must look after Cornelius Rufus as well, which makes Lucius snort. Tia adds:

Yes, do take care of Cornelius Rufus – anyone who volunteers to travel with you deserves high consideration. Do you remember the journey to Cicero's when we were little, and you had to run off to be sick every two minutes?

Of course, Lucius is very pleased that Tia is making jokes and is coping with the death of Caecilius so well, but he is a bit annoyed that she has chosen to remember the same journey as he has, with the detail he had forgotten.

His mother writes with news that so far the family have carefully kept from him: Quintus Caecilius' funeral was held two days after the murder. Lucius works out that he would have still been in Rome, at Albinia's, and already too far away. It had been very grand for such a young man, but Quintus Caecilius senior had decided to spare no expense. Cornelia had stayed at home with the girls, on the grounds that Caecilius' sister and mother would not be there.

I am actually quite relieved that this is how things turned out as regards the funeral. It would have been terribly upsetting for Tia. As it was, she slept at home with me in her room in case she should wake up. I admit that I made her drink some of that sleeping draught the doctor gave you. The only thing I regret is that Caecilius' mother and sister could not reach the city in time – we really couldn't wait any longer. The poor boy went to his funeral with no womenfolk to lament him, apart from some family slaves, and the mourners we hired. His father and yours were the family, which seems sad. The plan now is to take his ashes back to Capua and I think this is best. I don't want Tia spending her life at the side of a tomb, and she'll be able to get over it much more quickly with no reminder of Caecilius nearby. I hope, dear Lucius, I don't sound too hard, but we cannot help the poor boy now, and our lovely Tia is my concern.

Lucius has always respected Cornelia's judgement, and he thinks she is right in this case. He notes that it seems that life can go on perfectly well back on the Caelian Hill without his presence.

After four very comfortable days being pampered by Cicero's devoted and highly-trained entourage at Pompeii, they decide that they must leave. Lucius is not entirely reluctant. Cornelius Rufus has regaled the household with tales of the wicked city, and in return the housekeeper has remembered some of Lucius' more embarrassing youthful exploits. Cornelius Rufus is therefore able to annoy him over the next few weeks by suddenly saying, "Blackberries!" and chortling to himself. The story isn't even that funny, and it isn't as though blackberry juice leaves much of a mark.

They make a leisurely journey as they follow the coast back up to Puteoli. The weather is still mild and warm, and the sun spreads a fine golden net over the hills and cliffs of the coast. Even if you hadn't known though, you would have guessed that it is the light of autumn. It has none of the newness and energy of spring; in his regret at leaving Rome and Italy, it seems fitting to Lucius that even the sunshine is tinged with the anxiety of knowing that there is not much time left. With such fanciful thoughts, Lucius pictures himself, a smart-arsed Forum brat, with Cornelius his Subura rat in tow, as they ride along between the perfect sea and the grey bulk of Mount Vesuvius and come to Puteoli.

As this is one of the main ports of Italy, they hope that it is big enough to get lost in, though by now they are convinced that their travels are of little interest to anyone in Rome apart from their loved ones. They arrive at evening as the sun sets between a sea of amber and a sky one shade lighter. The hills around the bay seemed to grow into the dusk, and the lights of the town are harsh and unnatural.

As they go through the town, the roads slope down until they reach the harbour. Conversely, the inns get more respectable and a little quieter than those catering directly to the ships' crews as Lucius and Cornelius retrace their steps away from the harbour. They choose the largest inn they can find and are rewarded by finding that it serves a magnificent local wine. Such a discovery demands celebration, and they treat themselves to a good meal with ample quantities of the wine. Feeling as relaxed as he can remember since Caecilius' death, Lucius makes jovial remarks about Cornelius' snoring and is rather surprised to learn that he himself had snored like a donkey during the night they had spent in the stables on the Appian Way.

"How do you know what a donkey snoring sounds like?" Lucius asks, determined to cross-examine this hostile witness, and not realising that he is a little too drunk to understand any answer he might be given.

"Lad," says Cornelius Rufus, "I know what a donkey's snore sounds like 'cause I've heard you – right?"

Lucius acknowledges himself defeated by this logic and allows Cornelius Rufus to help him upstairs. He tells him that he (Cornelius Rufus) is like a father to him. Cornelius Rufus says he doubts it. Lucius cries.

In the morning, Lucius does actually awake as Cornelius

Rufus is getting dressed but feels so terrible that he shams sleep. He lies in misery hoping that Cornelius Rufus will get lots of important matters organised for him so that he won't have to think too hard that day. He feels no qualms about using Cornelius in this way, for he has already proved that he is by far the better at arranging these sorts of things. He says that Lucius' senatorial accent doubles the price of everything, so Lucius has become accustomed to staying silent until the bargain is sealed. Haggling a price with the ship's captain is definitely Cornelius Rufus' task – and he will probably discover that he is related to the captain's mother's first husband and wangle a discount. Such calm reasoning, though, proves of little use in dealing with Lucius' immediate distress. Once Cornelius Rufus has slipped out, Lucius is overwhelmed by guilt and nausea, and, stumbling out of bed, experiences one of the more revolting half hours of his life in the public latrines on the corner opposite the inn. After which, he asks weakly for the nearest baths.

When Lucius catches up with Cornelius Rufus towards noon, he is already bored with the sights of Puteoli. The town caters for travellers and not much more. Still, at least the baths are up to standard. He can see that he will be spending a lot of time there if there are no boats going to North Africa in the next day or two. Cornelius, however, has his smug look on.

"Tomorrow evening all right?" he asks in mock deference.

"I'll just check with my secretary – no, it's all right, I don't have any appointments tomorrow," Lucius answers with that touch of arrogance that marks a true Roman gentleman. "What's the ship like?"

"You ever been on a merchant ship before?" asks Cornelius carelessly. Lucius detects an undertone of mirth and his heart sinks a little; but he decides that Cornelius Rufus is not going to get any laughs out of watching him turn up his nose in horror at the conditions on board.

"No," he answers mildly, "but I have made the crossing twice in crowded troop transports, and the second time I was still recovering from a wound in the arm. Why – do you think I'll find it uncomfortable?" He wonders if he has made it too pointed.

Cornelius does not answer at once – a minor but satisfying triumph. Troop ships are not known for their luxurious fittings. "I reckon you'll survive, lad," he concedes. "Especially if you keep that sense of humour. Now – where are these baths?"

In the middle of a long afternoon when he has had as much of a siesta as even a hangover requires, Lucius decides that he can bear Puteoli and idleness no longer and goes for a walk. Cornelius is very disturbed by this; Subura rats have to walk everywhere in Rome, so the thought of doing it when it is not strictly necessary appals him. Lucius has to admit that most of his own friends would agree; yes, you walk in Rome, because it is the easiest way of getting anywhere in the crowded streets, but as all good citizens know, Rome is an exception. So exceptional in fact, that Romans rule the world, and they did not decide to rule the world so that they could take irrelevant, non-profit-making walks in the defeated countryside.

Sometimes, Lucius wonders if he really is Roman – he may understand exactly what Cicero feels on looking down on the Forum in a summer dawn, but Lucius also sees so many things that are wrong with his city and the people who live in it. Albinia would have been of great help at this point – he could have talked to her about things like that. But, regardless of the undoubted madness of such an act, he goes for a walk that afternoon. He decides not to head for the mysterious Phlegraean Fields where nothing grows, and where, they say, there is an entrance to the Underworld. He needs colour and life and sun, and the road climbing up away from the coast stretches those muscles not yet toughened by riding.

The countryside around Puteoli is displaying the washed-out greens and browns of the end of summer, and very little activity from the local soil-tillers can be detected. Rabbits bounce from field to field, nibbling at the dried-out grass, and generally having a good time, unaware that the rest of the world looks on them as food. Lucky, stupid rabbits. Lucius wonders if Caesar sees him as something soft and harmless, jumping into his way by accident, but easily and usefully disposed of. Usefully? He scolds himself for taking the metaphor too far (a common fault in young orators). You can eat a rabbit, use its skin for gloves or a cap, but Lucius Sestius is never going to be of use to Caesar again.

On the way back down into the town, he is passed by two horsemen and immediately feels apprehensive. They ride with the straight-backed confidence of cavalrymen. They are dusty, and the horses looked pretty tired. They give him a careful look as they pass and though he drops his gaze, he knows that they are checking him out. They come from Rome, and he doubts if they have been sent by his father to see if he was all right. He keeps his head bowed, and they disappear along the road.

When Lucius gets back to the inn he tells Cornelius Rufus, who scratches his head and can offer no comfort. Lucius is uneasy enough to insist that they move to a different inn that night, and they stay indoors there during the next day. After an early dinner, they creep out and make their way to the harbour; Lucius' skin itches all the way, and his fingers keep hovering over the knife he wears on his belt.

The Carthaginian Queen is an ambitiously named craft. Fifty quick paces and you've covered the length of the deck; the few scruffs on board amble aimlessly to and fro, gazing with wonder at the various ropes and levers, so Lucius guesses that they must be the crew. The captain is not actually related to Cornelius, but after one look at him, Lucius insists on going below and checking the hull. It all seems watertight at least, and he decides that it would be better not to investigate the cargo if he wants to be taken on the journey. The sailor sent below with him ("in case the gentleman trips") gives an approving nod as he goes back up on deck.

Cornelius and he make a nest of their belongings at the front of the boat, and manage to rig a little tent over it, then as the activity on deck becomes slightly less leisurely, they keep out of the way. The ship suddenly moves and there is a shout of what seems like surprise from the captain. One of the sailors is dragged away from the rope he is holding, and a quarrel breaks out so Lucius and Cornelius Rufus politely turn away and look back at the land. Whether by man's intention or not, the ship is slipping away from the quay, and the men at the nearest dockside bar are turning and waving as is the natural human impulse whenever one sees a ship sail. Lucius waves back feeling suddenly cheerful, and one man smiles right at him – and Lucius knows that the smile is for him, as the man turns and speaks to another man, and points him out. Suddenly Lucius feels that he is alone on the ship, the focus of all attention from the land. For one long moment he cannot stop looking back at the two men, and he knows that they know who he is. They seem relaxed at least, not worried that he is moving away from them.

"Cornelius! It's the men I saw coming into town yesterday!" Cornelius Rufus moves closer to him and he does not feel so large and vulnerable.

"Easy now, lad – they're not after us," he mutters. "They're seeing us off – that's all. Though they will be able to work out pretty easily that we aren't going to Rhodes."

As if they can hear him, the two men wave again, and laugh, and they all stand and look at each other until the ship is well out of the harbour.

Chapter Thirteen

In Africa Vetus, Old Africa, Lucius is able to relax. They reach the town of Utica, the province's capital, after a smooth crossing from Sicily that takes less than two days, and he spends the first few days on land doing nothing more dangerous than gaining some first impressions of Africa and helping Cornelius Rufus with what he vaguely refers to as "my business contacts." As far as Lucius can tell, Cornelius Rufus is setting himself up as a sort of go-between, promising to put likely businesses in touch with useful people in Rome. Lucius is impressed by the breadth of Cornelius' knowledge, but all those days down at Rome's docks, sorting out cargoes for Rubria have not been a waste. Lucius himself tries not to think too much about anything, but he cannot help wondering about the two men in Puteoli. It feels very strange, knowing that Caesar knows of his whereabouts; and while he had been afraid at the thought that the Dictator considered it important to make sure of his departure, the casual mockery of the two men and their complete openness, anger him. It looks like he is just worthy of Caesar's notice, but not considered dangerous.

The town of Utica lies along a softly-rising ridge that stretches away from the sea. The plain behind it is covered in neat parcels of olive trees and vines, and hills rise in the distance. South of the town a lazy little river runs muddily into the sea, and the marshes need some serious drainage. In the midst of this calm green landscape, Utica is a truly Roman city. Not only does it have the necessary theatre, baths and racetrack, but the enterprising city planners have at one end of the ridge laid down a small grid of streets to delight the heart of everyone who loves a right angle.

Villas and blocks of apartments mix with shops, temples and a water system, and down at the north harbour lurk a military base and the governor's mansion; a couple of days' strolling covers all the sights. In fact, it is little different to the towns they have just left in Italy, Pompeii and Puteoli, though Lucius and

Cornelius both feel that the wines available in the dozen or so bars are not quite up to the standard of the Bay of Naples. The sea is as blue as the sky in Italy, the occasional rain falls out of the same sky, the same mix of people walk the streets. Utica has been Roman for over a hundred years, and it shows. They hear a lot of Greek and the occasional Latin, and Lucius doesn't have a clue as far as any other language is concerned. Shopkeepers manage to understand him, and Cornelius Rufus never has any trouble getting what he wants.

The only thing that makes Utica stand out is the space being cleared for a statue of Cato, leader of the opposition to Caesar in North Africa after the Battle of Pharsalus and up to the Battle of Thapsus. After Thapsus, Cato committed a horrific suicide, the story of which seems to grow more gruesome every time Lucius hears it, and everyone they meet wants to tell it to them. Apparently, Cato's first attempt to stab himself went wrong, in that he was still alive with a gaping wound in his stomach when his son found him.

A doctor was hastily summoned, and he sewed up the wound and stopped the bleeding, but once left to himself, Cato ripped open the wound again and pulled out his own guts to make sure of the job this time. Not a single person can tell or hear this story without wincing at the least, and Lucius is filled with a reluctant admiration for the man who once was his enemy – or at least, was on the side opposite to his own.

He had asked his father about Cato, and according to Publius Sestius, Cato had never been a lovable person. "Arrogant, prim and totally devoid of any sense of humour" is the memorable description. But his courage and decision to stick firmly to his principles were never less than admirable. Cato, for example, would never have left Rome merely to appease Caesar. The people of Utica, in appreciation of this courage, have asked permission to put up a statue of Cato, and Cato's enemy has graciously agreed.

And so, while lacking any other common ground with him, Lucius shares with Cato the honour of being an unwilling recipient of Caesar's famous mercy. Cato would have scorned this clemency as weakness, Lucius thinks, but does not say out loud, for he now lives in a Rome where the arch-conservative is called a rebel, and Sittius, once from Nuceria, is rewarded for his loyalty. The statue is not yet finished but Lucius would not take any bets on its having a stern and forbidding expression. It will stand in a square just off the harbour, and Cato will be able to gaze his disapproval over towards Italy for centuries.

They stay in a little inn just south of the governor's mansion, but Cornelius Rufus is keeping his eyes and ears open for a small house they can rent. They know that they will be there for several months at least.

One evening, after concluding what Cornelius considers a very satisfactory deal, involving a local dye which he says Rubria would kill to get her hands on, they sit over a celebratory meal in the inn. Lucius asks Cornelius Rufus why, with all his talents, he chooses to scrape a Subura living.

"Less of the scrape if you don't mind! I do all right, and you don't know the half of what I do to earn a living," says Cornelius Rufus mildly. Then, "Use your head, Lucius." His age and Lucius' new-found respect for him allow that, though Lucius does not think that he can ever call Cornelius Rufus by his first name. Cornelius takes a good swig of Utican wine and continues, "I enjoy it, don't you see? I actually like knowing other people's business – not quite gentlemanly, I know, but let's face it, I'm just the same as most people. I admit it, that's the difference, and I make money from it; other people call it gossip, pretend that only women do it, but they listen to it whenever they can. And I've always liked working for lawyers – that's how I got to work for your father."

They have been in Utica for several days and mention of his father reminds Lucius of how much he misses Rome and the family. He has had a letter written to tell them that he has arrived safely but knows that it will be a long time before his letter reaches them even though he has been lucky enough to find a man, a junior official on the governor's staff, going all the way to Rome. And October is now well under way, and the sailing season is drawing to a close. Although the journey between Sicily and Africa is as straightforward as you can get, in the winter the weather can be horrible – Lucius remembers the crossing he had to make when he followed Caesar to Africa for the campaign there. In a couple of weeks' time, the ships making the crossing will be few and expensive.

Cornelius Rufus insists that they keep busy. Not only does he conduct long and complicated negotiations with the locals, he asks Lucius many questions about his own time in Africa, all five months of it, and decides that they ought to go sightseeing. They take walks along the shore, because walks are all right when under the headings of "Tourism" or "Business" apparently, and they even manage to navigate a little way down the marshy River Bagradas, borrowing a tiny little boat from a local farmer, and using a combination of oars and poles to punt their way through. In Lucius' opinion, this expedition is not really worth the effort, but Cornelius Rufus finds everything of interest. Everywhere they go, thanks to him, they make friends, and Lucius does wonder how he manages to make himself so welcome around the town when they haven't been there more than a couple of weeks.

He is certain that his own lordly accent and moderately upper-class birth come into it; he knows that Cornelius plays upon these senatorial credentials for all they are worth when it suits. "Gives the deals a bit of class," he explains. Lucius supposes that this is true, especially as he is acting as Cornelius Rufus' secretary. Needless, to say, Cornelius enjoys this immensely, and being referred to as "my young friend" so often gets a bit tiresome. After their recent enforced familiarity though, and the debt Lucius owes him for all the help he has given, it is not surprising to find that although lots of little things still grate, he can more easily put up with Cornelius Rufus and even be amused by watching him in his business dealings. Lucius has never seen anyone who changes tactics as quickly: Cornelius Rufus' armoury is well stocked, and he can plead or patronise, show interest or boredom, thunder or whimper, all at a moment's notice and with an acting ability that has Lucius convinced every time. With a more refined vocabulary, he would make a splendid speaker.

When it comes to making the acquaintance of Governor Calvisius, however, Lucius insists on doing things the proper way. On the third day after their arrival in Utica the two of them set off from the inn, newly shaved and wearing togas, and they walk down the main harbour road which at its western end hosts the governor's residence. Lucius takes his letters of introduction from Cicero and his father, and they are immediately admitted to a moderately impressive entrance hall by a well-trained door-slave. Another slave runs off to find someone to whom they can present their credentials, and in no time, three young men practically run into the hall and introduce themselves as the governor's junior legates. Lucius feels like a lost coin lying in the street, such is the eagerness with which they fall on him. It appears that they hate Africa (especially its governor), and their job (especially anything they are asked to do by their employer, the governor) and their impatience to be told all the news makes him more homesick himself. Utica is large and comfortable and as Romanised as one would expect from a capital, but it is not his city. But he doesn't have to work very hard to get an invitation to dinner, and two days later, he and Cornelius Rufus get their chance to meet the governor himself.

Gaius Calvisius Sabinus has taken some time and effort to make sure that his residence reflects the glory of Rome, and Lucius and Cornelius Rufus have the honour of a personal tour of the wall frescoes after a dinner given in honour of local businessmen one evening. The frescoes are indeed very nice, covering the walls of the dining room and the official reception room where the governor meets the locals, and they must have cost a lot. In the reception room, a tumble of stylised villas balancing on improbably thin columns march down a hillside to a harbour, while the dining room is enlivened by a head-high frieze of youthful deities, dancing and flying, flirting and hunting incredibly sweet animals. The details are humorous and clever, the craftsmanship excellent. Lucius wonders how Governor Calvisius paid for them and holds out no hope that the money for the work came out of the governor's own pocket. Publius Sestius knows Calvisius very slightly; Lucius is glad that it is only slightly, for Calvisius does not appear to him to be the sort of person who is going to inspire confidence in the local community especially after Sallust's little spree next door in Africa Nova. The businessmen at the dinner do not seem convinced either, and Lucius sees that they watch the governor carefully, and speak only enough for politeness. Calvisius eats very well at that dinner and shows signs of enjoying his food on every possible occasion. His big square face is flanked with folds of flesh that drag at the sides of his cheeks and chin, pulling his wide mouth down at the corners. His eyebrows on the other hand join in the middle and so seem to be pulling the two sides of his expression together at the top of his face. His dark hair is greasy and thinning; he blames the latter on the African sun.

His manners are dreadful – he talks about the people he governs as if they are slaves and ignores his slaves as much as possible. In fact, Lucius notices that Calvisius never addresses a slave directly, even to give an order; he just states what he wants to happen, and the nearest slave makes sure that it happens.

What is also clear is that his three legates are scared of him; they do not speak unless spoken to and concentrate on making themselves take up as little space as possible. They all have full heads of hair, at which the governor looks frequently and enviously, and Lucius approves of their good sense in keeping those heads down. Calvisius makes Sallust look like a carefree clown, and Lucius wonders how much poorer Africa Vetus will be at the end of his governorship. Surely, given that Sallust is just about to be prosecuted for mismanaging his province, Calvisius will go easy on his provincials?

Cornelius, who has come to the dinner as Lucius' assistant this time, spends the time chatting to a couple of corn merchants. He is not addressed by Calvisius at any point in the evening but doesn't care. He has no time for Calvisius, and instead is scheming. He has decided that developing grain production and transportation is the future, as far as Africa is concerned, and this apparently entails journeying further afield. He has made all the necessary contacts in Utica and has now drawn up an itinerary that will take the two of them all over the two provinces of Africa and includes room for tourism. As a true patriot and wise supporter of Caesar, he wants to see the site of the famous Battle of Thapsus (where Lucius gained his not-so-famous war-wound) and to look around the site of Carthage. He has heard rumours that Caesar wants to build a new town there so Cornelius reckons the detour worthwhile on business grounds.

"It's on the coast, lad," he explains. "It's got these sheltered lakes just like Alexandria, so it's going to develop harbour facilities, with grain storage no problem – it is bound to take over from Utica. Just look at how that river is silting up the commercial harbour here. And grain is what Rome has needed ever since I can remember. Free corn doles don't come cheap or easy and for a long time Italy hasn't been able to keep up with what Rome needs. We've got Egypt of course, but we can only rely on Egypt as long as Cleopatra is in bed with the Dictator, and anyway here we are nearer, and it's a much easier journey."

"Doesn't Africa already export corn to us?" Lucius asks, feeling ignorant. His family may not be the richest in Rome, but he has never had to worry about where the next loaf of bread will come from.

"Of course," says Cornelius, with great scorn at Lucius' ignorance. "But we're going to need more. Think about it – what's the best way to get the great unwashed masses on your side? Feed them! Clodius started the permanent corn dole, and now we can't stop. Caesar's trying to cut the numbers eligible, because it's so expensive, but he'll never abolish it completely. And what happens the next time someone needs a favour from the people? They'll put on a procession, some games, a big meal – and they'll give away corn. And the man who can sell corn at a good price gets a contract worth thousands, maybe millions."

"Cornelius, what did people do before they had the corn dole?" Lucius asks curiously.

"Had smaller families," he answers. Then more impatiently, when he sees Lucius' face, "What you'd call 'infant exposure'. Too many mouths to feed already, but Ma has another baby anyway. Little blighter gets left somewhere where only the gods can decide to save it. Or a friendly passing childless couple, as happens in all the best comedies. Don't say you've never heard of it?"

"Heard of it, yes," Lucius said. "I just never met someone who actually did it. Or admitted to doing it."

"Not something you put in a letter to all your relatives at Saturnalia," says Cornelius Rufus. "Now, when do you fancy seeing Thapsus?"

"Never," he says gloomily. "It didn't look pretty last time I saw it, and I don't suppose it's changed."

"When was it? April? At least you had good weather for it. It wasn't freezing your socks off or worse," says Cornelius cheerfully.

"Oh, it was the end of winter, because we hadn't got the new calendar in," Lucius says, and pauses. As a battle, Thapsus had been a big mess as far as he could see, although the right side (his side) had won. He remembered the captured elephants lined up in front of Roman troops; he remembered the battle proper beginning because he and his fellow officers had been unable to stop the men charging; he remembered the slaughter of all the prisoners. He still could not remember being wounded. Of Caesar's famous rapport with his troops, he had seen no evidence. What had struck him is how little control anyone had over this vast number of men, and he certainly had felt no confidence that any squaddie was really listening to his orders. He later heard that people on his own side had been attacked and even killed by Caesar's soldiers in the heat of battle; when the enemy surrendered, and asked for mercy, Caesar could not persuade 'his' men to spare them. Five thousand enemy casualties were recorded. Or ten thousand, depending on who you asked. Maybe it is difficult to tell when so many of the casualties were Roman, no matter which side they were on.

"We weren't there very long," he tells Cornelius and leaves it at that.

Chapter Fourteen

Needless to say, they go to Thapsus.

It doesn't take long for Cornelius Rufus to organise horses and even less time to ride out of the little town. South of Utica, the road leads through marshy, muddy country, and the River Bagradas slips almost unseen into the bay. They turn further south rather than going straight to Carthage, saving the site of Rome's greatest enemy for the return journey. As they head south to Thapsus, the road passes marshland, rivers, cliffs and green plains looking ripe for Cornelius' plans to exploit Africa's grain production. The road is recently repaired – Caesar again, of course – and on horseback the journey takes a comfortable seven days. The weather is clear and they are always able to find a farm with a stable to sleep in if no town beckons. Little villages, no more than a scattering of farms, pass by regularly but there is so much more space when compared to the journey they made several weeks earlier from Rome to the Bay of Naples.

And the traffic is virtually non-existent, except when they are approaching a market day. Lucius supposes that there is no real reason for many people to be on the road at this time of year, but they meet up with enough farmers to give Cornelius Rufus the chance for a gossip about the state of agriculture in the province. When they stay in Ruspina, north of the battle site, they have a chance to see at first-hand what the fertile hinterland can produce as they wander around a large and prosperous market square. Africa has potential all right, although the soil, according to Cornelius Rufus, isn't nearly as good as that around Pompeii and the Bay. The farmers produce respectable olive oil, loads of fruit and vegetables, and some decent wines along with the all-important grain. And now that Caesar has brought peace of course, the farmers of Africa are all cautiously looking forward to being able to rebuild their irrigation systems and open up further markets. Once Cornelius Rufus has told them that they are, anyway.

125

Two years previously, Ruspina had been practically Lucius' first sight of Africa, and it is strange to look around the almost cosy scenes in the market and see imposed upon them in his mind's eye the military fort that he had known. Lucius had arrived first in Sicily on the way back from Cilicia in the East, where he had been on his father's staff. Caesar had of course already sailed to Africa, arriving from Sicily in three days, but much of his squadron had been split up on the voyage and not everyone was as lucky as him, with troops arriving in Africa in messy little parcels of ships and men. At Lilybaeum in Sicily, Lucius had found a second wave preparing to follow the general over, and it seemed relatively straightforward at first. The sea didn't look that bad as he examined it from the harbour, and it was still autumn in fact, though the as-yet-unreformed calendar said it was January; but once out at sea, the winds and waves drove many ships off course, and once they got to Africa, nobody seemed to know where to land. Some headed to the northern coast and Utica, Lucius' ship was one of those which went south-east to Hadrumentum, only to find that the harbour was held by the opposition. Finally, they had found a cove along the coast where they could safely land. Ruspina had been where they had caught up with Caesar, troops and ships straggling in over the course of the old year's end. Here the Dictator had made his headquarters as he set up the blockade of Hadrumentum, and there was the feeling that he was tapping his feet impatiently as he waited for the rest of his army to catch up. The marketplace had been full of officers with scrolls and note-tablets, and along one of the long sides of the open area there had stretched a line of temporary stalls and tents as the supplies people set up with what they could salvage from the scattered ships. Caesar had already set to work cajoling whatever grain he could find out of the locals, again frustrated by the fact that his opponents had had so long to get their own supplies in order. Piles of wood lay in huge stacks along another side, and Lucius remembers that there had been a smithy in the corner, pumping out noise and warmth. Now, in exactly the same place, there is a brand-new bakery, doing much the same thing.

Ruspina also has some decent bars, and that night Cornelius

Rufus and he are in luck. Down an unpromising little alley is The Shield, the ex-soldier's den of choice, marked by a genuine and very battered legionary shield hanging up over the door. It is packed with army veterans now living the life on their own little parcels of Africa, donated by a grateful Rome. Once he has given his credentials and been judged (toff, but on the right side, and has the scar to prove it), they are treated to an evening of reminiscing which holds Cornelius Rufus in thrall as the Africa campaign is fought all over again, from the point of view of people who had not had a clue what was happening the first time around.

"What you've got to remember, that no one does," says one grey-haired ex-centurion, sitting straight-backed on his bench, "is that Thapsus, the actual Battle of Thapsus, was just the end of it. Day after day, for three months at least before your actual battle, we faffed around, chasing Labienus all over the countryside, then running back to defend Ruspina."

A quiet farmer, who had served under Caesar since the Dictator first went to Gaul, stirs and nods his head solemnly.

"And we never had quite enough to eat. Sometimes seemed like we spent all our time foraging and hiding from Labienus' cavalry."

"And what cavalry we had were useless, because they ran out of fodder for the horses. Do you remember we had to go and collect seaweed from the beaches for the horses?"

There is a silence as they all, including Lucius, remember that horrible task – and having to wash the seaweed in fresh water so the horses would eat it. Their hands were dried out by constant immersion in water, salty and fresh, and as the weather worsened, they were always looking for remedies for chapped skin. Lucius hadn't realised before how much the average Roman legionary cared about his skin, but a pot of goose-grease or even a nub of bees' wax could provoke fights. The centurion sighs as Lucius mentions this.

"My optio used to swear by a mix of olive oil and honey. He had to wait until he was sure he wouldn't be needed for anything, then just slather it on his hands and sit near the fire to keep it warm, not hot, mind, just warm. Complete waste – he got a spear right through him at Thapsus, poor bugger."

A brief silence reigns, for they all know someone who took a spear at Thapsus. The centurion's memories move on though, for after a minute he smiles and says, "But the number of people who came to Ruspina just to see Caesar! And then there were the deserters from Scipio and Labienus, loads of them, couldn't bear the thought of fighting against Caesar any more. All the provincial high-ups as well, complaining about Cato and Labienus and Scipio. They hadn't made themselves popular while they were making their preparations for Caesar's arrival. I reckon that's why we went straight into a proper campaign, never mind the winter. Caesar knew that the troops on the other side would come over to him if he just scored one victory, and that the locals wouldn't support the opposition any more than they could help. And he pulled it off, bless him."

"Might as well get on with it, that's what he thought, the general," agrees the farmer. "Our ships were taking a right beating as well, attacked as they arrived, attacked as they tried to get out of the harbour to forage, and couldn't sail along the coast for two minutes before someone decided to have a pop at them. Bloody useless really."

"Do you remember that hailstorm? Near that horrible little hill in the middle of nowhere we had to fortify?"

"Uzita," says the farmer. "Yes, I remember that. Nasty. I had a mate in the Fifth Legion, swore the storm had set fire to their spears."

The centurion thinks carefully and pronounces, "Mind you, the Fifth were all bloody liars."

Lucius needs to laugh at that point but doesn't dare, as the only ex-member of the Fifth legion in the bar that night. The centurion catches the twitch of Lucius' mouth and raises his cup in apology, "Begging your pardon, sir."

Lucius waves it away. "No need – you're right, we were all bloody liars in the Fifth."

This, combined with a round of drinks on him, brings the evening to a good-tempered close. As the old soldiers limp off into the night, Lucius silently wishes them all the luck the gods give.

Next morning, as they ride out of Ruspina on the last leg of the journey to Thapsus, he sees the remains of the fortifications, stretching between the town and the sea. No wood is left of course: anyone with any enterprise would have taken those nice chunky stakes and re-used them. But the ridges of thrown-up soil remain, with a covering of grass that tells him that soon you would have to look very hard for any traces of battle lines.

Like Ruspina, Thapsus is enjoying the benefits of peace and there are some decent-sized houses and a very good inn, where they lodge. Cornelius tells everyone they meet that Lucius fought in the battle, and the inn's clientele look at him with curiosity. The innkeeper's wife even smiles and gives him a very large slice of her game pie. But unlike Ruspina, Thapsus is not keen on refighting old battles. Several of the men who come into the inn during the evening are introduced as soldiers who have settled in and around the town after receiving their discharge, but though they exchange nods, and shake hands, and Lucius of course buys drinks for everyone, they don't sit and discuss the battle. Lucius doesn't mind at all. He has had enough of military chat at Ruspina, and none of these men seem too anxious to rehash it all. So, he saves his breath for the next day when he is due to give Cornelius Rufus his guided tour.

They ride west out of the town, and Lucius can hardly believe that this landscape is where it all took place. The countryside stretches away, so much bigger than he remembers, and so much more colourful in the absence of marching columns of grey and brown, churning up mud and dust. He is surprised when he realises that there are mountains in the far-off distance, having no memory of them. In the end, there is nothing which gives any indication that the decisive battle of the African campaign was fought all over the plain and under the town walls.

After a couple of miles, he finds a small rise and turns the horse around in a complete circle to get his bearings. Cornelius Rufus, who has been very quiet, looks at him and asks if he is all right.

"I don't know," Lucius says.

"It's a long time now," says Cornelius. "Last year was a long

129

year, remember – it's," he frowns and concentrates, "April to April plus two months, plus five months, nineteen months, I make it. Plenty of time for the grass to grow. I bet you hardly recognise it."

And with that, strangely, the landscape falls into place. Lucius begins to talk, first explaining the chaos of the troop-gathering and the preliminary fighting.

"We didn't just march up to Thapsus and have a battle. It was a lot more confusing and messy than that. Most of us only just made it to Ruspina in the January, to find that Caesar was well ahead of us and champing at the bit to get going. He couldn't bear the thought that Cato and company had been in Africa for over a year and were settled in. There were skirmishes around Ruspina, then a fight round a hilltop at a town called Uzita that seemed to go on for weeks. Then a load more troops arrived from overseas and you knew that the big one was coming. Thapsus was holding out nicely under a man called Vergilius and so Caesar decided to have a go at taking the town."

Dutifully, Lucius answers Cornelius' questions and illustrates the strategy of the battle – as far as he can remember it – with a twig and a patch of dry earth. He points out where his own legion had been drawn up in the middle of the battle line and shows him where the extravagantly-named Quintus Caecilius Metellus Scipio had lined up his elephants. Ever since Hannibal, Romans have loved being attacked by elephants. Together, Lucius and Cornelius Rufus work out where Juba the Numidian king and Lucius Afranius had tried to block Caesar in, and then they ride over to the coast to see where Cispius had sailed with Caesar's fleet to give Scipio a shock. Scipio had fled, followed closely by his fellow generals, and Caesar had been unable to stop a massacre. It had been muddy and bloody and truly horrible.

As they return to Thapsus, around the little town, the grass, green and brown and straggly has grown back, and flocks of goats and sheep keep it trimmed. Lucius wonders where the thousands of dead are buried; he had been shipped off pretty quickly after the battle, along with all the other wounded, which had been a great relief in many ways, despite the disadvantages of a sea crossing and an army doctor. Better the discomfort and rough-and-ready care than watching the final indignities of the defeated Cato or persuading tired men to bury those fellow Romans they had lacked the decency to spare. Looking around this peaceful place, he is glad that he never saw Thapsus surrender.

Back up the coast towards Utica they travel, in the steps of Caesar until they turn off for Carthage. It is all a bit of let-down: after one look, Lucius decides that he has seen enough and even Cornelius looks a bit disappointed as he takes in the sight. Lucius doesn't know why they expected anything else; after all, creating ruins is one of the things Romans are good at. Carthage was a city that had really annoyed them. For years, she had not only held out against Rome's undeniable charms (wholesale slaughter and slavery – what an offer!) but ruled her own empire and fought against the Romans to protect it. This had rankled so much in Rome that one old lunatic had started ending every speech he made in the Senate on a note of gloom and doom if Carthage was not destroyed. It didn't matter what was actually under discussion at the time – Rome had to destroy Carthage. Over and over and over, until, Lucius suspects, Rome went to war just to shut him up. So, Carthage was destroyed. Slightly to the north of where the original city had stood, the Gracchi brothers had built a small and short-lived colony, Junonia. The colonists had taken most of the stones of the old city, but a few remain, half-hidden in the long grass, and Lucius can still make a guess at where the main streets ran by the thinness of vegetation on the old road surface. Carthage had been a large city – not as big as Rome, of course, but mistress of her own empire then, just as Rome is now. Lucius sits on a stone at the edge of a small grassy heap of stones, watching Cornelius Rufus tramping off into the distance, and wonders what disaster would turn Rome into a grassy bog surrounded by seven, stone-littered hills.

Chapter Fifteen

"Pretty, isn't it?"

Lucius opens his eyes and blinks. After a few moments, the scene in front of him comes into focus, and his ears are filled with soft noises, the grasses rustling and sheep bleating. He feels the warmth of the sun and as he looks the words make sense – it is pretty. Governor Calvisius could have it depicted in a painting for his residence. In front of Lucius, standing on a pile of rubble about fifty yards away, a boy of about ten counts a small flock. He looks like a tribune on the speaking-platforms in the Forum; his face is fierce, and his lips move, although Lucius cannot hear the words. The sheep bleat and bump around him, just like a curious crowd muttering and wondering what the latest bright young spark has to say. Eventually the boy stops and looks relieved and sits down. The sheep, after looking at him expectantly for a while, start moving away, searching the brown scraps of vegetation for something green and juicy. Their guardian keeps a careful eye on them and leaps up to chase one sheep that wanders too adventurously far. Lucius laughs as the boy runs after the trotting sheep, and he turns to look at the man who spoke, remarking, "I had always imagined that shepherding involved a lot more lying around and tootling on rustic pipes."

The man next to him smiles. He has a very pleasant smile. His face is weathered and tanned and lined, but the lines fall so easily into amusement. He looks like a very contented Italian farmer, sitting on a heap of stones at the edge of his land and thinking of how good the harvest has been this year. A brown tunic of no quality and a great deal of use reinforces this idea, though it is merely dusty, not dirty. A broad-brimmed hat lies at the man's feet, along with a small sack, and a walking stick. Maybe, thinks Lucius, he should pass this man a long stalk of grass to chew on as he talks. But this man is definitely Roman: his Latin is flawless and his accent places him as from north of Rome, maybe as far as Cisalpine Gaul, but no further.

132

"I think that we Romans are so fond of the thought of the countryside that we have forgotten the reality. When did you or I last think to ask how wool is gathered?"

"My teachers used to say that I was rather good at wool-gathering," Lucius replies, smiling to show that he understands how poor the joke is. The man keeps smiling back.

"Then it would appear that you have changed considerably since you were in the schoolroom, Lucius Sestius, for you certainly have not been idle recently, have you?"

The voice is pleasant, and the face still amused. Lucius looks around for Cornelius Rufus, but he has vanished while Lucius slept. The innocent scene in front of him is still the same but has distanced itself from him – no room for warmth in this suddenly more dangerous conversation. Suspicion wells up familiarly and he deliberately pushes down the cold, sick feeling of being pursued. He is not going to let it win. Instead, he allows anger to take its place, and feeling that grow inside and growl softly under the surface gives him a kind of satisfaction, and control.

"Who sent you?"

The man gives a little chuckle.

"I'm glad we don't have to spend time on preliminaries at least! Not even a "Who are you?" No one sent me, Lucius Sestius. I live here in Africa. I served Caesar for many years, culminating in the African campaign – in which I understand you also served. Strange to think we might have met then. After the liberation of Utica, I retired and stayed behind. The Dictator generously made me a gift of some land and I farm that, in a rather leisurely fashion, I am afraid. I still could not tell you anything about wool, although my farm manager tells me that my flock is prospering. However, that is of no importance to you. You want to know why I have decided to come and see you for myself."

Lucius says nothing. The boy still sits on his vantage point, though Lucius thinks he is finding it more and more difficult to keep awake. Lucius wonders what the boy's reaction would be if he strolled over and offered to keep an eye on the sheep while he dozed. Would the lad speak enough Latin or Greek to understand?

"Please pay attention," says the man beside Lucius, rather sharply. So, he can be riled! Lucius is a little surprised that it can be done so easily and unintentionally, and it is gratifying. He tries to stir things up deliberately.

"I beg your pardon," he says, yawning. "It is hot, and I had not realised that you were about to say anything important. So many of my elders like to talk about their own affairs and I really find it difficult to concentrate sometimes."

And he yawns again, carefully looking to see if this has worked. But his deliberate insolence has failed – the man is laughing, with the same indulgence with which Lucius' father or Cicero laughs at Tia when she makes some unintentionally funny remark.

"I have always enjoyed listening to a clever speaker," says the man. "It is one of the best things about our system of education that we produce so many people who can really entertain with a speech. Even those of us who do not have the skill can usually appreciate it in others. Young men of course are not as funny as they like to think, but they can still be very clever. Now, I am of the age to really admire Cicero and his generation. They are so good at involving one's emotions – sometimes even against one's intellect, judgement, will. Did you ever hear Hortensius?"

"Yes, of course," Lucius says, admiring the deceptive skill of this stranger. He is by no means as humble as he seems. "When my father was prosecuted, Hortensius was on the defence team."

"You have impressive friends. But I think that those two, Hortensius and Cicero, were always best when set against each other," he said. "They disliked each other so intensely, it seemed to sharpen their differences when speaking. I have to say, Cicero nearly always won, in my eyes, at least. Ah, well, I shall have you dozing off again, if I don't come to the point. The captain of the ship that carried you here was kind enough to deliver a letter to me."

Lucius stares. "You mean those men we saw at Puteoli – they were delivering letters? I thought they were there to keep an eye on me."

"I doubt if they were there just to do that, though I expect they thought it a bonus to catch up with you. The letter makes it clear that you were expected to have left Italy by then. We thought you might try Athens, Rhodes or, as a trailing third choice, Africa. Rhodes was favourite. I gather that your legal work led people to believe that you would take the opportunity to get some higher education."

"Really?" Lucius says bitterly. "Well, as you can't possibly have been present at these fascinating discussions, I suggest that you just deliver Caesar's message. What does he want?"

"I must be more accurate in my speech," he murmurs, gazing at the now sleeping shepherd boy. "You're right. I was quoting my master. But look at that boy there – doesn't he look peaceful and so oblivious? Tell me, what do you think of this place?"

He is obviously determined not to come to the point, so Lucius resigns himself. He is not going to get annoyed by this man.

"This? It's rather depressing really, when you think of what it was and how powerful Carthage became. Is it true that Caesar intends to build a town here?"

"Oh yes, he's mentioned it before, when I first settled out here," says his new friend. "The only real trouble is the superstition still attached to the place. People don't like disaster, and this was a disaster on a large scale – we weren't merciful, in those days, were we? And this poor little ruin is still thought of as Rome's greatest enemy – look at it, completely abandoned, even by the gods. The mighty Carthage! Junonia didn't flourish either, despite being so carefully situated not quite on the original site. But there are many people, I believe, willing to risk the wrath of some obscure Carthaginian curse for a new chance here. We need colonies desperately, what with the end of civil war, and our rather shaky economy. The Dictator has cut the number of people eligible for free corn, but he knows that other policies must be brought in to deal with the poverty. Colonisation is an excellent solution, if the land is available, for it helps without making people dependent. Quite the opposite, in fact."

"Do you think that the poor want colonisation?" Lucius asks.

"There are very many who would be excellent colonists," the man says earnestly. "Not all of our Subura slums are filled with hopeless drunks and filthy beggars. Or do you already know that, because you have walked through the streets so often? Or maybe you know many inhabitants of the Subura? If you do, then you know that what I say is true. There is a spirit in Rome – a spirit of adventure and aspiration. Our people know how to work hard, how to persevere. They can learn new skills, they can adapt to different conditions. And then there's the army – think of all those newly discharged soldiers about to flood the city, all those trained, disciplined men with nothing to work for. We can make them feel that they are still of use to their country, which is why many of them joined up, after all. With a core of dedicated veterans, a colony here could flourish. Isn't that a better alternative than the corruption of a corn dole? It isn't even as if the grain handout was set up to help the poor – it was a bribe, when Publius Clodius Pulcher needed massive popular support. Caesar wants policies designed to restore dignity and pride."

As the man pauses, he smiles again; a smile which is confident that Lucius must agree with this impassioned outpouring. Clearly, listening to all those Forum speeches has made a powerful impression.

"I can't imagine why he let you retire here," says Lucius admiringly. "He should have you back in Rome, walking around telling people how marvellous he is."

That is a hit; his new acquaintance stiffens a little and sits with tight lips. Silence falls between them, as Lucius feels slightly uncomfortable that he does not walk through the Subura if he can help it, and knows nobody who lives there, except Cornelius Rufus. But he is damned if he is going to let this man know that anything in his speech made a point.

A breeze sweeps over the ruins and ruffles the shepherd boy's tunic; he wakes and scrambles up, looking around anxiously. Another counting session relieves him, and soon sheep and shepherd are on their way back to whichever farm they came from. Lucius can't see where it might be – there are no buildings in sight, from where they are sitting.

The man stands up, gazing after the little group, and says, "You are not really in a position to appreciate this, but he is good for Rome. How long did we have to put up with a Senate that is selfish and useless? How long has the city been swept along in the wake of one charismatic, grasping man after another?"

"How long, O Catilina, how long..." The words of Cicero's speech from years ago, taught to him in the schoolroom, runs through Lucius' head. That opening phrase has had an impact if it is being aped by this man of Caesar nearly twenty years later. And Lucius remembers the last time he thought of that famous opening line, declaiming it in tandem with Quintus Caecilius and laughing with him.

Meanwhile his companion is still trying to persuade him. "The top people have been so busy undermining each other that no one has done anything of real value for our citizens for years, nor have they dealt with the practical problems of running an empire. Governors don't rule their provinces, they plunder them, while the city populace is kept quiet with corn doles. It is no life for a true Roman, and Caesar sees that."

Lucius thinks that a supporter of Caesar should be more careful about criticising charismatic, grasping leaders but does not say so. This man is a dedicated admirer. And even the Sestius family had sided with Caesar in the civil war for the less-than-noble reason that they thought he would win. It is time he said something.

"My father kept the province of Cilicia for Caesar at the beginning of the war, and I went out there to help him," Lucius says. "I fought for Caesar. I was wounded here in Africa, and now I have returned to escape being killed on Caesar's orders. My friend is dead, and my family is terrified. Why has your Caesar sent you to me?"

"To talk to you," he says, sounding surprised. "He regrets the death of your friend, you know. The people he set to watching you were more enthusiastic than he had anticipated and misjudged the situation."

"I don't believe you," Lucius says.

"Why should he kill you? Frightening you is the most he

137

intended; unfortunately, your friend was in the wrong place at the wrong moment. You mustn't feel that you are doomed; in a few years, maybe less time than that, all this will have been forgotten. And in the meantime, there will still be wars to be fought and offices to be filled. I think you would make a very good quaestor, in the office of the praetors maybe as you have a legal training, or on the consul's staff, like your father was. If you spoke more enthusiastically about your time fighting here in Africa under Caesar, I might suggest that you take a junior legate's position, especially now that..."

He tails off and Lucius wonders what he was going to say. Parthia, probably. Everyone thinks Caesar's next campaign will be Parthia: there is a small matter of dishonoured legionary standards. Just after Publius Sestius' trial, Caesar's colleague Crassus set off on a venture into the Far East, into Parthia, a large, looming empire left over from Alexander the Great, made up of many different peoples and tribes and with a geography ranging from sand to mountains to two legendary rivers, the Tigris and the Euphrates. Lucius doesn't know all that much about Parthia itself, but he knows what happened to Crassus, and it wasn't pretty. Not only was virtually the entire army wiped out, but Crassus' head was used as a theatre prop. There aren't that many plays in the repertoire which demand a human head be carried on, but fortunately Euripides' <u>Bacchae</u> was playing that day in Parthia. The bronze eagle standards which were the souls of three Roman legions were captured by the enemy, and rumour has it that captured Roman soldiers are still enslaved in Parthia. Caesar will be more than just popular if he successfully thrashes the Parthians and gets those legionary standards back.

Lucius decides that he does not want to listen to any more job offers from Caecilius' murderer. Even if that murder was a mistake.

"If you do not leave me now," he says very clearly, "I shall hit you."

The man sighs and gets up, moving out of reach, but not quite ready to go.

"Don't let it all build up against him. You think about what

138

he is trying to do for Rome and the Empire. All he wants you to do now is to keep out of trouble and consider whether there might be a future for you serving Rome. He does regret your friend's death. He says that in his letter, and he is not a liar. He doesn't need to be."

Lucius looks at the ground. "So, all I have to do is stay here and keep my head down and I won't be killed or prosecuted for my friend's death? My family won't be harmed? My sister's husband won't find his career suddenly cut short?"

"Oh no, of course not. What on earth makes you think of these things?" He sounds shocked.

Lucius thinks of that letter Caesar wrote to Cicero. He would like to throw it in this stupid little Caesarian's face, but instead he asks, "What exactly did you do before you retired?"

The man smiles again, confidence re-established. "Nothing very important."

And then he turns and walks away. Lucius doesn't watch. "Well," he thinks to himself. "I have just met a member of Caesar's famous spy service – retired."

When Cornelius Rufus turns up, the first thing he says is that he has met a very interesting man who took him on a little tour of old Carthage.

"Nice bloke," says Cornelius. "He couldn't give me very much time, had some business to get on to, but he knew a lot. Gave me lots of tips on what to see. Apparently, he moved here after the war, runs a farm. I got the impression he'd been in the army. And he says the new town here is definite."

"Did he smile a lot?" Lucius asks.

"Smile?" Cornelius is puzzled but thinks about it. "Yes, he did. Like I said, he was a nice bloke."

Chapter Sixteen

Back in Utica, the inn has a message for them. Cornelius Rufus' enquiries have borne fruit, and they have been offered some lodgings with a young merchant who wants the favour of Rome (and, as he quickly realises, the expertise of Cornelius Rufus).The house is about half the size of Lucius' family home back in Rome but the merchant, Cyprius, (Lucius can't pronounce his real name; Cyprius is his alternative name for Romans to use) is young enough and unmarried enough to know how to enjoy himself. The three young tribunes attached to the governor's staff, Latinus, Venuleius and Horatius, soon begin to call round and Lucius and Cornelius find that their lodgings have become fashionable.

Lucius also finds that he is beginning to be drawn into Cornelius Rufus' plans, which are growing more ambitious. Now that there are two provinces here in North Africa, Cornelius Rufus thinks that they need to improve their share of the Roman market for food, luxury and wild animals.

Lucius' burgeoning interest in Africa is based on many things, and his interest in Sittius as a character in the drama is a large part of it. The Catilinarian Conspiracy seems a long way off, and yet it is here, just a few months ago, that Sallust did something that rang alarm bells back in Rome. But his journeying has made Lucius think more widely than just his own concerns. He is now thinking about how Rome treats her Empire and about her attitude to her foreign friends. The northern coastline of Africa has been of interest to Rome for hundreds of years and gradually her interest has turned to ownership. Rome already has Egypt and the two Africas, Nova and Vetus, under her imperial wing; she also enjoys friendly relations with many of the local kings who rule along the coastline between Alexandria and the Pillars of Hercules. Gradually those kings will become official friends and allies of the Roman people, and then, one by one, the kingdoms will be taken into the Empire proper, either because their rulers have bequeathed them to Rome in their wills, or because they show unwelcome signs of independence. Control of the north coastline of Africa makes Rome's domination of the Mediterranean much neater, and Lucius doesn't give much for Publius Sittius' chances of holding on to his little plot of land in Numidia. Lucius can see how this narrative will unfold, and for the first time in his life, he is wondering if Rome has got it right. Does she actually need so much control over this land? He doesn't have an answer, but it is interesting. Cornelius Rufus approves of all this deep thought, as it means that Lucius is showing enthusiasm during the preparation for their journey to New Africa. He knows that Lucius also has an ulterior motive for the journey, but it doesn't seem to bother him.

"I think you have to find out what's going on for your friend's sake," he says. "You're in no danger any more, that's obvious, so your family aren't going to suffer, and you needn't worry about them. So, find out what you can – you don't have to do anything about it, but you want to know, right?"

"Not that it'll help Caecilius," Lucius says.

"You don't know that. He was your friend, and a sensible sort of man, wasn't he? Are you telling me he now doesn't want you to find out, as long as you don't get into trouble yourself?"

The beliefs concerning the afterlife underlying this statement are too deep for Lucius, but he doesn't argue. He is not so sure either that to pursue enquiries is completely sensible, but the need to know is irresistible. He doesn't want to examine his own motives too much either; it isn't as though he can parade a neat list of sensible reasons, and he doesn't know if he is doing this for Caecilius or for himself. Resolutely, he tells himself to stop worrying, and for once finds it easy to take his own advice. Autumn in Africa is a pleasant season, and he is able to enjoy himself.

One evening, the merchant Cyprius and Cornelius Rufus are out cementing the bonds of friendship between African and Roman commerce, so he invites the three legates over for a drink. Venuleius is on duty, and can't make it, but Horatius and Latinus escape, and they have a cosy evening, quietly getting drunk and toying with the idea of finding a house of ill-repute and sampling its wares. Latinus actually knows of an establishment in Utica; he has had to accompany the governor to a house near the harbour on several occasions but admits that he was left outside on guard.

"Which is foolish of Calvisius really," points out Horatius. "I mean, if there is an emergency, it would be very useful to know the layout of the place. How could you rescue him from a raging inferno if you didn't know which room he is using and how to get there?"

"He's never in there long enough for a fire to start – I reckon that he can't do it," says Latinus. "You can tell by the look on the madam's face when she lets him out – all fawning flattery until his back's turned and then contempt."

There follows a rather tasteless conversation on the virility (or lack of it) of Governor Calvisius. The general opinion seems to be that brothels are wasted on old men, especially when the young could show them a thing or two, if only they had the time, the money or the nerve.

"I wonder if there's any way we could find out what really happens with Calvisius," says Horatius wistfully. "We could bribe the madam or the girls. I bet they all hate him as much as we do. They'd probably thank us if we set fire to the place while he is in it."

"I'd certainly be tempted to leave him, fat bastard that he is. But a conviction for murdering one's governor, while on provincial brothel patrol, would ruin my career," says Latinus sadly. He and Venuleius are both the sons of Roman knights, but where Venuleius is convinced that everyone overlooks him because of this humble background, Latinus takes the view that he is as likely to get into the Senate as anyone and if he doesn't, he will just make lots of money instead. Knights form the equestrian class, the next class down from the Senate, so they're not exactly the dregs, and everyone knows that many knights are richer than most senators.

"None of us has a career at the moment and we won't have until we get shot of that lump up in the governor's residence and get someone decent in his place. And that won't happen, because the men with any drive will get proper provinces," says

Horatius with an air of one who knows. He is a minor member of a family that boasts a famous ancestor, that Horatius who defended the bridge and thus saved Rome. This same ancestral Horatius had also killed his own sister, which makes his namesake easy to tease on the subject of family ties, but he reckons he is an authority on affairs of state.

"Well, there isn't anyone outstanding at the moment, is there? Caesar's Master of Horse, Marcus Antonius, hasn't defended any bridges that I know of so he's no good," Lucius remarks. It is such a cheap shot, but as usual it works, and Horatius sighs as the two others snigger.

"You know very well what I mean," says Horatius raising himself up on his couch. "Nearly everyone at Rome is busy grovelling to Caesar or keeping well out of the way. What we need are men with the spirit to stand up to Caesar, challenge his authority, or the Republic will die."

Strange, thinks Lucius, that this arrogant young scion of a noble tree and Cicero the middle-class upstart from Arpinum should agree on such a gloomy prediction. He wonders what Horatius thinks of the orator, and asks.

"Why the sudden change of subject? I've heard Cicero, of course, he's a great speaker, but my father says that he's just a country nobody. As if anyone believes that stuff about Catilina anymore! If you ask me, I think Cicero is too busy crawling himself; he may not approve of what Caesar is doing, but he goes along with it all the same. And yet Caesar is far more of a threat to the Republic than Catilina ever was, so why isn't Cicero giving the clarion call, saving the Republic with his precious Union of the Classes?"

Latinus, older than Horatius by a crucial one and a half years, and a good deal more tolerant, stirs.

"The Union of the Classes is a jolly good idea," says Latinus, the knight's son. "In fact, the only strange thing is that it took a consul to point out that we should all be working together for the Republic, when it should have been obvious."

"Oh yes, of course, but Cicero as usual went on and on about it, as if it was all completely his idea, and made everyone thoroughly fed up with it. And now, he's abandoned it, because it doesn't fit in with what Caesar wants."

"You can't have it both ways," Lucius points out. "Either you want Cicero to stop talking about the Union of the Classes or you don't. Would you rather be fed up hearing about it, or disgruntled that Cicero's abandoned it?"

Latinus breaks in before his fellow legate can reply. "Why don't you just admit, Horatius, that discretion is by far the most sensible option at the moment? Caesar controls the army, you idiot – who is really going to try and defeat him? Everyone with any talent for strategy is dead."

His tone, slightly amused and yet reasonable, is guaranteed to annoy. Like the rest of them, Latinus occasionally feels exasperated by Horatius' assumption that the older the family, the better the man. Lucius reckons that the only thing keeping the three legates from falling out with each other is the revulsion inspired in them all by Governor Calvisius.

"The army should realise that it is controlled by the Senate and people of Rome," says Horatius, putting on his obstinate face.

"Oh please, Horatius!" Latinus is getting annoyed now. "Grow up and admit that the army has not been under the control of the Senate and People of Rome since Sulla taught it that individual generals were a lot more generous with the booty. Very few men in the army give as much as the bits of fluff you're picking off that napkin for Rome. Most of them aren't from Rome – they only see Rome when they come for a triumph, and they spend most of their time in the great city getting drunk and burning down the prostitutes' street and looting as much of their so-called homeland as they can. They're as moody and capricious as our beloved governor having a hangover, with as much loyalty to Rome as their wages can buy, and no more. And that is why Caesar, who can control them for some reason, is Dictator. And that is also why anyone who tried to oppose Caesar would be a suicidal fool."

Horatius and Lucius gape for a bit, and then Lucius claps.

"I'm impressed!" he cries. "That deserves another drink – here." And a house-slave glides forward, wine jug ready. Lucius tells him to serve the wine, then go to bed, for by the look on

Horatius' face the political discussion is not yet over. They wait in silence while the slave, looking uncomfortable, tops up their cups and retires.

Horatius, to his credit, begins quietly.

"In my heart, I know that you are right, Latinus," he said. Latinus looks surprised. Horatius continues, and Lucius realises that this is more than three young men showing off in front of their peers after a few cups. Horatius is very serious and again Lucius is reminded of Cicero.

"I know that to oppose Caesar at the moment is foolishness to most men, including our revered senators who have given him all that he could have dreamed of. I also know that I am not brave enough to be the man who stands up to him myself, so I can't blame anyone else. But when I remember the stories I was told by my grandfather and my teachers, then I can't help thinking that this is all wrong! We are letting a monster rule us, a monster we have helped create, and it seems that no one is prepared to do anything about it. How can we just sit here and pontificate? It is happening now, and we are letting it. And yet, all it will take is one man to do what I am not brave enough to do – and when I meet that man, then I will follow him and be glad to be led."

There is a silence as Latinus and Lucius think about it.

"There seems to me to be only one thing a man like that would do," says Lucius slowly. "And..."

"No!" cries Latinus, suddenly seeing where the conversation is going. "You must be mad even to think it, and Horatius, I beg you, forget any such ideas at once. Lucius, you could be quaestor next year, if Caesar wanted. Don't you see? You are going to have to go along with the system he's set up – we all are. When it comes down to the boring truth, we three are nobodies – even you, Horatius, with your famous family, will get nowhere without Caesar's approval. Let those at the top fight it out – they have the most reason to fight. Don't get involved when you are too unimportant to be taken seriously."

"Caesar is very pleased with his great-nephew, Octavius, they say," says Horatius, shrugging off the slur of "unimportant". "By the time we are old enough to be taken seriously, it may be too late – the Republic will have become a kingdom, handed down from father to son, or great-uncle to great-nephew, ruled by force and allowing no opinions, no policies, no allegiances other than those approved by its king. That is what will happen – are you prepared to watch?"

"What else can we do?" asks Latinus. "No, I won't hear what you have to say, Horatius – apart from anything else, you'll only regret it tomorrow."

"But he's right," Lucius says. "About the Republic, I mean. It's dying, and we are just watching it die. But what I think we have to face is that we and every other ambitious man in the city will do that – watch – and no more, because we all know that we can do nothing about it. I am not prepared to kill Caesar, even for an honourable purpose. It's too dangerous. Not everyone would support me, and Marcus Antonius for one would almost certainly kill me. And I'm not sure I could completely agree with anyone who did such a thing."

"Why not?" demands Horatius. "It would solve our crisis of conscience, wouldn't it?"

"It would solve many things," Lucius says, and thinks of his home and family on the Caelian Hill.

"Of course it wouldn't solve anything!" snapped Latinus, ignoring him. "Haven't you been listening, Horatius? If Lucius Sestius here kills Caesar, he in turn will be killed. Let's suppose that he is prepared for that and goes ahead. What happens next? The Senate are left without a leader – can you imagine the pitiable mess they would make of trying to rule again? They'd fumble around and waste time, and while they were busy talking about it, several mini-Caesars would rise up and begin trying to gain control of the army. I can think of several without any problem, and Marcus Antonius will be at the top of the list. At that point, nobody will bother about the Senate at all, and we shall end up all fighting each other. We could have years of civil war again, worse than the last lot. Nobody would win, least of all poor old Rome."

Lucius pours the wine again and everyone suddenly finds the bottom of his own cup of great interest. Lucius' own words of caution come back to him. Caesar has made him into – what? A coward, or is that too simple? In a situation where he cannot win, or even retain his dignity, what word can describe a man like him, one who just accepts the situation? And he knows that the real reason he has not thought of killing Caesar is that he as incapable of doing such a thing as Governor Calvisius is of achieving anything of use in a brothel. He summons up the shade of Quintus Caecilius, wondering if that friendly ghost can fire him with courage and a desire for revenge, but Quintus just laughs at him and shakes his head as he fades away.

"Are you all right?" asks Horatius. "Look, we've been dying to ask, and you've dropped hints the size of elephants this evening – what is the real reason that you're out here?"

"I'm not really sure of the real reason," Lucius says. "Have another drink."

Chapter Seventeen

As they set off for Africa Nova, Lucius feels neither excitement nor fear, but a sense that soon he will find an answer. He is almost satisfied with life. Cornelius and he are in no hurry and there are many stops on their journey along the coastline.

The border between Old and New Africa is vague to say the least, but when they enter a village where the headman identifies himself as "The servant of King Juba", they know that they have crossed an invisible line. King Juba no longer rules Numidia – after running away from the Battle of Thapsus, he died in a mutual suicide fight with that pattern of the old-fashioned military hero, Marcus Petreius. Lucius' father knew Petreius: they fought the Battle of Pistoria against Catilina together. When Petreius' death was announced in Rome, Publius Sestius had sighed, but said, "A good end for someone like him." Petreius, a good man forced to make a choice, and dying because of that choice, is the supreme example of what is so wrong with civil war.

And now, King Juba's infant son has been taken by Caesar to Italy, and shown off in a triumphal procession, and the kingdom the little boy should have inherited is a Roman province. Africa Nova is not as Romanised as Old Africa; before they reach the capital, they encounter many settlements but few with an inn. Lodgings are easily available, though; they find the headman of each village and he points out one or two households where they might find a bed for the night.

The hospitality they find may be simple, but no mention is ever made by their hosts of the Roman occupation of their land, now well over a year old. Every day, someone sees them onto the road and sets them on their way with much pointing and smiling, as though it is a delight to be inconvenienced by their conquerors. But, as at that first village, the allegiance of the people is still turned towards a king who deserted them, and the old couple who put them up on the first night refuse their Roman money – very politely, but definitely. After a quick conversation in the corner, Cornelius and Lucius offer blankets, then food, but these too are refused. Rather unexpectedly, they are successful with a small scroll of Greek poems that Lucius has optimistically brought along to read on the road. The old man holds it carefully, and while he and his wife cannot read the poems, they like the strangely-marked papyrus with its neat red ribbon and tag, and from the reverent way in which it is placed in the household chest, Lucius thinks that it will be cherished for a long time. He wonders about the likelihood of anyone with a good knowledge of both classical Greek and the local dialect ever coming to the village to explain the meaning to them. Cornelius Rufus tells him not to be so patronising – well, he doesn't actually say "patronising", but that's what he means.

"You've got to remember," Cornelius continues, "Greeks have been in North Africa for hundreds of years – don't know why, but they have. What about our host back in Utica? You know his mother is Greek because you asked him how come he knew Greek so well, and where did he get a name like Cyprius. And hey presto! He chose Cyprius because his mum's from Cyprus."

He is right, of course. Indeed, soon after this they find one village leader who speaks enough Greek to hold a conversation and he suggests that wherever they stay, they should give a certain amount of money to the chief man, so that he can take it along whenever the governor's touring court-circuit is near. At such a gathering, even Roman money will be able to buy something for the good of the village, and King Juba, it appears, won't mind. Lucius wonders how many of his people have accepted that Juba is dead.

The main Roman town of Africa Nova is actually Greek – Hippo Regius or "Royal Horse". Cornelius Rufus doesn't think much of this name.

"The only four-legged friends here are the dogs and those scraggy donkeys," he points out. He has been very unimpressed with the horses hired for their journeying so far, and admittedly, the donkey Lucius has bought to carry the bags is scraggy. Africa has not lived up to its reputation for breeding good horseflesh so far, probably because the warring armies took all the decent animals. It takes more than a year to build up decent stock again, and Lucius thinks back to the cavalry horses forced to eat seaweed. Cornelius has also not been impressed with the local culture as they travel further and further from the relative civilisation of Utica. He still manages their journey beautifully: when he cannot converse fluently in Latin – or not so fluently in Greek – with the locals, he talks loudly and makes extravagant gestures while Lucius blushes. It works though; they can always make themselves understood and everyone they encounter loves Cornelius. Lucius asks him if this "shouting at the natives until I get what I want" attitude is patronising, but it isn't. Apparently.

The governor's residence in Hippo is in the southern end of the neat little town and is large. They arrive late in the day and decide to pay their courtesy call the next morning. They are hoping that the governor's staff can provide them with some information about the town; and if they are very lucky there might be rooms within the Residence itself. But for the moment, they carry on past and head for the forum to get their bearings.

Hippo Regius' forum squeezes itself in between two hills just south of a tiny harbour and Lucius thinks of the up and down life in Rome for just a moment. But Hippo's little hills cannot compete with Rome's. In fact, Hippo is a little place, though shiny and new. As the capital of the new province, it has a set of baths and a busy building industry. The brick houses and shops are all being plastered and painted. There is plenty of employment, and an air of purpose, and they find a little – yes, it is little – inn just on the edge of the forum which welcomes them with an interestingly spiced stew and clean beds.

When they left Rome, no governor had been sent out to replace Sallust, and so they are not surprised to be greeted by two legates, roughly the same age as Horatius and Latinus, but quieter and more serious. There are no grumbles from these two; they don't have time, running the province as they been for several months now with little assistance from Rome. Their names are Quintus Sulpicius and Lucius Plinius Rufus, and their delight on hearing that Lucius and Cornelius Rufus are Romans, actually from Rome herself, is evident, although they are too polite to weep in their arms at first acquaintance. Quarters are made available for the tourists within the official residence, and it is discreetly made clear that of course no payment is expected for lodgings. The two tribunes express great interest in Cornelius' ideas for reorganising the local grain supply and seem only too thankful that someone is prepared to help them manage something. It doesn't say much for Sallust's management style. Lucius also starts thinking about what he can do in this great enterprise, and as they wait for the housekeeper to arrive, he casually suggests that he too might be of some small help in administration somewhere, perhaps in a position where his legal training would be of use. The two legates exchange a quick look while Cornelius Rufus beams with pride, and they all agree that his help is appreciated. And so, his career in the provinces begins.

Much to the travellers' delight a well-trained house-slave leads them to a small suite of baths, as more slaves scurry to make ready a couple of guest rooms under the supervision of a wonderfully haughty housekeeper. She freezes off the most endearing leer that Cornelius Rufus can produce and treats the two legates to a scold for not warning her that there would be visitors. Arrangements are made to collect their bags from the inn they stayed at the night before, and as Lucius and Cornelius make their way to the baths, they can hear the housekeeper telling some poor skivvy not to drop anything, and grin with relief that they are safely out of her way. But when two cups of chilled watered wine arrive as they lie in the warm pool, they appreciate her efficiency. The slaves rub them down with large soft towels fit for the Dictator himself, and the masseur is very well trained. It occurs to Lucius that Sallust has spent (or misspent) his time in Africa profitably indeed if he has built up this excellent staff and not arranged to take it back with him. Perhaps he managed to pass them off as legitimate governor's expenses, but many of these slaves are not even native Africans; they are imported. What the locals of Hippo Regius think, the gods only know, but while he enjoys the luxury, Lucius doesn't find this example of Roman rule impressive.

The legates are all right, though. Quintus Sulpicius Galba is twenty years old, the son of a devoted Caesarian, hence the quick start to his career, though not everyone would have looked on Africa Nova as a plum in the pie. Lucius Plinius Rufus is in his late twenties, much quieter, distantly related to the late Pompey the Great, and so in more need of discretion than his younger colleague. Galba has only to live long enough to reach the required minimum ages – and maybe not even this, maybe Caesar will grant him office as a favour to his father – and political office will fall into his newly whitened toga folds. Plinius Rufus on the other hand is busy making friends wherever he can to ensure his appointment to the Senate. Sallust had probably seemed a good bet as one's boss two years ago when Caesar had clearly shown favour by helping Sallust back into political life. Now Rufus needs to find another patron, and unless he is very lucky, in the right place at the right time, and an eagle is flying backwards and reciting Sibylline verses over the Capitoline Hill, he will enter the Senate and then stick on the bottom rung of the ladder for the rest of his life. Money would help enormously but his family have less than the Sestii. Lucius feels great sympathy; his own career has never looked that full of promise and recently has looked to be more and more of a prostitute's dream of weddings. A quiet life as a lawyer – contracts, land disputes, marriage settlements – awaits him in some distant future, and is actually quite attractive.

On the morning after they move into the governor's residence, they are given a tour of the capital of the new province, and as towns go Hippo isn't a bad little – there is that word again – place. One-storey houses gleam in the sun, and Lucius can't help noticing how clean everything is – no notices or graffiti. Hippo Regius hasn't yet got around to the vandalism of electioneers and too-clever layabouts, dying to show off their unfulfilled literary aspirations. Galba and Plinius show very un-Roman enthusiasm for this place, and even know people's names, calling greetings and enquiries as they go down the streets. Cornelius is impressed.

"These two know this place properly," he says approvingly. The two of them are standing politely to one side in the forum while the two legates are brought up to date on the nefarious practices of a local thief by an angry shopkeeper.

"Their contacts are going to be good," continues Cornelius.

"We ought to do all right here." There is a pause before he adds in his most casual tone of voice, "Ever thought of an alternative career?"

It takes a moment to realise what he is getting at, but it is no surprise, and echoes Lucius' own recent thinking. He can't live on the money supplied by his father and Cicero for much longer, pride will not let him ask for more, and he cannot just wait for Caesar's death, no matter the wild talk of the young legates back in Utica. He has volunteered Cornelius some casual help, but more seriously he can use his legal training to some advantage in a place where Roman law has not been in place too long. If he wants to make money, he must go into business. It might be sordid and low, but it is practical. Tia would understand, he thinks, and feels a brief blast of homesickness. For one moment, he wonders about the practicalities of bringing his family over here to live, but he knows he is just being selfish and Cornelius needs a reply.

"Yes, I have thought about it, and I'd like to talk about it with you, and possibly those two as well sometime. Why don't we treat them to dinner tonight? Do you think you can arrange something special – use your charm on that housekeeper?"

"Sure," says Cornelius, blissfully confident as usual. The discussion with the shopkeeper over, Galba and Plinius return and entertain them with an update on the battle against Hippo's only known shoplifter.

"This place has a lot of potential," says Galba earnestly at dinner that night. He looks at Plinius for confirmation.

"We supply quite a bit of grain as things stand now," says Plinius, "and that is despite the farms here not being the most efficient. We have been working on getting the local farmers to realise that we are now a province and that their market has opened up, just a bit. Hippo's growth has taken them a bit by surprise, and at the moment we are managing to sustain the local population, which includes the military, with some surplus. A couple of the bigger estates have got together to hire a ship every year. They sell to a man in Ostia. I can't remember his name, but he isn't one of the big players. There is definitely room for improvement. Galba and I have only just started thinking about it really, but now that we have you here, we'd like to get things moving before the new governor arrives. We don't yet know anything about who it might be, but Galba's father is going to write to us the moment it's decided. His letter has a good chance of arriving first."

"You're right about the potential," says Cornelius, leaning forward. "The whole of North Africa needs to think about how it's operating. You could do with thinking bigger, so why not get in touch with the people in Utica, the legates? Don't bother with the governor there – he's a slob."

"He's a friend of Caesar," says Plinius dryly.

"Lad," says Cornelius, "he's still a slob, no disrespect to the Dictator intended."

Plinius grins, though Galba looks shocked at hearing his respected colleague addressed as "Lad". He is probably not sure whether his father's friend, the Dictator, has been insulted as well.

"All right," says Plinius. "We'll get the <u>lads</u> in Utica on to this."

"And I'll let the corn merchants in Utica know," says Cornelius. "I've got some good contacts already through the merchant Sestius and I stayed with. Lucius, why don't you get a list to these two?"

"I'd like to get working on something, and I'm going nowhere in the foreseeable future," Lucius says. "If I can make some money from it, I'm in on any scheme."

Galba is shocked at such vulgarity; Plinius understands too well.

"How do you plan to make money and be a senator?" asks Galba. There is a silence while the rest look at him. He colours and says defiantly, "Well, it's forbidden, so you'll have to show some discretion. How will it work?"

Lucius claps Cornelius Rufus on the back. "My new colleague and I have worked out a mutually beneficial arrangement. Don't worry, it won't ever cast aspersions on you. And it needs to be done if you two are to make something of this posting."

They plan late into the night and start the next day.

Chapter Eighteen

Paperwork first, so they draw up a basic plan of action. Lists of merchants, farmers and ship-owners are compiled, and then they move to the land. They discuss who owns what; they talk about plains, mountains and marshes, about who will work with whom, and who won't touch the scheme; they plan routes from farms to ports, tot up the numbers of available transport carts and the necessary animals to draw the carts. They consider barges, and sea-going ships, and which skipper can be trusted to get to Ostia, without sinking or ending up in Britannia. Lucius drafts specimen contracts, and a secretary is co-opted to make copies of the agreed wording, so that there will be no delays waiting for agreements to be drawn up. They know that they can make no official promises on behalf of the state until the new governor arrives, but there is a lot that private enterprise can get going, in anticipation. And at the end of several days' thinking and scribbling, Lucius writes it all up and sends a copy off to Utica to Venuleius and his colleagues, with a request for their ideas.

The idea is very simple: we get everyone to agree to coordinate. We want farmers to get into groups and transport grain together to save costs; then proper liaison with ships' masters should make transport more efficient. Do either of you have a contact among the grain chandlers in Ostia? We need someone looking to expand, but not too small. We are ambitious... And that's where you come in. We think Old and New Africa should work together – can you persuade your governor that it is his idea and get the ball rolling from your end? There isn't any point in the provinces working separately on this, not when every ship is going to want to do the crossing from Utica.

Then they celebrate over dinner and cannot stop talking about their grand scheme. Galba in particular is very pleased.

"If there's the framework for a good, profitable system up and running when he arrives, it stands to reason the new governor will be more likely to let us organise the state contracts. We have to get in some decent managers and keep them under control, though, or this will all be for nothing. They remember Verres here, and having Sallust as governor just confirmed their worst fears as far as the locals are concerned."

"What province doesn't remember Verres?" asks Cornelius. "He's what most of them still think Rome's about – beat 'em up, then make 'em cough up."

"And that's why they were so quick off the mark with Sallust when he started," Plinius says. "After three months, they had a deputation organised and sent off to Rome to complain. They even wondered about contacting Cicero first, to see if he wanted to help prosecute, as he did with the Verres case."

"It's twenty-five years since Cicero prosecuted Verres," Lucius says. "I don't think he'd take on another case like it now – he's too old, and he never did like prosecution work. But he would have supported the province, I'm sure. He's very keen on not using one's office to make money." He gets a couple of accusing looks for that but doesn't care. He isn't in office and has no intention of being in office for the foreseeable future, and he is going to use some of his limited means to invest in this scheme. Galba and Plinius are the ones who cannot make money from it, but then, it is supposed to be their job anyway.

As midwinter approaches, the two legates start to travel all over the new province to explain their plans. Rome is forgotten in their new enthusiasm for this warm, lovely and fertile country. It seems very strange to many of the New Africans that these upper-class young men should spend so much time on such a task, but nobody in Africa Nova is going to stop their fun. In Rome, the political situation tightens and tenses as Caesar takes on more honours and offices; in the pale sunshine of Africa Nova they are only concerned with corn, the basic material that keeps the politicians in power. The legates hire translators, hold meetings, visit tiny villages, cajole merchants, nod sympathetically at tales of woe and loss; they organise, persuade, and suggest remedies for a stream of problems. Sulpicius Galba, it turns out, has a knack of getting on with farmers; his youth, as well as his undeniable good birth, means that they always give him a hearing. He is always careful to let them talk first and stands and looks impressed with their superior wisdom. He isn't as ignorant as they might have supposed either, for his family estates are extensive and he has spent every family holiday since he can remember on prime agricultural land in Campania. He knows how to defer to the African farmers (which they love), and when to drop the odd suggestion or comment that lets them know that they can't fool him. When he pleads with them to "just try", they can't resist.

Back in Hippo, Lucius tackle the ship masters and the middlemen, the merchants. Cornelius Rufus comes along to their meetings, supposedly as an adviser, but actually to point out ways of overcoming the many problems put forward by those unwilling to cooperate. He attacks them in one of two ways: blistering scorn or no-nonsense contradiction. Opponents to the scheme either wither or flounce off in a huff, and the whingers and the scoundrels are discovered.

Once they have done the preliminary reconnaissance, the legates decide to hold a series of meetings in Hippo Regius at the governor's residence. There are two major problems they have to solve – transport inland, and investment. Getting the grain from the farmers to the port is going to be expensive as there are few rivers of any use, and all along the chain of supply, the people of Africa Nova are unwilling to part with cash. They have to be persuaded that the risk is worth it. And of course, all the way the legates have to pretend that they will have the full confidence of whoever is coming out to govern. Several weeks after Cornelius and Lucius first arrive in Hippo, they decide to hold a series of dinners, inviting all interested parties in the weeks leading up to the December festival of the Saturnalia. And the inevitable happens as plans for a suppliers' meeting with dinner are being discussed.

"Publius Sittius wants to come over from Cirta," says Plinius. "I suppose we had better offer to put him up."

"Publius Sittius?" Lucius can't help echoing the name.

"He has a big estate in Cirta, south and west of here," says Galba. "He should be very useful. He got on well with the governor last year, and you must know how he helped Caesar in the war, Lucius."

"I do indeed," says Lucius, and wonders how to make the most of this opportunity.

He and Cornelius Rufus go off to a little wine shop the next morning and hold a council of war. The enemy is coming to them.

"You need to tell the legates," says Cornelius Rufus. "Your name must not be mentioned." He sees Lucius' face and says, "Well, you can't go to the dinner and introduce yourself now, can you?"

"No, I suppose not," says Lucius, abandoning dreams of watching Publius Sittius gasp and pale as he realises who is seated next to him at dinner...

"I'll go because he doesn't know me," says Cornelius Rufus. "And we can prime the youngsters to steer the conversation a bit, see if we can get anything out of him. He might be willing to talk a bit more freely on home territory, and he won't see the legates or me as anyone important."

"Well, it must be pretty common knowledge that he has been away, and I bet everyone knows that he went to Italy, so you can start there," says Lucius. "And if he is staying here overnight, then I am going to see if I can have a nose round his room."

"No point," says Cornelius Rufus knowledgeably. "He isn't going to bring anything incriminating to a meeting about grain supplies."

"I know," says Lucius. "I just want to."

He doesn't say out loud that he wants to violate some small part of Publius Sittius' life, just to see how it feels.

Now all they have to do is make sure that Lucius' presence goes unnoticed. This may be tricky. He has already been introduced around Hippo Regius as "Sestius the lawyer", and any one of a number of people could mention the name to Sittius. They have to tell the legates why Lucius left Rome, and the part played by Publius Sittius.

"Ye gods and heroes! You did what?" yelps Sulpicius Galba.

"Left Rome to show Sittius that I was no longer going to investigate and so was not a threat," says Lucius patiently.

"And you came here because...?" Plinius Rufus' tone is sarcastic.

"All I've done here is tour Carthage and help you with the grain project," says Lucius. "But obviously, I don't want to meet Sittius."

The legates exchange glances.

"Will the slaves keep quiet?" asks Galba, then answering his own question, "Yes, probably if we warn them and make it worth their while. We shall get Galatea to organise that."

Lucius thinks that if he were told to do something by the housekeeper, Galatea, he would definitely obey orders.

"And we had better make Sittius the only guest at this particular dinner," says Plinius. "Just in case someone asks where that nice young lawyer is. It is a good thing that you have stuck to Hippo all this time – I see now why." He shakes his head. "What on earth are you doing here, Lucius Sestius?"

"I need to keep looking," says Lucius.

"And are you sure that you will be safe?" Galba asks Cornelius Rufus.

"I'll be fine," he answers with no sign of any strain in his voice or expression. "He's never seen me, and I'm not generally well known in senatorial circles."

"He might have seen you at the docks with Rubria," Lucius points out.

"But," says Cornelius, "he probably didn't. And if he did, there's no reason for him to remember me. He'd have been looking at Rubria anyway. She's quite something." And he sounds wistful for just a moment.

"And you need us to ask him if he went to Rome, because obviously we are desperate for the latest news from the big city. And what are we actually hoping to hear? A confession?" Plinius still thinks this is a mad idea.

"If you can get him to admit he met Caesar, that would be good," says Lucius, refusing to be riled. "And if you can get him talking about his valiant role in the Catilinarian Conspiracy, I'd like to hear that."

"Because you are going to be hiding behind a curtain, listening to everything?" asks Plinius.

Lucius laughs. "No. I'll be busy elsewhere."

Plinius groans. "You're going to snoop in his room, aren't you?" He turns to Galba. "This is going to take a lot of bribing. We had better get a good story ready for Galatea and the other slaves."

And so, this is organised. Galatea is told that Lucius is an agent of Caesar spying on Sittius, a suspected traitor. Cornelius Rufus rolls his eyes when he hears this, but it does work: Galatea is thrilled and loses no time in rallying the staff. Promises of extremely generous Saturnalia presents are made. Lucius moves into a little suite of rooms at the back of the governor's residence, far away from the public rooms and guest quarters. As long as Sittius behaves like any normal guest, there is no reason they should meet. Lucius determinedly squashes a rising feeling of doom inside himself.

When the day comes, Lucius stays in his rooms, and listens, though he cannot tell any difference in the background noise of the governor's residence as the day goes on. At mid-day, Cornelius Rufus brings in food and wine and the news that nothing has happened. Lucius spends the afternoon imagining ways in which this evening's drama may go wrong. Eventually, he tries to work on the grain project, planning possible routes for transporting grain from somewhere inland, like Cirta, to the little port of Hippo Regius. Road transportation, then sailing along the coast looks good – two or three days by cart, then less than one day by sea; factor in the loading and unloading. What about if a ship can be persuaded to go along the coast to pick up the load and then straight to Rome...?

"He's here," says Cornelius Rufus, elegant in his best party tunic. "Give us time to settle him down to dinner before you start your life of crime."

"Which room is he in?" asks Lucius, as all problems of transportation fall away.

"The other side of young Galba's," says Cornelius Rufus, and winks. He doesn't wish Lucius luck.

Knowing that he is about to do something dishonourable, Lucius finds the short journey through the residence overpoweringly and ominously quiet. He has never realised how dark the short corridors are and wonders why he didn't bring the lamp from his desk. He meets nobody, and the curtain which separates the small bedroom from the corridor is already slightly drawn back, obligingly inviting him in. There isn't much to do once inside. He checks the cloak – camel-hair and wool, very nice – hanging on the peg and the small leather travel bag on the bed, but there is nothing to mark their owner as a murderer. He feels under the pillow and even checks under the mattress. Publius Sittius has some good quality clothes, sleeps in a nice soft wool tunic and likes to ward off the chill of a North African winter. He also likes to have nicely manicured nails: a small roll of material on the washstand reveals a dainty set of clippers and files, all in bronze and polished lovingly. Lucius sits on the bed and wonders what else he expected. As he stands to go, he glances at the bedside table, and he sees that there is a scroll lying next to an unlit clay lamp. Surely that must belong to Sittius? What sort of literature does a man like that bring with him on a jaunt to the big city?

Lucius takes the scroll and sits down again as he unrolls it – to find that it is a speech by Cicero, the speech made in defence of a man called Sulla. Lucius skims the text, vaguely remembering a series of lessons in which he and Caecilius had pulled the speech apart in order to tell his father what the orator was hoping to achieve. The speech had worked, he remembers – Sulla had been acquitted. He realises after a while that this is a much-read volume. Small cracks are attacking the papyrus at some points, and the ribbon on the end of the wooden spool has lost its seal and is fraying at the end. And in one passage the letters are faded: maybe Sittius has left it open in the sun, or maybe he has just rubbed at the text for some reason. Lucius realises that it is a passage in which Cicero is discussing Sittius himself, and seems to be defending him:

"And now I must not desert the cause of my old friend and host. Can we really believe that a man like Publius Sittius would, thanks to either background or conviction, even want to wage war against the Republic?"

And next to this passage, in the margin, someone has drawn a grinning face, no more than a few scribbled curves and dots.

Lucius reads it again. "Old friend and host"? Cicero has never mentioned this. Is this just the inflated rhetoric of a defence lawyer, or does Cicero actually know Publius Sittius a little better than he has admitted? Lucius memorises the passage, then rolls up the scroll and replaces it.

Lucius makes his way back to his own rooms without incident, though as he enters he is glad to find that Galatea has left him a tray. He isn't really hungry, but the relief of getting away with his snooping makes him want to eat and drink just for the satisfaction of knowing that he can.

When Cornelius Rufus eventually comes along, Lucius has too much going around in his head. But Cornelius Rufus is relaxed and grinning.

"It went fine, lad," he says, with just a hint of slurring. "But he can drink all right. The two youngsters are properly done in. So, I've told Galatea to make breakfast late tomorrow, and I'll let you know when Sittius has gone, and then we can fill you in. All right?"

Lucius needs to sleep. He agrees and goes to bed.

Water, oil and bread have appeared by his bedside when he wakes the next morning, and he blesses the wonderful Galatea. He has no sense of the time of day but knows that it can't be too late and that he must be patient. Sittius must be out of the way. Sure enough, a slightly bleary-eyed Cornelius Rufus walks in and informs him that a proper breakfast is being served now that Sittius has gone, and he and the two legates are dying to update Lucius on their evening.

Galatea has prepared a hearty but plain breakfast, and while Sulpicius Galba can only nibble dry bread with a look of queasy trepidation, Plinius and Lucius dig in. Cornelius Rufus says he has already had breakfast with last night's guest.

"Well, someone had to see him off," he says, and the two legates look slightly ashamed. Lucius is struck by the wonderful thought that to all intents and purposes, Cornelius Rufus is now a member of the governor's staff in Africa Nova...

"Did you get into his room?" asks Galba, abruptly.

"Yes, and there wasn't much, just as we thought," says Lucius. "But he had some interesting reading material by the

162

bed – a copy of Cicero's speech in defence of Sulla, with a passage marked."

"Most people have at least three or four Cicero speeches in their libraries," points out Plinius. "Though I personally wouldn't bring mine along for an overnight stay."

"Good for getting you to sleep," mutters Galba.

"It mentions him, Sittius, I mean. By name," and Lucius recites the passage he found marked.

"An old friend, eh?" says Cornelius Rufus. "Marcus Tullius Cicero kept quiet about that, didn't he? How unlike him..."

"It could be nothing though," points out Plinius. "Orators say anything which suits their case."

"Still should have mentioned it," says Cornelius Rufus.

"My father didn't mention it either," says Lucius, suddenly worried.

"When was the speech?" asks Galba.

"The year after Cicero's consulship," says Cornelius Rufus. "He was in demand, what with all the post-Catilina fallout. Sulla was charged with involvement in the conspiracy and having Cicero defend him really impressed the jury. You know – if Cicero, of all people, said Sulla wasn't guilty, then he couldn't've been."

"My father was in Macedonia," realises Lucius. "So that probably explains why he didn't remember it."

"And how much of the speech was actually about Sittius?" asks Plinius.

Lucius thinks back. "A few lines. Not much more than the bit I quoted to you."

"Easy enough to overlook," says Cornelius Rufus. "Though I would still expect Cicero to have said something."

"And what about you lot?" asks Lucius. "Did he come out with anything juicy or were you all too merry to notice?"

Galba winces. "I certainly was," he admits. "All I remember is that he seemed a nice, ordinary farmer type. Once we had discussed what his estate produces, I got a bit hazy."

"You were hazy all right," says Plinius cheerfully. "And I was only a bit better. Good thing we had Cornelius with us! Though even so, he didn't admit to much, did he?"

"He trotted out a story about being Cicero's spy during the Catilinarian crisis," says Cornelius Rufus. "And – get this – he started off as Caesar's spy. Caesar knew Catilina was dangerous – got Sittius to infiltrate the conspiracy for him, then when they realised how serious it was, told Cicero. Cicero took over running Sittius as a double agent and arranged for him to escape to Africa as things hotted up."

"It was a great story," says Plinius. "Who would have thought old Cicero was so cunning? A spider controlling all the threads. No wonder the conspiracy failed. According to Sittius, Cicero knew everything the conspirators planned within a day of them planning it."

"And you believed him?" asks Lucius.

"I did," answers Plinius. "He had no hesitation, and it all hung together. Even if you account for the usual sort of exaggeration, it sounded convincing."

Lucius looks at Cornelius Rufus, who thinks, then slowly nods.

"Yes, that's it. Convincing. He's either a really good actor or it happened like he said. Which leaves me still wondering why Cicero hasn't mentioned it."

At that moment, Galatea sails into the room, a maid in tow, and all the men straighten up automatically. Galba hastily drinks a cup of water, then looks as though he wishes he hadn't.

"Gentlemen," announces the redoubtable lady, "this is Chrysis. She helps in the kitchen mostly, and she has something to tell you."

Chrysis, barely into her teens and skinny to the point of boniness, looks very excited but keeps her eyes fixed firmly on the floor in front of her. Galatea draws her gently into the centre of the room.

"Go on – what you just told me."

Chrysis needs no further encouragement. She keeps her gaze down, but her tone is anything but humble. She can't wait to tell her story.

"I was talking to this man that Publius Sittius brought with him last night, his freedman. He's called Messenio." This all comes out in a rush and she takes a breath and continues more

164

steadily. Nobody prompts her or stops her with a question. "He was boasting about how important his master is, and we got a bit fed up and were teasing him and saying if he's so important why is he stuck out here, sort of thing. So, he got annoyed. He wanted to impress us. So, I said why didn't he tell us what sort of people visited his master, and of course he couldn't say anyone because he lives miles from anywhere and no one visits but he said his master was always getting letters."

Lucius feels the interest in the room quicken. She continues.

"So of course, we asked who wrote to him that we'd heard of and he came up with some names, and we were all dead impressed, but then he knocked over his cup, and we talked about other stuff. And this morning me and the secretary Hermes got together, and he wrote down as much as we could both remember, and here it is."

And she produces a small wax tablet and passes it to Plinius. He looks at it and his eyes widen. He passes it to Galba, who passes it to Cornelius Rufus. Lucius feels he must say something.

"Thank you very much, Galatea, Chrysis, we really appreciate this. Chrysis, we may want to talk to you again about this. Is that all right?"

She looks thrilled and nods her head. Galatea ushers her out and Cornelius Rufus passes the wax tablet to Lucius. On it are four names:

•Caesar
•Marcus Aemilius Lepidus
•Marcus Antonius
•Marcus Tullius Tiro

The Dictator, his second in command Lepidus, his friend Antonius who is already lined up to be consul the next year – and a freedman secretary, faithful servant of Cicero: Tiro.

Chapter Nineteen

The Saturnalia is one of the happiest times in the Roman calendar. It comes at midwinter, just as everyone needs cheering up, and no one is left out or forgotten. This year, the legates have decided to combine the festival with a grand dinner for the most important figures in their scheme to expand Africa Nova's grain supply. This will be held on the night when the slaves are invited to recline at the dinner table and let the masters serve them for a change, traditionally a time of carefully judged misrule. Too much wine will flow for all the residence's staff to be on show, so the legates have planned a big party for most of them; a select half a dozen will be at the dinner. While Galatea the housekeeper presides over the noisy jollifications at the back of the building, the reliable few will act out the Saturnalia for the benefit of the guests, who will be able to see Romans enjoying themselves. More importantly, the festival gives the Romans a chance to show how approachable they are. If any of the slaves get drunk or go too far ("They won't," says Galba confidently), they can say it is all part of the festival. To Lucius' surprise, Cornelius Rufus is the least enthusiastic about this great idea.

"It'll be fine as long as everything goes exactly as to plan," he tells Lucius. "But the whole point about Saturnalia is that it doesn't go to plan – everything is topsy-turvy. It's supposed to be unpredictable and silly. All it'll take is one rude slave and you've lost the respect of a lot of people. They've all heard of the festival of course, but suppose our guests don't get it and decide that they want to talk business over dinner? Bang goes all your ideas about having fun, the jovial face of Rome and all that twaddle."

"We'll just have to educate both the slaves and the guests," Lucius says firmly. "We shall say that this is an ideal opportunity for the Africans to get a valuable insight into the Roman character. And we'll stress that they're here to enjoy themselves. Business will have to wait until the morning."

"When everyone will be hung-over," says Cornelius dryly. He sighs. "I still don't like it. Which slaves will be there?"

"The secretaries, the librarian, the cook," says Lucius. "That's five, the five most senior and reliable."

"Who's going to cook then?" asked Cornelius. "It should be our two lah-di-dah legates, but I can't see it myself. Or have you volunteered?"

"We didn't think that would be a good idea," says Lucius smoothly. "The cook has a friend who also cooks."

"What a surprise," says Cornelius.

"The food is organised," Lucius says. "Stop worrying."

"Thank the gods," says Cornelius, with a pious glance to the heavens. "For one moment, I thought I was going to have to save the day again. "And he winks and strolls away.

As he makes preparations, Lucius thinks about the party they will be having on the Caelian Hill at home. Saturnalia is always a huge success in his house – his mother says that it is because they have relatively few slaves and they have all been with the family for years. Decius will head the slave family for the day, while Publius Sestius capers along in Decius' footsteps with pen and wax tablets at the ready for dictation. Decius will stop every now and then and say, "Now take this down – Happy Saturnalia everyone!" Cornelia will cook a carefully planned meal, which is served by the family; and, on behalf of the slaves, Decius will invite the family to join in the meal. Saturnalia dinners, Lucius recalls, always end with everyone except Publius Sestius and Decius creeping out, leaving the two of them to their tipsy recollections of bygone glories. The whole household sleeps in very late the next morning, and then everything goes back to normal. There was one never-to-be-forgotten Saturnalia when Tia, then aged about six, and Paulus the house-boy, who was even younger and hadn't started his household duties properly yet, had both crawled under the table and managed to get drunk on the lees of the wine in all the cups. When people around the table had begun to play a word game, Tia had joined in, loudly, with a very rude word she wasn't supposed to know. Lucius smiles as he remembers the look on his mother's face as this extremely vulgar comment had floated up from underneath the table.

"What's the joke?" asks Plinius as he comes up to consult, holding a stack of wax tablets filled with his scribbled ideas.

"I was thinking about home and the parties we had at Saturnalia, and all the silly things that happened – you know."

"Saturnalia's a good time for doing things people never let you forget," says Plinius. "Once, my father put his foot in a half of a huge yellow squash, and it wouldn't come off. We all laughed ourselves silly while he hopped around the dining room getting madder and madder, cursing us all and ordering us to help. And of course, everyone just said that it was Saturnalia and they weren't going to help."

"My little sister entertained us with her repertoire of swear words," Lucius says.

"Did she indeed? A woman I'd like to meet then," Plinius remarks, as he hands the top slate to Lucius. "This is the seating plan. Two tables, three couches to each table, with the open end of each table together. There are the five slaves, three of us, if we get the chance to sit down, the corn merchants' representative, those two farmers Galba dug up, and the master of the <u>Diana</u>. We can share two to a couch. You and Galba and I will be up and down serving the meal anyway. Is that all right?"

Lucius hastily stops wondering if Plinius is a good match for Tia and resolves to talk to his mother soon – or, rather, when he gets back to Rome. He looks at the seating plan and immediately sees the flaw. Plinius has forgotten Cornelius Rufus. Without saying anything, Lucius scratches the name onto the tablet. Plinius looks puzzled at first, then guilty.

"I'm sorry," he says quietly.

"I used to do it all the time," Lucius replies, and they leave it at that.

Lucius and Cornelius Rufus have decided to leave speculating about Tiro and Cicero and Sittius for a few days. They and the legates have hammered on the question over and over and have come up with no satisfactory answer. They have questioned Chrysis and the other slaves and come up with no further information, other than that the slaves were impressed by Caesar's name being on the list. Finally, everyone has to admit that they have no clue as to why Sittius should be receiving letters from Tiro: it is bad enough that the three top men in Rome have contact with him. But Cornelius Rufus makes sure that the slaves are rewarded generously, and in advance of Saturnalia. Chrysis the maid goes around the residence with a selection of bright ribbons in her hair and a big smile on her face. Lucius is amused to see that both legates have taken to smiling back at her.

Three days before the Saturnalia festival, one of the secretaries – Lucius can never remember which is which – announces that a man is waiting in the main hall. This man has given no name but has made it clear that he wishes to see Lucius in particular. The secretary likes his clothes and his Latin, so has gone to tell Lucius. Thinking that one of his merchant contacts is being a little mysterious, Lucius strolls into the huge atrium, and recognises the visitor at once. The man smiles.

"How do you like Hippo Regius then?" he enquires, enjoying the surprise he has caused.

For a quick moment fear washes over Lucius' skin, making it cold and prickly, and his stomach tightens. He has not thought about that meeting at Carthage for weeks; he has been so taken up with trying to understand the role of Publius Sittius. But does he have any reason to be scared? Or, come to that, polite?

"What are you doing here?" he asks and makes it as unwelcoming as he can.

The man is much cooler than he was amid the ruins at Carthage. He makes no attempt to convert him this time and doesn't get upset at the thought that Lucius might not like him. He has progressed.

"I'm checking up on you of course," he says. "Did you think we wouldn't?"

"I see no reason why you should continue to be interested in me." Try as he might, Lucius is worried that the words sound like a whine. "What am I doing here that is so alarming? Or don't you think the corn trade needs a bit of organising? Has it occurred to you that if you leave us all alone we might get something worthwhile done?"

"Why do you say <u>we</u>?" he asks. "I'm only interested in you. If you've been putting your time here to good use, I am of course delighted, as I'm sure the Dictator would be."

He sounds so pompous that Lucius almost laughs and with that feeling something inside him relaxes.

"Come along then," he invites. "We'll have some wine in the small dining room, and you can question me there. Do you have a name?"

His visitor raises his eyebrows at such amiability, but makes no answer, following him into the study. Lucius shouts for Chrysis – yellow ribbon today – and gives her instructions, and they wait for the wine to arrive before getting down to business. The man takes his drink well-watered and makes sure that Lucius notices this.

"You seem well established here," is his opening comment, and Lucius takes up the explanation, making sure that he emphasises how lax the Senate has been in their care of the province. He emphasises the part played by the two legates and even Cornelius Rufus comes in for praise. Lucius' own hard work, although he does not refer to it directly, is therefore made clear. His own modesty warms him and at the end of the little speech he sits back and admires himself.

In return, his Carthaginian friend makes some polite remarks of approval and for a time they do not fall out as they discuss the farming and trade situation in North Africa. As the visitor speaks, Lucius remembers that the man owns an estate himself; he is certainly familiar with the region's agriculture. He even suggests a couple of names, Roman knights with interests in Old Africa, who might be persuaded to invest in this particular venture. Lucius is grateful for the information, but after a while begins to wonder when the man is planning to leave. When at last the man gets to his feet, Lucius is quick to get up and smile him into the atrium once more. It is as they are waiting for a slave to bring his cloak that the man finally hands over a small package from Lucius' father. Lucius is astonished.

"I was visiting the Governor Calvisius," explains the visitor, "and it happened that an adventurous captain had just docked in Utica harbour with this letter for you. Naturally I offered to bring it."

"Naturally," Lucius answers, and takes the letter, pointedly examining the seal. Nothing immediately strikes him as amiss, so he smiles at his visitor and bids him a firm farewell. The man sighs at this evidence of lack of trust, allows the slave to drape his cloak around him, and walks out of the residence without saying anything further. Lucius stands holding the package and staring after him until the slave with trampling delicacy asks if he requires anything. The questions Lucius wants answering dance around his head in frustration.

Back in his room, Lucius discovers that the package holds several letters from the family, among which Tia's breathless account of Caesar's Spanish triumph is an unconscious masterpiece. He reads it with a huge grin on his face.

My dear brother Lucius,

I hope you are well. Our mother and father are well and send their regards. I too am well. There, that is all the politeness I can summon.

We went to Caesar's triumph yesterday and it was – astonishing! I know that the triumphs he held last year were very good too, but as you know, Mother only let me go to the one about Caesar's victories in Gaul, and I really can't remember much about it, because we watched it from the terrace at Uncle Marcus' house, and had to wait forever. I didn't even get to see that Gaulish leader with the unpronounceable name that everyone was talking about, but Uncle Marcus gave us date rolls, and his lovely Tullia was with us, pregnant and happy. I miss her a lot, Lucius. And what happened to Caecilius just reminds me of it even more. But that won't help you, so I shall cheer up and tell you about the triumph!

Father let Paulus go to see the soldiers lining up on the Campus Martius first thing in the morning, and we didn't see him again until it was dark. He had a great time, because some soldiers let him help them get ready, and they showed him their tent and all their gear, and now he says he wants to join the legions when he grows up. He ran alongside them, and it sounds like they made him their mascot, because when they went off to the feasting they took him with them and fed him all sorts of amazing food and too much wine... It was nice of them though. Melissa had to put him to bed and let him sleep for the whole of the next morning. Nobody really minded, as he is still young, but Melissa is worried that he really does want to become a soldier, and hasn't realised that he can't.

We didn't go to Uncle Marcus' house this time. I don't know why, but I expect he was already busy. Father was walking with the Senate of course, so Decius and Mico took me and Mother. We found a really good place to sit on the steps of the Temple of Portunus in the Forum Boarium, and we remembered to bring cushions and food so although we had to wait for a long time it wasn't too bad. And all the people around us were so interesting! There was a baker from the Subura who was very polite and gave Mother some honey rolls for us. Then there was a family from the Aventine, with a girl who looked my age and every time her brother said anything, she rolled her eyes at me and made me laugh. I thought of you of course! As the procession approached everyone bunched together a lot more, and I could hear what everyone was saying: and I realised that many of them were not very pleased with Caesar. One man kept saying in deliberately loud tones that it was wrong to celebrate fighting other Romans. We all knew what he meant but of course we all still stayed and watched it, so that was slightly uncomfortable if you thought about it too much.

We were in a good position to see the procession when it first came around the Capitoline Hill and crossed the Velabrum to the Circus Maximus. I didn't see any prisoners at all which I was really glad about because I hate thinking about what is going to happen to them. And any prisoners would have to be Roman, and that would be horrible. I suppose even Caesar realised that. There were only a couple of floats with captured weapons on them as well, and the loud man said, "Roman weapons! How do we even know they are from the other side?" But there were lots of pictures of Spain being carried along, and some Spanish people dressed in gorgeous outfits. The women all wore dresses in bright colours and had long black hair and lots of jewellery, and the men had beautiful leather tunics and belts and boots. They were smiling and waving, and Decius said they were a tribe who had supported Caesar. So, we all cheered them, even the loud man.

Then came the Senate in their best togas, all trying to look very serious, but Father saw us and waved. He was walking with Titus Fadius Gallus who came to dinner that time, and he waved too. Mother said that she expected that Father and Titus Fadius had spent the whole walk gossiping. By now it was after noon, and a crowd of lictors in red cloaks came marching, looking very fierce – they were Caesar's bodyguard. And then the most beautiful horses came along drawing the chariot. They were all white and so well-behaved, even though the cheering suddenly got very loud. And there was Caesar in the chariot, a lot smaller than I thought he would be. His red-painted face was very strange; I had forgotten that triumphing generals have to do that, and it spooked me a little. His purple robe was beautiful, though, and we were close enough to see the gold embroidery. It actually glinted when it caught the sun. Can you imagine having that much gold, just on a robe? Behind him came lots of men on horseback, then came the soldiers. They weren't in armour, but they were singing marching songs, so I knew they must be the legionaries. They all had wreaths and garlands and looked drunk, but I had to pretend that I didn't get all the words of the song they were singing, and Mother said she couldn't hear properly either. I'll tell you when you get home, but let's just say they seemed to admire Caesar's – er – prowess. The crowd was certainly appreciative! Then Mother said we should try to slip away while the procession returned to the Forum for the sacrifice, and we left just as the two white oxen for the sacrifice were led past. Instead of going to the Circus Maximus, they went off up the Velabrum to be ready on top of the Capitoline Hill when Caesar arrived. We had to fight our way through the crowds, and it took ages to get home. All of our usual shortcuts were crowded, and Decius had to keep thinking up other ways around. I was glad to get home; after a while, watching men marching along the road can be less than thrilling. It was interesting to see the Dictator because I can't remember seeing him last year, and of course he is hardly ever in Rome. He is quite old, isn't he? I was surprised that he still fights in the battles alongside the legionaries. And I really liked the pictures and the people from Spain.

We had a lovely meal that evening, and Decius said there was a massive feast around the Forum and Campus Martius and anybody could go. And Paulus did go, of course, and missed our dinner, which made Melissa cross, but I think she was actually a bit worried about where Paulus had got to. And then there were some gladiatorial games and chariot racing, but we didn't go because, frankly, we didn't want to. I stayed with Albinia for a couple of days instead and she took me shopping for a new dress and we talked about how to choose a new maid. She is going to ask her friends if anyone has a suitable girl they can recommend. She says that is better than going to the slave market and choosing a complete stranger you know nothing about. I think a new maid is a good idea, and Mother agrees. Oh Lucius – she and Father will do anything for me at the moment. They are lovely.

This letter will take weeks to get to you, I'm afraid. Father won't say where, but you must be overseas. I hope you eventually read it all right, Lucius. Take care, wherever you are. We miss you loads. Everyone sends their love.

With all good wishes from your sister Tia

PS Mico and Melissa have just come back from the market and guess what Caesar has done? Apparently, he didn't think the feast after the triumph was good enough and he is going to put on an even bigger one! I bet Paulus tries to go again. I can't imagine how much that will cost Caesar. It is just getting silly.

Lucius hopes that Caesar's spies have read this and sent a copy on to the Dictator – especially the bits about him being old and short. He reads between the bright, chatty lines and can see Tia recovering slowly. There are hints of her old cheerful cynicism. Immensely cheered, he turns to his father's letter.

After assuring him that his family are all well and still love him, Sestius senior starts reporting the news from the Forum, with as much discretion as Tia's description of the aged little Dictator.

Caesar's latest triumph passed off in the usual style, although he's had so many triumphs now we're all getting blasé.

One of the tribunes even risked annoying the Dictator by not standing as he rode past, and they say that Caesar is furious. He's certainly been making childish comments about it ever since, which is tiresome of him.

Lucius hurriedly re-checks the seal – it really does look as though no one has tampered with the letter, but is it within the realms of possibility that his smiling friend did not read it and reseal it? Lucius acknowledges that there is no hope, and that Caesar probably already has a copy of this letter on his desk. His father continues:

And at last we have had some elections! Forty quaestors this year – if the trend for huge numbers of useless junior officials continues, we should be able to get you in without any trouble, in a few years' time, when you're back, of course. Caesar has made it clear that he does not intend staying in Rome for much longer, and certainly it is a long time since we paid serious attention to the East. Parthia has captured Roman standards in her keeping, and to get those standards back is a popular as well as patriotic move. Everyone expects that the Dictator will start campaigning there next spring.

Lucius notes the huge number of quaestors – after four years of civil war, Rome does not have that many men of the right class and age, so where is Caesar getting all these young officials from? Promoting outsiders is the obvious way, but it is not too popular. He also wonders why it is that Caesar seems unable to stay in Rome for any length of time. Soon he will be too old to go campaigning – what then? Lucius cannot see Caesar residing by the fire and smiling generously while younger men go to war to gain glory. Caesar has enjoyed military success for too long, gaining his power by soldiering successfully all those years in Gaul, sending back enthusiastic reports of his progress and ostentatious displays of captured wealth. Perhaps he is going to make sure that he has done all the fighting necessary before he retires. He would certainly find a young imitator very hard to tolerate.

As you can imagine, this longing of Caesar's to be away from us all is taken almost as a personal insult by some in the Senate and there is a good deal of grumbling going on at the moment.

Why doesn't Decius censor his letters? Lucius shudders and reads on.

Not to put too fine a point on it, Lucius, and this is absolutely confidential (Lucius groans and would have closed his eyes if it doesn't make reading rather difficult) the word "King" is being whispered around the Forum. Caesar and Marcus Antonius are to be consuls next year, and the story is that Caesar will have the title of "King" offered to him on the grounds that it is the natural progression for one who has been Dictator for so long. I don't myself believe that Caesar is really that confident yet, but it is worrying that the thought has occurred to other people.

Lucius thinks of Horatius back in Utica, burning with indignation on behalf of his Republican ancestors, and agrees.

However, that is enough of all that. We hope to hear from you soon and everyone sends their love.

Cornelius Rufus comes in as Lucius is nearing the end. He clearly has something to tell but waits for him to finish and then reads the letter himself, pleased that Lucius offers it to him. He says nothing about Sestius senior's freedom of speech.

"Had to happen," he comments as he hands the letter back to Lucius. "Dictator, king, consul, whatever'll get him where he wants to be, that's what Caesar will choose. But, look, this thing has turned up – I've found someone interesting."

"Who?" asks Lucius, humouring him with the required amount of eagerness.

"Someone who used to work for our old friend Publius Sittius, no less. His freedman, to be precise."

Cornelius Rufus is right – this is interesting. "Do you think he knows something then?"

"He was his secretary or something for years – including during the time of the Catilinarian Conspiracy," says Cornelius Rufus. "If anyone knows who is writing to Sittius and what about, it'll be him. And he gets drunk very easily."

Lucius grins at him. "Which wine shop?"

"The Horse. Another brilliant piece of original thinking on the part of the locals," says Cornelius. "He's been there every night for the last three nights and has had to be helped home twice."

"Looks like we'd better go drinking tonight then," Lucius says.

He does not tell Cornelius Rufus how the letter arrived. He does not know why, except that the funny little man from Carthage has the knack of making his teeth ache with gritting them. He does not want to think about him anymore.

Chapter Twenty

Lucius is surprised that a man like Sittius frees his slaves at all. Sittius has had a colourful career, outside of Roman bounds of respectability, so surely a secretary would have known far too much? He has a feeling that this man will turn out to be either simple or not as important as Cornelius Rufus hopes; too unimportant to matter.

The Horse is quite a nice bar. It is on the main street leading to the harbour at Hippo, but not actually on the waterfront itself. It has clean white walls inside and out, and a pot of leaves and flowers stand on the scrubbed serving bench. Lucius thinks of the wine shops in the Forum back in Rome that could be improved by showing an interest in a similar attitude towards hygiene. The owner has obviously not given up on all things Roman though and has adopted the practice of keeping the wine cool and the food hot by sinking huge jars into the bench top. Drawn up to the bench are a couple of tall stools, and three tables with more stools are crammed into the rest of the space inside. More tables are outside, and when they arrive, Lucius and Cornelius Rufus pass two old men keeping their places with fierce, if unnecessary, determination. They are obviously set to stay there as long they can endure the cool night air, and maybe even until the lights inside the bar are put out, leaving their patch in darkness. Their jug of wine is still half-full and they look obstinate enough to stay there in a snowstorm should anyone foolishly suggest that they come inside.

The bar is empty when Lucius and Cornelius arrive, except for the flowers, so they have to stand at the serving bench making loud and unconvincing coughing noises until a woman appears from a back room, wiping her hands on her apron, and smiling. She looks them up and down and addresses them in very respectable Greek.

"Sorry about that, he was just getting the bread out of the oven next door. If you'd like something to eat, there's the bread, soup, and lentils in wine and oil."

"Sounds wonderful," says Lucius, and he isn't just being polite. He can smell the bread and thinks he can manage just a bit of it.

"But," says Cornelius Rufus firmly, "a drink first."

The Horse relies on its regulars to make a living. Every man who comes in is greeted by name by the woman at the serving bench, and most customers eat something. One or two even get a plate of some sort of stew with the lentils. All the food smells wonderful and is eaten with appreciation. After a while, Lucius can bear it no longer and indulges in soup, still-warm bread and the famous lentils. Cornelius angles after the stew but is told with a smile that special dishes were only for very special customers. He promptly leers and asks how you become a very special customer, but she just laughs and pats his cheek and tells him to sit down like a good boy. It is wonderful to watch. Lucius is emboldened to ask why Cornelius' famous charm never seems to actually work on the opposite sex.

"Well, my heart's not in it," explains Cornelius Rufus. "I keep thinking of Rubria, and women can always tell when your heart's not in it."

Lucius applauds his devotion and wonders what he would have to do to get the woman to pat his cheek.

They are slurping their way through the soup, when Cornelius raises one eyebrow at him in the most annoyingly obvious manner and nods energetically in the direction of the serving-bench. Lucius refuses to turn around, purely to be contrary, but when he takes the bowls back to the serving bench, he is able to get a good look.

Needless to say, the man propping up the bar is as ordinary as everyone else in the town. Lucius puts him down as of Greek extraction, not especially rich, no great family background there. Not that many people would actually bother to look at him that long to begin with. Lucius realises that Cornelius Rufus, since his arrival in Africa, has developed into a man one notices as he walks past in the street. It is the way he looks at everyone and everything so carefully, as if sizing them up for inclusion in one of his schemes, which he probably is. The point is that Cornelius offers people a view of themselves as potential successes. The man at the bar doesn't look at other people at all so other people will not look back at him. Lucius had thought that the easiest way of scraping an acquaintance would be to offer him a drink, but having seen him, doubts that this will work. Instead he gets another jug of water for the wine and hurries back to their table.

"He looks completely useless," he hisses at Cornelius Rufus. "Nobody who enjoyed life would let him anywhere near them, let alone entrust him with dangerous secrets."

"Well, he's the nearest thing to Publius Sittius we've got," Cornelius hisses back. "He'll have to do. Drink up so I can get another jug of wine."

And he moves in.

He begins by making another half-hearted attempt on the woman at the bar, and as before, she laughs at him, adding a few words to their man, and making him smile a little. At that, Cornelius changes direction and starts talking to him. The man replies with an expression that indicates that he is merely being polite, but within a few moments his attention is trapped as Cornelius treats him to a diatribe about something or other. Lucius watches anxiously, convinced they have lost him, so when the man suddenly looks right at Cornelius and laughs and nods enthusiastically, Lucius' relief is equalled by surprise. They go on laughing, Cornelius gets some more wine, and they toast each other cheerfully. Then Cornelius looks at Lucius, makes encouraging faces and drags his new friend over to the table, while Lucius tries to look relaxed and friendly.

"Here, young Lucius, is the first person I've met in this place who knows a good joke when he hears one," announces Cornelius Rufus in embarrassingly loud tones.

Lucius stands up politely, and Cornelius drags a stool over for their guest, so he, looking slightly bewildered, can hardly do anything other than sit down and accept another cup of wine from the new jug.

"So, what's your name?" asks Cornelius.

"Messenio," says our new friend. "Publius Sittius Messenio."

The name hits Lucius. Messenio is the boastful freedman

who showed off to the residence slaves about how important Sittius was.

"A fellow Roman!" cries Cornelius, overdoing it of course. Africa Nova isn't that much of a backwater.

Messenio looks a bit wary.

"I used to be a slave actually," he says. There is a pause while he waits for cries of disgust; when they just nod as men of the world who have known lots of ex-slaves, he cheers up and swigs a good mouthful of wine to be on the safe side. Feeling chatty, he then confides, "In fact, when I was born, I was named after the slave in Plautus. The Menaechmi Brothers is the play. One of the brothers in the play has a slave, you see."

"Called Messenio?" asked Cornelius.

"That's it!" Messenio is delighted.

"Well," Lucius jumps in before the two others realise what a banal exchange has just passed, "I'm Lucius and this is Cornelius."

"You're from Rome, aren't you?"

"That's right," says Cornelius. "We're here to help reorganise your corn trade."

"Oh yes? What needs doing?" asks Messenio politely.

"Ah well, it's your channels of communication," says Cornelius easily, now he is an expert on the subject. "You need facilitating here, you need contacts there, you need someone to show you how it can be done, overcome the problems, that sort of thing. What we're doing is tying up the knots in all these little bits of string until we've got one long line from the smallest farm in Africa Nova to the Aventine wharves in Rome. And when that line is all tied off, then we'll all get rich."

Lucius recognises the rhetoric and grins. Cornelius is an expert at ridiculous imagery and has actually persuaded one of the more obstinate shippers with that particular piece of cynicism. Messenio's eyes have lost their focus.

"Oh," he says. "Really?"

"Never mind all that," Lucius cries cheerfully. "Tell us about you – what do you do?"

Messenio blinks several times as he thinks this one out.

"Well, I don't really have a lot to do nowadays," he answers. "When I was freed, my master was very generous. I have a bit of land, near Cirta, and it's run along with his estate and I get the money made from it. I live here in the town pretty comfortably." He looks up at their intense faces and adds hurriedly, "Not that it's that much, you understand – just enough to live on and it gets to me yearly in January, so I haven't got that much left at the moment."

Cornelius roars with laughter and bangs Messenio on the back.

"Jupiter save us all from thunder, we don't want your money! There's no need to worry about us – we're too respectable and we need to get on in this town. We can't afford to foul this particular nest, if you see what I mean?"

Messenio looks blank.

"If we got into trouble here, that'd be all our good work ruined and our backers in Rome would be very upset with us," Lucius explains in very calm tones. "Honestly, you've no need to worry about us, you can check at the governor's residence if you like. They can vouch for us."

Messenio looks relieved, although Lucius knows that someone like Messenio will never go to the governor's residence to check on a couple of strangers he has met in a bar. Now, they need to make sure that Cornelius tones down the friendly touch. It is beginning to annoy Lucius and must be scaring the Furies out of Messenio. They all have another drink, and Cornelius and Lucius chat about the impressions they have received from their journeying and ask Messenio how being turned into a province has affected life here in Africa Nova.

"Well, I haven't lived here in Hippo very long," says Messenio. "I've lived and worked in and around Cirta for the last twenty years or so. Sittius brought me over here when I was about twenty, and I like it here. The country, the people, even the heat – they all suit me, I suppose. It's all so clean and small and unhurried – life here is on a different scale to Rome. Conquest hasn't changed anything really."

As he speaks, the nervousness falls away, and he smiles as he thinks about something for a moment.

"The only thing I'd like," he continues, "is a theatre. I heard about Pompey building a theatre out of stone on the Campus Martius, and I've often thought that that is why I might go back, if I ever do go back now – to sit in that theatre and watch some Plautus, perhaps even see the other Messenio. That would be fun."

"Sounds like a good ambition to me," says Cornelius, his heartiness gone and a wistful expression on his face. "In fact, you can count me in – I'd like to see Rubria again."

Lucius thinks of Quintus Caecilius. Suppose he returns to Rome, finds out that it is all a mistake, and Caecilius is waiting there to drag him off down the hill to the baths, teasing him all the way. Lucius has had enough of Africa.

After a pause, the three of them laugh a bit, and make vague promises to meet in the bar again sometime. They all leave together, and as they go out of the bar, the cool winter air streaked with tiny shards of mist curls politely around them and makes them all draw their cloaks around themselves. Lucius is automatically turning towards the governor's residence, when a voice calls from the doorway opposite, "Messenio!"

As Lucius glances towards the voice, Cornelius Rufus suddenly pushes past him and grabs a handful of his cloak to start dragging him up the street. Lucius starts running, but stumbles, confused. It takes the few moments he spends in looking back at Messenio for everything to make sense, but the pathetic mixture of pride and eagerness on Messenio's face suddenly registers. That voice is known to Messenio, indeed, he has been expecting it. The boring little man, at whom nobody would take a second look, steps into the darkness and disappears, as several shapes come forward, forming out of walls and doors into men, and Cornelius Rufus and he are running, pounding the dusty street with the stamping sounds of feet echoing all around them. Cornelius only speaks once.

"Get to the residence!"

Lucius turns to question, but Cornelius Rufus drags him around a corner and pushes him with such violence that he staggers back several feet before connecting very definitely with a wall. He crouches in a little heap at the foot of the wall and feels bewildered. After a very long few seconds, he gets his bearings. He is lying in a narrow alley in the dark and mist. He listens but can hear nothing – the pursuit has gone past him and into the blessed distance, and he realises that Cornelius Rufus has saved his life and given him a chance of getting away.

For a moment he is furious with Cornelius Rufus – how dare he? Lucius doesn't want to be saved, not like this with Cornelius Rufus acting as bodyguard, risking his life for him. He wants to be treated as he would undoubtedly have treated Cornelius Rufus; not once did Lucius think of his companion as they turned and ran. Feeling scared and resentful, he crawls to the entrance of the alley and puts his head into the street, at ground level, where hopefully no one will be looking for it. Silence. He sits back and gets his breathing under control.

He spends more time crouching than upright like a normal, dignified human being as he makes his way along the three streets to the governor's residence. The darkness shifts as he peers into corners, and moulds itself into shapes which could be those of men; Lucius hides in doorways and feels both ridiculous and afraid.

Stumbling back into the governor's residence past the astonished doorkeeper, he looks around and can hardly believe that it is all real. In the soft light, the furnishings and decorated walls seem to melt at the edges, and for a moment he panics that it will all vanish and leave him vulnerable in the dark town. It seems so insubstantial, whereas the imagined demons of his scrambling journey back from the alley are real. Lucius is struck by this curious contrast and gawks at the doorkeeper, who comes to ask him what is the matter. He clutches at the slave's arm to make sure that he is real.

Lucius goes out with the search party. The memory of his fear has to be put away for the moment; Cornelius Rufus needs more than a gibbering incontinent. The two tribunes and he each lead a small party of the residence's slaves and they search the town street by street, calmly, methodically, quietly. There are no traces of Cornelius, or a group of men, or on the roads out of the town, horses. They even call on a few of their merchants and they provide more slaves and a network of friends who know acquaintances who know people Lucius has never heard of. They are looking for a house that might be being used by Publius Sittius of Nuceria, but nobody will admit to knowing of such a house.

At dawn, they trail back to the palace, and no one offers any words of hope. Lucius goes to bed and falls asleep to the rhythm of a single thought: he should have told Cornelius Rufus about Caesar's spy. He is awoken in the late afternoon by the news that Cornelius' body has just been taken out of the harbour. He has been killed with a single knife-thrust to the heart.

Chapter Twenty-One

Lucius is reading in the study he has been given to use at the house in Tusculum. When he looks up, Marcus Tullius Cicero junior is standing in the doorway watching him. Behind him is Cicero's nephew, Quintus.

"Did you know," Marcus observes, "that you've been sitting there, only moving to unroll the book, for absolutely hours and you never noticed we were here until just now?"

"Why should I have noticed?" Lucius asks ungraciously.

Quintus grins, but Marcus' face can't help showing his hurt for a moment. Then he shrugs.

"Letters have arrived from your papa and mine, again," he announces. "They must be important because my cousin Quintus has brought them – fancy that!"

Quintus punches him. Marcus grins, throws a package of letters at Lucius and wanders off. Quintus leans against the wall without actually coming into Lucius's room and raises his eyebrows.

"You've had fun, I hear. Actually, I'm sorry not to meet Cornelius again. He was all right. Or should I shut up about that now?"

Quintus is good at this, thinks Lucius, and can't help smiling. Yes, Cornelius Rufus had been "all right". Hastily, he looks for something else to say.

"I think your cousin is finding Sestius-duty a touch tedious and unromantic," he says.

"Give him a chance," says Quintus unexpectedly. "It probably doesn't help that he's that bit younger than us. He'll learn. And like all of us he suffers from not being my uncle. Are you going to open that letter?"

"In a minute," says Lucius. "Can I have a word with you first?"

Quintus raises an eyebrow but comes in and finds himself a stool.

"You look awful," he says. "Do I gather that it did not go as planned?"

"I need to ask you about what you said that night when we walked to the stable and met Cornelius Rufus."

Quintus looks cautious. "All right. But I don't want you to say anything to Marcus. I like Marcus and the way things are going I want to hang on to my family. I could have lost him so many times already."

Lucius remembers that both Quintus and Marcus fought at the disastrous Battle of Pharsalus, while he was in Cilicia with his father. Technically they had been on the opposite side to the Sestii at that point. How strange. And Marcus can only have been about sixteen. Lucius shivers, and Quintus looks at him with concern.

"What is it?" he asks.

"When you left me that night, you said that I shouldn't trust your uncle. I need to know what makes you say that. Please."

Quintus blows out his cheeks and stares off into the distance. "The minute I said that, I wondered if I should have. But I said it. So – yes, I don't think my uncle is completely trustworthy. You know he and my father had a huge row after Pharsalus, don't you?"

Lucius nods. He can understand rows after Pharsalus. Civil war does that to families.

"Well, that brought all sorts of things out into the open between us all." Quintus frowns. "It was not pretty, and we didn't speak to my uncle for months. And that was really strange because for as long as I can remember, I have treated Uncle Marcus' house as my own home. I kept up with Marcus, but the two of us just didn't talk about our uncles in front of our fathers. Doesn't that in itself sound strange? It sounds as if we don't have the vocabulary to describe it. Anyway, I had a long time to look back and it was quite revealing. From my point of view, my father has done everything Uncle Marcus wanted, all his life, and that hasn't always been to his advantage. Uncle Marcus always needs money, and my father has bailed him out often enough to make a real impact on us. But the thing I found I really resented is that we – my father and Marcus and I – were not allowed to choose Caesar until after Pharsalus. Have you any idea what it was like, having to crawl to a man I've always admired, and explain to him that I hadn't sided with him in the first place because my uncle persuaded my father and my father persuaded me?"

Quintus has no good memories of that time; Lucius can see the bitterness in his eyes.

"Anyway," says Quintus, "my uncle will only ever think of himself first and foremost, especially now Tullia is dead. He is charming, he is clever, he would be generous if he weren't always in debt, but you cannot rely on him. If he makes a promise, he will deliver as long as something better doesn't come along, and he will change his politics to suit himself because he is a coward."

There is a pause. Quintus says, "It was no fun saying all that. Now – tell me what you have discovered."

Lucius tells Quintus about Publius Sittius, and the letters received from Rome, from Caesar, Antonius, Lepidus and Tiro. Quintus is clearly surprised by the last name.

"Well, Sittius fought in the African campaign, so I can sort of see why the Dictator's people would be writing to him. But Tiro? That only makes sense if Uncle Marcus were in touch with Sittius, and I can't see why that should happen. Not that I've ever heard Uncle Marcus talk about Publius Sittius, and come to think of it, that in itself is strange. Uncle Marcus has been yattering on about all things Catilina ever since I can remember. Do you want me to ask Tiro?"

"No," says Lucius, wearily. "It probably doesn't matter."

"That is so clearly untrue I'm not going to bother any more with this conversation," says Quintus. "Read your letters. But I warn you, you are going to have to come up with a bit more than you have done so far. See you at dinner and be prepared to spill."

He vanishes from the doorway, and Lucius turns to read his letters in peace. First is a short note from his father:

My dear Lucius,

Things are bad here and you certainly should not dream of trying to sneak into the city limits – just in case you were contemplating such a thing. Caesar is behaving in a most peculiar manner and I cannot imagine what he is planning – apart from this dreadful Parthian campaign, which is boring everyone to death. Cicero is writing to you and has asked if he may describe the latest fiasco; I suppose that he has thought of a good ascending tricolon or something and wants to show it off to someone.

The family are well, on the whole, although Tia remains very quiet, and your mother is worrying about her. I think that it is only five months since Caecilius died and it is going to take time.

I am sorry not to be more encouraging, but things are tense, and so you must be patient. We may not always think of it in such terms, but we are very lucky that Caesar has allowed you to return in Italy at all.

Lucky? Yes, he is indeed lucky. He isn't dead, and he is probably safe. Once back in Italy, he told only two people about that last night in Hippo Regius. Cornelius Rufus, as far as the world is concerned, has disappeared after cheating a local merchant. The official story is that he is presumed to be in Africa still, but has probably moved on in search of new lambs to fleece. It is a pity after all the work he had appeared to be putting in to help the legates in Africa Nova, but what else can you expect of a man who is basically still a Subura rat?

Sulpicius and Plinius and he had been quite pleased with this in a warped sort of way, sure that it is the sort of thing most Romans of their own class will readily believe, and they are right. Nobody in Rome has shown the slightest bit of interest in the mundane squabbles of Africa, grain or no grain. The legates' official report has mentioned the affair; maybe it has already filtered through to Cornelius Rufus' family and friends, and what they think about it, no one knows. No one official cares. There is very little anyone can do now – Cornelius Rufus had not been on official business and no one in government is responsible for his safety or whereabouts. Maybe the new governor of Africa Nova will scratch his head over the disappearance – when such a person is appointed.

As for Lucius himself, he is not officially anywhere in the Empire so cannot be contacted. He has left Hippo but is not in

Rome; if anyone is so interested as to bother with an investigation, they will have guessed that once more a Cicero house is involved – that is easy enough. The Great Man has come to the aid of the Sestius family yet again, negotiating a truce with Caesar and standing guarantor for Lucius' good behaviour. All Lucius has to do is stay in the house at Tusculum, just outside Rome, and keep out of mischief, until he is sent for. He has decided that he is definitely no longer that interested in anything to do with Caesar. His feelings about both Caesar and Cicero have undergone such a change that he is still wading through bewilderment. He hates Sittius. That is simple. He has never thought of hate as a worthwhile emotion – rather the opposite. It takes up a lot of energy and accomplishes nothing as far as he can see. He has been rather proud of this civilised attitude and cultivated it. But three men are now dead because of his involvement with a normal, messy lawsuit and behind it all is the Dictator, Publius Sittius and maybe, Cicero. Lucius, as always, does a little mental sidestep to avoid that last thought and concentrates on Sittius and Caesar. Caesar did not give the order to kill Cornelius Rufus; in fact, Lucius rather doubts if Caesar controls what Sittius does in Africa at all. The fact that Lucius has had to risk Caesar's famous clemency again, just to escape Sittius himself, makes him seethe.

Cicero's letter begins badly.

You know more than most, my dear Lucius, of the complete lack of respect with which Caesar has chosen to treat our state and its institutions.

Lucius sighs. He really does not think that he cares any longer for the Republic or its institutions; Caesar has been trampling on Republican institutions for as long as Lucius can remember – it is normal. But friends being murdered is not normal, and that Cicero still has the nerve to complain about Caesar while supporting him, is infuriating.

You remember the fiasco of last year's consulship. Fabius Maximus, having held office oh-so-gloriously since the beginning of October, decided to die on the last day of the year. Instead of mourning him decently and leaving be, Caesar decided that a replacement should be elected, sorry, selected, just for the day! Never mind that that useless lump Caninius didn't do anything while he is consul, we were just grateful that he didn't have the time to do anything! But I digress.

He did indeed digress, especially as Lucius has been brought up to date on that particular incident many times. Apart from anything else, he has grown so tired of hearing complaints and snide comments about Caninius' consulship, that he no longer thinks that Caesar has acted so outrageously. Caninius seemed harmless enough, and at least provided the opportunity for a series of jokes along the lines of what didn't happen in Caninius' consulship. Cicero himself enjoyed even the ruder ones and has scrupulously passed them on in his letters.

For some time now, as you know, the word "king" has been whispered among the Forum loiterers. Many believe that Caesar intends to bring back that title and make himself the first king of Rome since Tarquinius Superbus was driven out, all those hundreds of years ago. I myself would not believe that Caesar could be so arrogant and foolish, but it seems clear now. After all, he has been busy building that new temple to Venus, in his new forum, and it's specifically a temple to Venus the Ancestress to remind us that the Julius family claim descent from the goddess. Yesterday's little incident shouldn't really be so surprising.

"Jupiter!" thinks Lucius crossly, wishing that he'd just get on with it.

We celebrated the Lupercalia, with all the usual high spirits. I've always thought it a rather vulgar festival, especially as so few people bother to remember its origin and purpose, and yesterday my opinion was not changed. Needless to say, the worst offender was Marcus Antonius, our beloved consul and Caesarian arse-licker extraordinaire. I know Antonius is a priest, but really, one does not expect one of his age and rank to claim the privilege of actually going around and whipping giggling girls with wolf-skin. It's because the whole thing is associated with fertility – it gets his mind running along well-known tracks and he can't stop. And it does mean that he gets to find out which women are actually wanting to have children. He can eye them all up, and then arrange to get them in a

191

suitable condition himself. We shall have a crop of children with the Antonius nose by the end of the year, poor little bastards.

Lucius has to grin. It isn't often that Cicero indulges in such a fit of the sulks, but his dislike of Antonius is justified.

So, there is our consul racing around the Forum making eyes at every female in his path while Caesar in full regalia – which we had voted to him of course! – sits and watches. Suddenly, before anyone realises what is happening, Antonius is kneeling at Caesar's feet and offering him a diadem, wreathed in leaves. One of his slaves had been carrying it, hidden, but ready to be passed to him. Antonius stayed like that, on his knees without moving, for some time, and likewise Caesar did not move. I suppose they wanted time for everyone to notice. It was like a backwards ripple – people's heads turned towards the Rostra and there was a gradual turning and shuffling towards Caesar, and then everything fell still. Suddenly someone shouted, "Don't take it!" and the crowd roared at Caesar. Antonius took no notice and pushed the diadem towards Caesar again, and this time, Caesar looked up and at the crowd. The noise was tremendous – they didn't want him to have it and they knew he wouldn't take it. He sat back in his chair, very relaxed and smiling a little, and pushed Antonius' hand away. Everyone cheered and then quietened down to let him speak. He was very clever. "Jupiter is the only king in this city," he said. "Offer it to him in his temple." And that's what they did. For some reason, nobody minds Antonius' part in all this, they're all too busy praising Caesar for his restraint.

I don't know what will happen now though; I suspect that Caesar's supporters will wait until after the Parthian campaign, which they are sure will be victorious. That will then spur them on, and then Caesar will be king – Life Dictator, it would seem, is not enough for him. I know that to some people it is just a matter of what he is called, but, Lucius, you know the significance of "mere" words as much as I do. There cannot be a king in Rome again – that has always been our ancestors' vow, and it is clear that the people of today still do not want it. And yet – one of the shrewdest men of our age is ignoring all that tradition, all the weight of public opinion, he is so set on it. I do not know whether he will succeed, and it frightens me that he can even dream of it. And yet, I am not surprised.

How sad that your safety depends upon this man, Lucius! I feel sure that you are safe, by the way. He is very proud of his acts of mercy, and while this one is not generally known, he has still some respect for me and for your father as well, and he will not go back on his promise. I see your father or Decius every day, and I can assure you that your whole family is safe and well. I hope young Marcus is looking after you."

Marcus junior enters just as Lucius is reading this letter through for a second time. Trained by his father, he waits until Lucius has finished.

"May I read it?" he asks. "Father only sent me a short note – he says your letter will bring him up to date, and so I waited for ages and then couldn't wait any longer."

Lucius hands him the letter wondering if he has ever been that young, and watches while Marcus reads it through. He reads quickly and without moving his lips, which impresses Lucius – it's the sign of someone who does a lot of reading. Looking at him and trying to work out why Marcus irritates him so much, he is suddenly struck by the thought that he probably wouldn't have got on with Marcus' father had they been contemporaries. This is an uncomfortable thought to entertain and adds to his sense of unease. After all, Cicero has been instrumental in gaining his pardon from Caesar and has given him shelter. And Lucius' father is his friend. The young man in front of him now is just a fairly typical example of his class: he is well educated, and enjoys hunting, and suffers from not being as brilliant as his father would have liked. This is something for which Lucius can feel pity, if not exactly sympathy, as Sestius senior has never demanded anything from his son but showed the greatest delight when he had chosen as his father would have wished. Lucius waits and thinks about his father.

After Marcus has finished, he sits for a while, before looking up and asking, "Is this really what Caesar wants, do you think? I mean - to be king...."

Lucius shakes his head.

"Don't ask me. I've given up second-guessing the great and the good. I never thought that Caesar would let me be in peace once he knew I was back in Italy, but he did."

Marcus shifts around a bit and looks at the floor. Then his shoulders go back as he makes a weighty decision, and he says, "Er...can I ask now why you actually came back? Father said I wasn't to pester you, and my cousin Quintus says it has to be fairly shady, but you've been here two weeks now and I don't think it's shady. So, may I ask? Did you do a deal with Caesar?"

Lucius thinks about his one and only meeting with the dictator.

"I didn't do a deal," he says bitterly. "But I accepted one. Look, I don't want to go through it twice. Can I tell you and Quintus together? At dinner?"

Marcus of course agrees and slips out. When he has gone, Lucius realises that the younger Marcus Tullius Cicero has taken the elder's letter with him. He decides to let him keep it.

Chapter Twenty-Two

The deal? Caesar had put forward his terms, expecting them to be taken up, and Lucius had agreed, on the grounds that it seemed the most sensible thing to do, even if the shades of his friends wept. With that disconcerting thought he goes to dinner, ready to tell the story, with certain passages edited of course.

"On the day we discovered Cornelius Rufus' body, Plinius and Sulpicius and I threw a plan together," he begins.

His overwhelming desire had been to get away to safety and to keep the whole thing quiet, and this they had managed pretty well. They had covered up the circumstances of Cornelius Rufus' death, as it was bad publicity to advertise the arrival of Rome-style gang warfare in Hippo Regius. And so, Cornelius Rufus was cremated the same day as his body was found, and after a night's cooling, his ashes were buried very swiftly by the three of them. The master of the Diana had been paid well to give up his Saturnalia dinner in order to take one passenger to Utica, and once there, Lucius got in touch with the young legate Horatius. Horatius had put him up in a room in the guest wing of the governor's residence until he could be smuggled onto the next ship to Italy. They had had to wait for what seemed to Lucius an age before any ship was willing to make the voyage, but Governor Calvisius did not even realise he was there, and the slaves were well recompensed for their silence. It had been very efficient, and all the legates had shown an admirable knowledge of the options for travel to and from their particular provinces. Lucius would have been impressed if he hadn't felt so dull and lost. The days spent in that little room were long and empty, and he found it difficult to talk about anything, even to Horatius.

Lucius pauses in his story and Quintus and Marcus paste on sympathetic expressions, while clearly avid for more. They think he is overwhelmed but Lucius is instead taking the sensible decision not to discuss that time of growing suspicion that Cicero was somehow involved in all of this. Tiro's letters to Sittius may have been from years ago, and do not prove that Cicero knows anything about Cornelius Rufus' death. Probably.

Lucius carries on with a description of the sea-crossing in winter. The ship had taken a cautious seven days to cross to Sicily and make its way up the coast, and he had landed back in Puteoli at the end of December. He had considered no other option for he was tired and just went where the ship took him. From there, he had gone straight to Cicero's house at Pompeii, and his worries about Tiro and the letters to Sittius were not allowed to trouble him. That could wait – he needed familiar things and there he had found a refuge. A message was sent off to Rome, to be answered in a few days with the instruction that he was to ride to Tusculum and wait at Cicero's house there just outside the city.

"When I at the Tusculum villa, your father, sorry, Quintus, uncle, and my father were waiting," and Lucius remembers the almost overwhelming relief at seeing Publius Sestius – and Decius – again. Seeing Cicero was strange, but Lucius just ploughed on. In the midst of his unexpected return in winter with the death of Cornelius Rufus weighing on him, his concerns about Cicero were not yet ready to be examined too closely. And every time he looked at Decius, Lucius thought, "We really must free him."

"You two," says Lucius, "are now the fourth and fifth people to be told about Cornelius Rufus' death – outside of Africa, that is. My father, of course, was very shaken and was worried about Cornelius' family and girlfriend until he realised that he didn't know whether Cornelius Rufus had any family; we didn't have the name of any friend apart from that of Rubria. I suppose we could find her, if we really wanted to, by going to the docks and asking around, but I think that the thought of explaining everything to her and getting her to keep quiet about it all was too much for Father. He has actually met her, and says she is a good woman, and he does not want to lie to her. In the end, we just hoped she had already found another man, and left it there. That feels absolutely..." Lucius does not finish. More wine is poured by Quintus.

Lucius then told them about the decision they had made that the Dictator should be informed about those final few days in Africa as well as Lucius' return to Italy. Cicero thought that if they put the story to him as another example of Sittius' lack of control, they could even make Caesar feel a certain degree of responsibility towards Lucius. It would be a neat irony.

"Sittius is Caesar's creature – supposedly," said Cicero. "If Caesar can't control Sittius sufficiently for you to go into exile without being killed, then it is up to Caesar to do something about it. After all, he guaranteed that if you left Italy, you would be all right."

"Did he?" Lucius asked.

"I can make him think so," said Cicero firmly.

At this point in the story, Quintus laughs and takes a large mouthful of wine. "I love the idea of Uncle Marcus off to be all rhetorical at Caesar of all people and Caesar not noticing!"

Young Marcus colours, and his cousin adds kindly, "Oh come on Marcus! We all know your father is brilliant, but you know how clever Caesar is. He can't be manipulated like that."

"Well, Cicero thought it .was worth a try," says Lucius. "I stayed at Tusculum and Father and Cicero rode straight back to Rome, which was good of them. I think your father, Marcus, was keen to get right in there and enjoyed the idea of having a good talk with Caesar. And of course, of reporting back on Africa. I doubt that Sittius bothered to send a letter announcing Cornelius Rufus' death. Your father worked quickly, anyway, because I got a note summoning me back to Rome the next day. I was to enter the city once it was dark and go straight to Cicero's house. I waited a couple of hours before setting out, while you, Marcus, kept telling me how lucky I was to be going back to the city." Lucius toasts Marcus and grins at him to show that this is a joke. He does not mention that he had to be sick twice on the journey and endured the humiliation of the accompanying slave's tangible discretion.

"So we got to your father's house and I have to say even he looked a bit apprehensive," Lucius continues. "It turned out that Caesar was expecting an interview with me straight away, and after making me drink a cup of neat wine – very nice wine too – your father and Tiro took me to a house I've never visited before. I didn't even know who it belonged to, just that Caesar was dining there that night. I have never seen your father going out armed in the city before, Marcus, but he and Tiro carried daggers openly, and the slaves we took had cudgels. It was unreal. And all the way there I kept thinking over and over that I was going to meet Caesar, and I didn't have a clue what to do or say."

And, as any good orator would, Lucius pauses. In his case, it is because he needs a rest after the strain of telling this story without saying anything that implies criticism about Cicero. Young Marcus' eyes are fixed on him, and Lucius is aware of the debt he still owes the Cicero family, despite the mysterious letters to Publius Sittius. He eats a little and drinks some wine, and Quintus and Marcus keep silent.

"Well, it turned out that we were going to the house of Marcus Antonius," says Lucius. "And we were expected and shown into a rather nice library to wait. I tried to distract myself by finding reasons to criticise Antonius' literary taste, but he has all the usual Greek and Latin classics, with only a few scrolls of dodgy poetry. He likes plays, especially comedies, I'd say, and there were all the signs of use: tangled labels, scrolls with ruffled edges, the images on the library seals rubbed into blanks."

"I hear he likes actresses as well," says Quintus. "Particularly the ones that show signs of use."

Lucius enjoys the pause for sniggers and drinks more wine. This next bit is going to be hard to recount, and as it flashes through his head, he shudders. It is all horribly clear.

As footsteps were heard coming across the atrium towards them, Cicero gave him one look – what he was trying to say, Lucius could not tell – and he and Tiro ducked under the leather curtain in time to hold it back for three men, the Dictator and Marcus Antonius, and one other, unknown to Lucius. Without even realising what he was doing, Lucius backed into the corner opposite the desk. He watched as Caesar and Marcus Antonius headed straight for the two chairs, with Caesar choosing the one behind the desk. Antonius pulled his chair back so that it would not block the Dictator's view of Lucius, standing as far away as was possible. The third man stayed standing at Caesar's shoulder, and Lucius suddenly knew exactly who he was,

without ever having seen him before. About fifty-five, skin
weathered and tanned and lined, Publius Sittius of Cirta in
Numidia looked very contented with his life. He had more hair
than Caesar, and it was cut in a very regular line across his
forehead. It grew down the sides of his head in two straight
lines, so that the top of his face was beautifully squared-off. Not
quite fleshy, the rest of his face curved gently to a generous chin
under a very small and thin mouth. As he looked at Lucius, two
frown lines appeared between his eyes, but he did not speak.

Marcus Antonius leaned forward in his chair and studied
Lucius intently for a few moments. Then he grinned and relaxed
visibly as he shifted his weight back in the chair and stretched
out his legs in front of him. He glanced at Caesar, smiling.

"You won't have any trouble with him. He's wetting himself
already."

And at that, Lucius finally lost his temper. He stepped
towards Antonius, his arm already swinging back for the blow,
thinking of the mess he could make of this useless lump of flesh,
and the happiness he could give to his ghosts. He heard Quintus
Caecilius laugh but Cornelius Rufus was silent.

If only Marcus Antonius, veteran of a thousand fights,
drunken brawls and pitched battles alike, had not easily swayed
out of the way, sitting though he was. If only Lucius had not
stumbled as he overbalanced and put out his hands to break his
fall. If only he had not fallen against the desk, pushing it up
against the Dictator. There was a startled silence which
Antonius broke with a bellow of laughter. Slowly, Lucius
pushed himself back upright and retreated step by step into his
corner again, resisting the temptation to apologise. He gazed
steadily at a scroll poking out of the bookcase just above
Caesar's head, then at the Dictator's bald spot, and concentrated
his hatred on that small pink shining circle. Here were the
murderers, the people who had ruined his family's life, a slight
thin Dictator, with his lecherous ape of a sidekick and a well-
fed middle-aged merchant tagging along. Lucius waited.

The Dictator leaned forward and said, "We have not the time
or the interest to waste in discussing the events of the past.
Cicero has pleaded admirably on your behalf, and there were

even one or two points worth making in among the verbiage. I do owe you something, I suppose, and I'm prepared to make you an offer. I need your assurance that you will stay at the Cicero house in Tusculum until I am gone on the Parthian expedition. I was quite tempted to take you on my staff, but I don't suppose that you will be that eager. So, you will remain in Tusculum. When I have left Italy, you may return to the city, where you will find that you are a quaestor. You will be working for Gaius Cassius Longinus, the praetor in charge of foreign lawsuits. I imagine that the work will interest you, and that you will be quite good at it. Cicero assures me that your curiosity is fully extinguished, and I am relying on his word. Should he be mistaken, I shall have you removed from office and exiled formally – at the least. There are certain conditions besides: one, you will never again go to Africa, Old or New, and two, you will never make any public speech which criticises me. That is all – do you wish to have some time to consider?"

Lucius must have looked astonished, for Caesar's tone softened a little towards the end of this speech and the final offer of time for thought was not rehearsed. Lucius had never imagined this – public office, the first magistracy on the ladder to success. He needed no time, he discovered. He was going to accept the terms, very decidedly. But he could not leave it there without questions. And Publius Sittius was not going to like them.

"I have to know," he said. "Why do you let Sittius here have so much power? And I still don't understand why you are suddenly so against Sallust."

The Dictator looked at him warily.

"Firstly," he said, "I do not allow any power to Sittius and in fact dislike anyone who behaves in one of my provinces with such stupidity and lack of care." The man next to him looked down at him sharply with an expression of contempt on his face, but Caesar seemed unaware of him as he continued. "And if you don't know about Sittius and Sallust then I am not going to enlighten you. You'll probably guess – when I come back from Parthia if not before. Or maybe, Publius, you'd like to do the honours now?"

He pushed back his chair and looked at Publius Sittius for the first time since walking into the room. Publius Sittius made a sound like a suppressed sneeze but chose to remain mute.

"Why must I stay away from Africa?" asked Lucius. Not that he wanted to return, he was just curious as to why that particular condition had been set.

Finally, Publius Sittius broke his silence. "Because I don't want you there."

Caesar sighed audibly and with clear irritation. Antonius gazed at Sittius with a thin-lipped scowl. Publius Sittius did not seem to care.

As he comes to the end of a surprisingly detailed version of this sorry conversation, Lucius sees shock and sympathy on Marcus' face. Even Quintus looks worried. But Lucius no longer cares about their reactions, for he remembers the arrogant, despicable certainty in Sittius' eyes – and he also remembers that jolt of realisation. That was the moment when he saw the great secret at last. It was, of course, very simple and so small when compared to the lives it had cost to keep.

"So, the interview, such as it was, was at an end, and I accepted the terms, of course, and I walked into the atrium and asked Cicero to take me home. I have never been so pleased to leave a place, I think, but we could not relax until we arrived back at Cicero's house. I had a few hours' sleep, then we started off for Tusculum at dawn. My father was waiting there for us, and we spent the rest of the day and sat up into the night, going over the conversation with Caesar again and again, looking for traps and signs of displeasure, clues as to what Caesar really wanted, evidence that he was lying. On the following morning, Tiro and I wrote a letter to the Dictator, thanking him for the unexpected bonus of a quaestorship and hoping that the campaign in the East would go well." And Lucius finds that there he must stop. There is a pause around the dinner table and Marcus and Quintus look at each other.

Finally, Marcus says, "I'm sorry."

Marcus had been at the villa at Tusculum while all this had happened, but nobody had ever thought to invite him to discuss anything or had even told him what was happening. Now, as

Lucius sees the distress on Marcus' face, he feels a pang that the boy has been so left out. Marcus is quick on the uptake as well, for he realises that the most important thing has been left unfinished.

"So what is the great secret then?" he asks, once he has sat and thought about things, and has assured himself that Lucius won't mind the question.

"I'm still not absolutely sure," Lucius replies. "But I have an idea."

Marcus looks thoughtful.

"It must be something to do with what is happening now," he observes. "But as Caesar and Antonius didn't appear very worried about whether or not you guessed it, it also doesn't matter much. And by the time the Dictator returns from Parthia, it won't matter at all. So, it is something that will happen soon, and the nearer we get to the time the more obvious it will get. Is that incident with the crown important? Are they planning to bring back a king?"

Quintus stirs. "That must be their final goal," he says. "They are laying the way, aren't they? He and Antonius and Lepidus. They can afford to wait, but once Caesar defeats the Parthians – and he will; he doesn't lose – then they will be able to do what they like. There will be statues to King Caesar and Divine Caesar all over the East before they return. Look at Alexander – he couldn't resist the adoration he found in Persia. Caesar won't want to be far behind Alexander in any respect."

"Yes, the king thing is a part of it, I'm sure," says Lucius. "But the great secret that Sallust was going to discover in writing that book isn't that important when you look at it now." He looks at them both, eagerly awaiting the grand announcement, but there is no pleasure in finally saying it out loud. "It's just that Caesar was actually behind the Catilinarian crisis. He and Sittius had it all planned, including a back door through which they could escape if it didn't all work out. There was the perfect fall-guy in Catilina, because if he failed, as was most likely, that would give Caesar an opportunity to step in during the confusion and take on emergency powers. If Catilina had succeeded, I'm sure they had plans to get rid of him at some point down the road. In the end, Catilina failed but there wasn't the confusion that they'd hoped for, and in fact, the conspiracy was dealt with pretty efficiently, so they decided to abort their plan, and Sittius, the only one who was definitely linked to Catilina had to go into exile. Then Caesar got the consulship and went to Gaul, and built up his power there before trying again, a slightly different way, and this time, he managed to get a civil war started. The civil war went well – for him, anyway – and he got the Dictatorship, and then decided that it was time for the crown. He had Antonius try out the crowd last year." Lucius sighs. "It is nothing more than that. Pathetic."

"But it would have been quite something if Sallust had discovered it in September last year, before Caesar became Dictator for Life," says Quintus slowly. "Caesar persuaded the Senate to pass so many of his measures and reforms last year, and he wouldn't have succeeded if Sallust had found out and proved this. I mean, this last episode with Antonius offering him a crown – it's stirred up a lot of feeling as it is. If all this had become common knowledge then, it could have been disastrous. So Sallust had to be distracted away from his research, and Sittius had to be brought back to Rome to consult."

"But it doesn't really matter anymore."

Lucius sighs again and leans back on one of Cicero's extremely comfortable dinner couches, thinking about it. Last year, Caesar had been away from Rome for most of the time, and people had grumbled about that. He had come back and announced yet another triumph, and they had liked that, though not as much as usual – triumphs are cheap in Rome nowadays. If it had been whispered that the absent Dictator had nurtured plans to take power ever since the Catilinarian affair twenty years ago, then things would have been very different. No nice honours from the Senate, no new forum and temple, no Parthian expedition. Instead, a lot of suspicious questions and accusations of treachery; perhaps, if someone were feeling very brave, a lawsuit. Maybe even an assassination?

So the Dictator had recalled Sallust, held talks with Publius Sittius, killed a couple of innocent men, and sent Lucius and

Cornelius running off into exile so that he had a clear field for his steady progress towards becoming king.

Quintus says, thoughtfully, "Now he is on the final straight, he can afford to be generous, for the idea has been sown in people's minds, and he will just bide his time, waiting for an opportunity to push just a little more. And so on, until the day Rome wakes to find herself a kingdom, rather than a Republic. And, you, Lucius, are no longer able to get in the way, so you can be made quaestor, half apology, half bribe."

Marcus looks at Lucius.

"At least it's all over now," he says gently. "You and your family are safe, and you have the quaestorship to look forward to. I know," he goes on quickly, as he sees Lucius' face, "it's not what you want. You want to tell Caesar where to stuff his quaestorship, although he'd probably enjoy having it stuffed there anyway."

He waits until Lucius smiles and then goes on.

"You have to take this opportunity. Quaestorships are practically dictated by him nowadays, if you'll excuse the pun, so you would have to rely on him for the promotion anyway. And the one you've got is one of the more interesting ones, and he's right about it being the right post for you. And then you'll be able to go back to your own home, and I know how much that means to you."

Lucius has thought of this as well, and he has encountered a nasty little thought about it. His family have coped without him after all, and that is how it should be while his father is still alive. But what will they think of him when he returns, the exile home again, the quaestor-elect? Would they see why he had accepted Caesar's offer when he couldn't quite work it out himself? Quintus looks at him and sees it all.

"It will be fine," he says. "We've all compromised at some point or another along this road. Your family know that, and they will just be pleased to have you back. What else could you have done?"

"I could have refused the quaestorship," points out Lucius.

"A pointless act," says Quintus. "You aren't that stupid."

He holds up his wine cup. "A toast," he says. "To Parthia."

Chapter Twenty-Three

Life in Tusculum goes on pleasantly enough, and when Quintus returns to the city a couple of days later, Lucius begins to respond to young Marcus' eager-puppy offers of friendship. Marcus is a good hunter and takes Lucius out around the estate, and he enjoys the exercise and the feeling that he is free. Even Marcus' conversation is bearable, and he does at least have a sense of humour. Sestius senior writes often, and it seems that Caesar will be setting off on the Parthian campaign even sooner than Lucius imagined – the middle of March is looking likely. Caesar will go through the Balkans, briskly subduing as he goes, using it as a warm-up for the long journey to the East, and making sure that supply-routes are clear and established. Having served in Cilicia with his father at the eastern end of the Mediterranean, Lucius can picture the route in part, and acknowledges that this is good sense.

The early March weather wavers from chilly sunshine to spectacular thunderstorms, and the slaves report some bad omens in the town: sheep are giving birth to deformed, dead lambs and a statue in the town square at Tusculum has been struck by lightning. The day of the Ides is cold and misty all day, and the day after not much better – to hear the sound of hooves as it is growing dark is unexpected. Dinner is nearly over, and both Marcus and Lucius go out to the entrance where they find that Decius has arrived. There is news, clearly; but Decius' face breaks into a faint smile as he sees them. He doesn't keep them waiting. Decius has always been too nice to need that sort of drama in his life.

"Your families are fine," he announces, "but Caesar is dead. Yesterday morning, in a meeting of the Senate, he was assassinated," he announces. This is unexpected, and both Marcus and Lucius are taken by surprise. Neither of them had thought that Caesar would be killed, not now, not with the Parthian campaign coming up.

"I suppose," says Marcus slowly, "that someone just
205

couldn't take any more." A thought strikes him, and he takes a horrified step towards Decius. "My father – he wasn't involved, was he? He would never have done something like... He didn't, did he?"

"No," says Decius emphatically. "They were mainly the new league of Caesareans, funnily enough. Marcus Brutus, Decimus Brutus – people like that."

They gape again.

"But I thought Marcus Brutus is – well, they say he's Caesar's son!" protests Marcus. "And Caesar treated him like one. He is – was – doing really well under the new regime."

"Not well enough, it would appear," says Decius with a whiff of irony.

"I can't believe it," Lucius says. "Brutus is a fairly pathetic character, I always think. He's interested in money and getting in with the right people, and he has a keen eye on his own career. He's the last person to contemplate this sort of thing, I would have thought. Who else is involved?"

"Cassius, Trebonius, Casca – not a very grateful lot," says Decius. "Brutus is claiming that they did it to save Rome, and that whatever he may have thought of Caesar as a close friend, his duty was to kill the man who was killing the Republic."

He stands and waits, while Marcus and Lucius look at each other. It is Marcus who makes the decision.

"I think we'd better just sit and listen to the whole thing. I'll get some wine. Decius, when did you last eat? And we ought to get back to the city as soon as possible. If we set off really early tomorrow, we should be in time to see any action." He goes off and Lucius can hear him shouting for the steward. Orders are given and Lucius knows that he will find a small bag packed and ready in his room by the time he retires tonight. When Marcus returns, he has a fresh jug of wine, and they settle Decius down in the dining room for the story. Lucius sits back on his dinner couch and is reminded of the time so many years ago when he and his mother had sat and waited for a younger Decius to run back from the Forum with news of death. Lucius is struck by how much Decius has changed since then, not in looks, but in manner. He is now so at ease with the family, one of them almost. How long has he been part of the household? Lucius can't remember a time when Decius wasn't there. He must have been bought before Lucius was born. As he is wondering whether or not to bother him by asking, he thinks that the question of Decius' freedom must be raised with his father again.

"No one knows how long they have been planning it, or even all those who were involved in the plot," begins Decius, as he sits and cradles the wine cup appreciatively. "It seems to have been quite well planned, but on the other hand Caesar made it so easy for them. Really, it was all very straightforward. Yesterday morning, Caesar came to the meeting of the Senate at the Theatre of Pompey because of the Senate House being rebuilt still."

They know about the Senate House – it is forever getting burnt down and rebuilt. Decius sees and lifts a gentle hand.

"Ah, but, it really is significant. It adds a rather neat touch, which you'll see later. Well, all they had to do is get Caesar on his own, so one of them – Trebonius, I think it was – delayed Marcus Antonius outside, and once Caesar had got in, several men attacked him. The members of the Senate just sat, stunned – your father, Lucius, says that he couldn't move because he didn't believe what he was seeing, just like in a dream. When it was done, Marcus Brutus called out Cicero's name, but by that time most of the senators had fled. He and the others left Caesar to die at the foot of Pompey's statue."

It is very fitting. Pompey had been Caesar's son-in-law, political ally, and finally bitter enemy. By refusing to settle with each other, they had given a cause for war to the greedy, the dissatisfied and the selfish, and had led the country into the civil war. Pompey, one of the greatest generals Rome had ever employed to enlarge her Empire and increase her revenues, had been killed by treachery in Egypt. Lucius has a sudden picture of the statue crunching and grinding as it turns its head to look down (with whatever satisfaction is enjoyed by cold stone) on the destruction of Caesar.

"There was – not exactly panic," continues Decius thoughtfully. "Just a complete lack of organisation. No one knew what they should be doing. Antonius has disappeared but is thought to be alive, and the assassins have taken refuge in the Temple of Jupiter on the Capitoline Hill. The city is very quiet, as if a lot of the tension has been drained off. Now we're all just waiting to see what the important people do." He suddenly laughs. "The trouble is, no one knows who the important people are any more. Now that Caesar has gone, we're going to have to redefine important, and make do with second-best in a way."

"You mean, after being ruled by a dictator, we're not going to be satisfied by a mere consul?" Marcus has been well drilled by his father and sounds incredulous that anyone should see the death of Caesar as anything but the greatest piece of good fortune for Rome and the Republic.

"Decius is right," says Lucius. "Who are we going to accept now? And will anyone be content to be a consul and share power with his fellow consul? It might not be safe to try and restore a republic again. Do you think Marcus Antonius is going to keep his head down while Rome sorts herself out?"

"If the Senate get their act together, they should be able to keep Antonius under control and set up a proper republic again," says Marcus with confidence.

Decius and Lucius look at him in silence. He sighs.

"Yes, all right, the Senate have to want to set up the Republic again. Let's hope our fathers get things moving."

Lucius' father does not have that sort of influence; Cicero might. Lucius doesn't know what to think and decides that the future is too difficult. Marcus looks at him.

"I thought you'd be really pleased," he observes. "After all, doesn't this mean you can go back to Rome tomorrow?"

"Yes," Lucius says, and gets up. "And now I'm going to bed. Early start tomorrow, you two. Marcus, you'll see to Decius?"

"Of course," says Marcus cheerfully. "I've asked for a bedroom to be made up for you, Decius. Let's go and see where they've put you. Although you know your way around this house better than I do, I expect. I shall say good night, Lucius."

Marcus and Decius leave the room to find the housekeeper, and Lucius sits down again to pour another cup of wine. He has no desire to think any more about all this, but he will need help to sleep tonight. He must, he tells himself, regard all this as merely interesting, something happening very far away to people he doesn't know and having very little effect on him. He must not get drawn into anything. It is not his problem.

One thought does strike him before he falls asleep – will there now be a case for Sallustius Crispus to answer? That is interesting, for with Caesar dead, does anything that has happened since last September have a meaning? This seems a grimly suitable end to the whole messy business, so he sighs and shuts his eyes.

He cannot escape dreaming. In the middle of a circle of men, Caesar lies messily shrouded in his toga folds. Gradually the circle gets wider as each man steps back and further apart from his neighbours. They become individuals again, and their movements now are those of independent minds. They look around at each other, and, glancingly, at the red and cream heap of laundry in the middle of the hall. It is silent apart from the breathing, almost panting, from Brutus whose face wears an expression of exaltation. A neat row of tiny drops of blood cuts across one cheek and through the triumph.

"He called you 'child'," Lucius says to Brutus. "Why did he do that?"

Brutus can't hear him, but suddenly Cicero is standing next to Lucius, and saying, "Does it matter?"

He turns to the group of men and shouts, "Liberators! To the Capitol!"

In a welter of bathos, the men obediently turn for the entrance to the hall. After a couple of paces, Cassius turns back and lets his dagger fall next to Caesar's body. The others ignore him and clutch their swords and knives as they leave the safety of the hall. Cassius does not linger by the body of the man who had forgiven him but walks quickly to catch up. Lucius sees them walking down an empty street, waving their swords and shouting, "Freedom!"; then finds himself back in the hall, next to the statue of Pompey, and Cicero is there, looking at Caesar and saying, "I had him to dinner once you know – so much trouble..."

During the journey to Rome, Lucius is wrapped up in

consideration of this dream, so detailed and lucid. It is only when he walks through the Capena Gate that he starts to think ahead, and as they enter the city, there is an awareness Lucius has never noticed before. There are people milling around everywhere he looks, in little seething groups, but there is no purposeful stream of humanity. He realises that he is used to being in a sort of well-behaved mob, ribbons of people heading towards the Forum, the temples, the markets. Now it seems that people are tethered on long chains, staying within defined boundaries, close to home. They are not frightened, exactly, but they are unwilling to push beyond the boundaries they have imposed upon themselves. Lucius looks around for the obvious signs of civil unrest, but there is nothing out of the ordinary. No unusual litter lies in the streets, no signs of fighting, no suspicious red smears on floors and walls. Talking is subdued, and people look at him and Marcus and Decius as they pass with carefully blank faces. He feels as though he is the only person strolling through a gallery of waking statues. At some point they might all turn on him, he thinks, and he shakes the fancy out of his head with a scowl.

They make for the Forum of course. Where else? But almost unheard of, they find that though their way is not barred, they must enter the Forum between two rows of soldiers, clearly on official duty. Soldiers. In the heart of Rome. Once past the Regia, the groups of people get larger, and Lucius notices that the focus of these groups is often a building. Around the little circular temple of Vesta is a group of women, respectable matrons and their daughters and maids, swathed in cloaks and scarves against the chilly air. A couple of the Vestal Virgins are moving among this group, and Lucius realises that these women have lost their father figure. Julius Caesar was the Pontifex Maximus and therefore in charge of the Vestal Virgins, taking over the role of their paterfamilias. Until a new High Priest is chosen, the Vestals have no guardian. He looks carefully, hoping that his mother and sisters have stayed at home.

Their group naturally skirts this female gathering and Decius leads them to join a group of people milling around on the steps of the Temple of Castor and Pollux. This is a good place for views across the less built-up part of the Forum, though it is difficult to avoid looking at the building work that Caesar had funded. The Senate House still has a cladding of scaffolding, and the new Basilica Julia is pointedly half-complete. Even the buildings, thinks Lucius, are left unsure. More soldiers stand posted at important points, on top of the Rostra, at the bottom of flights of stairs and at the entrances of the basilicas. There are even a couple of men, posted at a respectable distance, keeping a watch on the Temple of Vesta, or as much as they can see of the little temple, surrounded as it is by circling ranks of women.

Decius has a few quick and quiet conversations and returns to update them. Marcus, who has kept absolutely silent since they entered the city, fixes all his attention on him, as though glad to have something else to look at.

"Yesterday," says Decius, "Brutus made a speech in the Forum which many people attended and then in the evening there were lots of small meetings. I shall get more detail about that if I can. Antonius called a meeting of the Senate for today in the Temple of Tellus, starting at first light, and that is still going on – people are waiting here for a messenger to be sent to update us all on what decisions the Senate are taking. If any." He lowers his voice. "People are cautious. They won't say anything which can be contested. I don't even know what to call the – well, Brutus and Cassius and so on. You can't use the words "liberator" or "assassin", there are people who would disagree with one or other – or both. And apparently, they are all – Brutus et cetera – still on the Capitol, camping outside the Temple of Jupiter. They didn't dare come to the Senate meeting. They have their own force of bodyguards up there, and they have more or less barricaded themselves against a possible attack."

Marcus is looking uncomfortable. "I'd like to go home but..."

Lucius doesn't think this is wise.

"Why don't you go to your uncle's?" he says, carefully avoiding names. "It's nearby, and you can get the news from your cousin."

Marcus brightens, and after a surprising and slightly awkward hug, he leaves, heading towards the Carinae. Decius raises his eyebrow in a silent question, then quietly slips after Marcus. Lucius settles down to wait, and he watches the crowd beneath him gently billow and recede, as people come and go very quietly. Time slows down as a watery sun climbs the roofs of the temples, and it is with an air of waking up that Lucius realises that the crowd are all looking towards the Capitoline Hill. He cannot see what is happening, but a murmuring grows towards him as men turn their heads to tell those behind them. A line of people starts to move up the hill, and Lucius descends the stairs of the Temple of Castor and pushes forward. Gradually he understands as the snatches of talk flow around him.

"Brutus is making another speech..."

"He wants people to come up..."

"I'm not going..."

"Someone has to," says Lucius, more to himself than anyone else, and he joins a shambling queue of those curious enough and foolhardy enough to see what an assassin has to say in defence of himself.

Chapter Twenty-Four

On the steps of the Temple of Jupiter stands a scattering of men, dressed formally in togas and purple-striped senatorial tunics. Lucius sees them first as a group, and for a moment he is reminded of his dream as the group resolves into individuals. But these men have no blood on their skin or clothes, and they seem calm and – ordinary. Lucius recognises Cassius, whom he has always admired for his courage and military exploits, and Marcus Junius Brutus, a man summed up by Sestius senior as a fawning prig. The others he doesn't know, though he can bet his father does. Lucius takes in the scene carefully, knowing that he will be describing it to his family soon.

Brutus stands waiting for the crowd to finish streaming in and settle. Whether consciously or not (it must be conscious, thinks Lucius), he stands at the centre of the group and slightly to the fore, on a lower step of the temple. This deliberate humility irritates Lucius, and again he looks at Cassius. He cannot help comparing them. Cassius is the war hero, his hair tidy, short and greying, his face grim and mouth wide as his large brown eyes gaze at Brutus with, almost, thinks Lucius, exasperation. Brutus is tall and thin, and his face is not quite gaunt, but you can see the bone structure. His eyes turn down at the outer edges and Lucius finds this fascinating. It gives Brutus a look of – what? Pleading? Whining? Again, Lucius looks at Cassius and this time the face is blank as the soldier stands to attention and does not betray any more feelings. Lucius realises that the wrong man has taken command of this enterprise. He stands with his fists clenched and looking around him he sees faces that are guarded, distrustful, unimpressed.

Then Brutus begins to speak, and Lucius is lost. The speech is gentle and regretful and noble. Brutus does not use long or complicated sentences or Cicero's exuberant rhetorical flourishes. He talks of his torn feelings and his agonised decision, of the horror of seeing Caesar's blood but knowing that this was something he had to do because he loves Rome more than Caesar. By the end of the speech, Lucius is convinced that Caesar had become two people and the person killed by Brutus was the cold tyrant, not the forgiving father. The men around Lucius sway with him, under Brutus' charm, and while there is a light hum of mutters there is also lots of nodding. By the end of the speech, there is a distinct lessening of tension in the atmosphere, and Cassius has relaxed enough to shift his weight onto one foot, hand on hip, as he listens as intently as everyone else to Brutus. Lucius sighs and his shoulders drop. He now knows what he is going to do with his quaestorship – that is, if he is still quaestor after the Senate have made their decisions.

Brutus ends his speech with a prayer to Jupiter and then makes his way down to the bottom of the temple steps. He walks unhurriedly and with a solemn expression on his face.

"Where are you going?" shouts Cassius after him, but Brutus does not turn. It is a planted question, and Brutus replies in a loud voice for all to hear.

"I am going to the Forum to wait for the consuls. They will tell us what the Senate has decided for the Republic."

And he makes his way through the crowd without having to push. The crowd hesitates, then turns and begins to trickle down the stairs. Lucius makes his way to the edge of the stream of people and then stops. He wants to see what the rest of the Liberators will do. They have a quick conversation on the steps, then come down to join the descent into the Forum. They keep together, and a band of their bodyguards fall in behind them. Brutus is out ahead and on his own, should any Caesarian feel like revenge. Lucius watches as they go past him, then follows. At some point he must speak to Cassius, but not now.

When he reaches the Forum, Lucius is not surprised to find that the crowd is looking expectantly at the Rostra. Brutus' timing was excellent – a small group of the Senate are there and Marcus Antonius is obviously about to speak. Lucius keeps an eye on them, as he slowly makes his way through the crowd back to Temple of Castor and Pollux. Sure enough, Decius is on the steps looking out for him.

"We have only just got here from the Senate meeting," says

Decius.

"It won't have been as interesting as the meeting up on the Capitol," says Lucius. "I think they might get away with this, you know, Decius. Brutus has got everyone convinced."

Decius looks unsurprised. "The Senate agree with you," he says. "Senator after senator has urged calm and reconciliation and no revenge. Cicero proposed what he called an amnesty, an act of forgetting. They liked the idea very much. There will be no punishment and no reward, and everything Caesar put into law will be respected. Congratulations, Quaestor!"

Lucius laughs out loud. People turn to look at him, but nobody comments. Decius looks a little surprised then grins himself, but it is forgotten as Marcus Antonius, the senior consul holds out his hands in the traditional gesture for quiet.

"Citizens of Rome! There is a Greek word amnestia, which means "forgetting". Your Senate has decided that this will be our watchword as we decide how to respond to the events of the last two days. This does not mean that we trivialise what has happened, but neither does it mean we approve. It simply means that for the good of us all we must keep the state working and for that to happen we must not hold any deed against any person. It is not forgiveness. It is not praise. It is forgetting. Do we then forget Caesar? No, how could we? His achievements are too many to forget. But we separate his end from his beginning, his death from his life. And we do not judge anyone. So, let all of Caesar's laws and appointments hold true. Let the calendar remain, let the provincial governors stand as he decreed, let building on his new forum continue. Let us honour everything good about him, while looking first and foremost to the continued health and prosperity of our nation."

Marcus Antonius does not look like the relaxed, sprawling figure who mocked Lucius just a few weeks before. He is a statesman and he judges the mood beautifully. A noble aim is offered to the crowd, one in their interests, and it extinguishes any desire for more blood. The crowd like it because, while they thought that in situations like this, revenge should be considered, their hearts did not want any more confusion and violence. Lucius sees that the Liberators are being ushered onto the Rostra and Antonius walks up to Cassius, takes his hand and says so that all can hear, "Gaius Cassius, will you dine with me tonight?" Lepidus has approached Brutus, and Brutus looks noble and shouts, "Yes!" and for some reason, everyone starts cheering. The other Liberators are approached by senators and they go off the Rostra in pairs, obviously heading for a series of planned suppers. Lucius and Decius watch in silence and when Lucius sinks down to sit on the temple steps, Decius joins him. Gradually the crowds around them drift away until they are left perched on their own like a pair of exhausted pigeons.

After a while, Decius puts an arm around Lucius, and they are still sitting in silence, when Decius realises that a man has come up the temple steps and is standing in front of them. The man is a senator, and so Decius gets to his feet, and shuffles as far back as the step will allow. Lucius looks up. In front of him is Gaius Cassius Longinus.

"Gaius Cassius?" he says uncertainly, as he too scrambles to his feet.

Cassius looks him up and down and says, "You look tired," and he pushes Lucius back down and sits next to him. Decius takes up a cautious perch on a step behind them.

After a silence, Cassius says, "I am exhausted. And now I am supposed to be having a civilised meal with Marcus Antonius. He has gone ahead to get things arranged, despite the fact that things have been arranged since late this morning when we got his first message. I suppose that he is really not yet ready to be seen with me. See those four soldiers over there? They are to make sure that I get to Antonius' house in one piece. I kill a tyrant but this act lets armed soldiers into the city, it seems."

Lucius looks at the unsmiling face beside him. A long time ago, or just a few months, in Africa, the young legate Horatius had summed up Lucius' own dilemma – "...all it takes is one man to do what I am not brave enough to do". How had Horatius gone on? "And when I meet that man, then I will follow him and be glad to be led. "Lucius is deciding whether or not to offer his allegiance to this brave man, the traitor who killed his own friend.

For a moment he looks into the sky and hopes desperately

that the gods will send him a sign, as here, surely, is where signs should be seen. A lone eagle would have done – he imagines it flapping easily across the heavens and his heart lightening as he realises that for once, he really is doing the right thing, no question. But no speck grows out of the sun, and he is left by the gods to go on by himself. He knows what he is going to do.

"I am Lucius Sestius Quirinalis," he says firmly.

"Yes," says Cassius. "You are one of the quaestors that the Senate have just confirmed in office. In fact, you were added to the list just a couple of weeks ago. I am still praetor, it would appear, and my province will be Syria. I'd like you to be my quaestor out there."

Lucius' eyes suddenly fill with tears, and he nods, and looks up into the sky, swallowing before saying, "Yes. Thank you, yes." There are no questions to ask. Cassius pats his shoulder and goes off towards the Palatine without any further word, and the four soldiers fall in quickly behind him.

Lucius has one last thing to do, and Decius, after a half-hearted attempt to get him to turn for home, falls in beside him, asking where they are going.

"We have to find Cicero," says Lucius, and, shadowing Cassius, they climb the Palatine Hill to Cicero's house.

Cicero's door-slave maintains with defiance that his master is not home, but Lucius pays no attention, and strides through a house which is hushed and waiting. He finds Marcus Tullius Cicero sitting in his study at that ridiculous desk and gazing into the tiny flames of the lamp-stand at his elbow. Without Caesar, there is suddenly a lot more room in Rome, but equally many things left undone. Lucius can see the list running through Cicero's mind, and the solutions being attached to each query, ready to be dictated to Tiro. He turns his head as Lucius comes in, but there is no change in his distracted expression – except that the little frown lines between his eyes deepen.

Lucius picks up the chair by the door to move it to the desk, then changes his mind. He will stand; it isn't as if he is staying that long.

"Where is Tiro?" he asks. "I have a question for him."

Cicero, instead of exclaiming at this abrupt start, looks wary.

"I don't know where Tiro is," he says quietly. "It has been a strange time. I feel I am not really alive. Maybe it is just that I'm asleep and dreaming."

Lucius has no time for this.

"This is real, and I need to know – why was Tiro writing to Publius Sittius in Africa?"

Cicero sighs as if disappointed with Lucius.

"He was writing for me of course," he says. "I have kept in touch with Publius Sittius for years. Ever since..." He stops and looks at Lucius, the calculation plain on his face.

"You don't have to worry about whether to tell me or not," says Lucius coldly. "Let me guess instead. This goes back to the Catilinarian Conspiracy, when Caesar came to you with news of a dangerous plot. But it turned out that he had a man on the inside, who was willing to stay on as a member of the conspiracy so that he could supply you with valuable details. And you realised that the only way Caesar and Sittius could have got involved was by being a part of the conspiracy, at least at first. So, what to do? Arrest everyone including Caesar and Sittius and let them take their chances in a law court with the other conspirators? Or pretend to believe that they are really patriots working on behalf of the Republic so that you could make a big splash out of putting a stop to the rebellion? And ever since then, you have been terrified that someone would find out what you did to protect Caesar."

Cicero has gone quite pale.

"I had to," he says. "The Senate would not have believed me, or if they did, they would not have backed me up. Look what happened even when I did have solid proof! I still got exiled for it! When Caesar announced that he was going to run for election as Pontifex Maximus I saw my chance and went around to see him. I only had suspicions that he was involved on the fringes – to discover that he was the driving force was terrifying. But we struck a deal. I worked to get Caesar the post of Chief Priest, and he persuaded Sittius to work for me on the inside. I have to say, Sittius was invaluable, he kept up the game to the bitter end, though part of the deal was that he would escape to Africa halfway through the year. He has never admitted to being my agent. There are still people who think he was Catilina's right-hand man and should have been executed."

"Maybe that's what you should have done long ago," says Lucius. "Why not just send a few soldiers over to Cirta to get rid of him?"

Cicero's eyes widen in disgust. "Don't be ridiculous, Lucius. That is how the people I fought all my life behave – people like Catilina and Clodius. And now, Marcus Antonius of course. He wouldn't hesitate about something like that."

"But you did," says Lucius. "And if you had not hesitated, three men would not have been killed over the last few months. Doesn't it bother you that Cornelius Rufus was killed by Sittius? And Caecilius?"

"Of course it bothers me!" snaps Cicero, suddenly standing. He waves his hands with a silly little shake which looks almost comical but is borne of frustration. "Sittius is out of control. He does nothing Caesar tells him unless he wants to, and Caesar does not seem to understand that the man is a liability! At any time now, he could come forward with the truth about the Catilinarian Conspiracy, and while I think we could refute it, it would be a lot of effort, and there is Caesar just swanning off to the East..." He remembers and sits down. "Not that Caesar matters any more of course."

"But you do?"

Cicero looks up at him, weary but yet not finished.

"Yes, I do matter at the moment, Lucius," he says. "I have to lead the pitiful remnants of the Senate so that Marcus Antonius does not succeed in taking over, so that Brutus and his friends don't suffer for what they did, so that the Republic moves on."

"My father fought against Catilina at the Battle of Pistoria," says Lucius. "If you had revealed everything you knew to the Senate, straight away, there would have been no fighting. You could have dealt with everything in Rome. Instead, you decided to let Catilina escape to become the ringleader, the focus of the rebellion, to distract attention from Caesar. And you have said nothing all these years, even when Caesar let you go into exile, even when Caesar started dismantling the Republic. Nothing."

"It was the compromise I made to make sure that Rome survived," says Cicero. "If I had broken the news about the conspiracy straight away, there would have been a mess. The Senate would have dithered, everything would have quietly been dropped, nobody would have been charged with anything. And then a few years later, Caesar would have tried again. And possibly succeeded. In fact, you could say he did succeed on the day he became Dictator for Life. For a while I thought of those years of keeping quiet, and despaired."

Lucius goes right up to the edge of the desk.

"Just one question then," he says. "Did those conspirators you executed really write those letters that convicted them? Or did you and Caesar arrange that as well?"

There is no mistaking the flush which crosses Cicero's face. He says nothing, but he looks defiant, and there is a hint of a smile.

"Or is it," continues Lucius, watching Cicero closely, "more complicated than that? The letters weren't forged, but they were written because you and Caesar and Sittius put pressure on the conspirators. You needed them to provide proof of guilt, so that you could execute them, and so you steered them into writing those letters. How did you manage it? What did Sittius have to do?"

Cicero snorts. "Sittius was long gone by then, and those men condemned themselves. They were trying to get a tribe of Gauls to join them in rebellion, and all I did was tell the Gauls to ask for the letters. It was ridiculously easy, and the conspirators signed away their lives themselves. Don't you dare try and make me feel guilty over that! You aren't the first person to attempt that, and nobody will ever succeed because I am not guilty of anything! I put an end to that conspiracy practically single-handed because the Senate were too busy sitting on their hands to do anything constructive, and then they all sat on their hands again when Clodius attacked me. And do you know why? Because I was born in Arpinum not Rome! Because I was born into a mere middle-class family! Because I am more intelligent than they are! Because I run rings round them all when I speak! The Senate is a mob of ill-educated, cowering, vain, snobbish, thin-blooded, puffed-up nobodies who think they count because their grandfather was once a consul!"

He stops for a moment, and takes several deep breaths while Lucius just stares at him.

"I'm going to do this, Lucius," Cicero continues. "I'm going to bring the Republic back. You can try to bring me down if you want, though you won't get anywhere. Do you think anyone cares about Catilina or Sittius at the moment? Look, Lucius, over the next year I shall either succeed in which case nobody is going to want to see me humiliated again over Catilina, or I shall fail, in which case I shall be dead, and you can tell anybody anything you like about me."

Lucius can hardly believe Cicero's singlemindedness.

"And Publius Sittius?" he says at last. "What will happen to him?"

"He can go back to Africa and live out his days in Cirta, as far as I'm concerned," says Cicero. "I don't care anymore, and I shan't need to write to him. He won't bother you as long as you don't bother him."

"No!" shouts Lucius. "It isn't that simple! You knew what he was like, you knew what Caesar was like and you helped them to get at Sallust. You knew that they wouldn't hesitate to kill, and you dragged us into it to be distractions, to draw their fire. And we were supposed to be your friends! Can you imagine how my father is going to take this?"

"Don't tell him if you don't want him to be upset," says Cicero, cool and collected once more. "Now, I am not prepared to talk to you about this anymore. I know you are angry, but you aren't going to harm me – that is one of the reasons you brought Decius, isn't it? So now you had better leave. Decius, will you see to it?"

And Cicero turns once more to the lamp-stand, gazing at the little flames, lost immediately in whatever he is thinking. Lucius almost envies him. It must be good to be able to let go of something so easily. But he has one more thing to say. He needs to hurt Cicero, just a little, to make the break between them complete.

"Look at you," he says. "You, the only man in Rome who

wants the Republic, are sitting here doing nothing. You have lost, Marcus Tullius Cicero. You lost the moment you decided to let Caesar off the hook twenty years ago. Look at you – you divorced your wife. You have lost your daughter. Your son feels guilty for not being you, and your nephew knows you only too well. You have manipulated everyone you are supposed to love, and now you have lost."

Lucius does not wait for any sort of reply to this but stands and leaves the room. Decius, after a moment, follows. There is no movement or sound from Cicero.

Lucius makes for Albinia's house with Decius beside him. They do not talk. Decius looks shattered, and Lucius is sorry not to have warned him. But he had been unable to tell anyone his suspicions right up until the moment he saw Cicero sitting at that desk.

Albinia and Apuleius are both home, and look, like the rest of Rome, uneasy. Albinia runs to hug Lucius and even cries, though she smiles too much for the tears to last long. When they realise that Lucius has something to tell them, they all go into Albinia's study, and there Lucius pours out his suspicions. He has had plenty of time to think it all out, and nobody to try it all out on until now.

Albinia reacts exactly as Lucius expects any member of his family to react. She is devastated and again cries, with disappointment this time. Heroes are not meant to crumble quite so completely. Apuleius is only slightly less stunned, for, like Lucius, he has grown up thinking that Cicero at least is the old-fashioned, reliable sort of senator, who loves the Republic and acts on principle. And that the great Catilinarian Conspiracy wasn't what it is supposed to have been is unthinkable. But Albinia realises that the Sestius family have suffered a more personal let-down.

"I can't believe it – Cicero has known all along what Caesar and Sittius were planning?"

"Yes, since he heard about Sallust's decision to write the account of the Catilinarian Conspiracy," says Lucius. "That would have been just before Sallust went to Africa Nova. Cicero told Caesar, and Caesar contacted Sittius and asked him to start collecting material to use against Sallust for a prosecution. Cicero used us to keep an eye on Sallust once he came back to Rome. He knew we would tell him everything about the case, and he could then trot off to Labicum and report to Caesar. He may not have realised that Caesar would recall Sittius. And I don't suppose it was his idea to have Caecilius killed to scare me off."

"But why get you involved and then get rid of you?" asks Apuleius, looking appalled. Lucius shrugs.

"Sallust would have asked someone to help his defence, so why not us? We were unimportant but easy to manipulate. Cicero would have pretended that nothing was going to happen to us, but people like Caesar and Sittius think nothing of two or three murders to keep themselves from being inconvenienced. And it made Sallust shut up, didn't it?"

Albinia starts to look thoughtful. "They didn't predict you very well, did they? You were supposed to go to Greece and lie low, furthering your education, and instead you went straight to Africa, and needed constant watching."

"Yes, Cicero misjudged that, and it was probably only when Caesar sent those men down to Puteoli to check up on me that they realised what was happening. Sittius decided to return to Africa, Caesar lined up a retired spy to keep an eye on me, and when people started asking about his role in the Catilinarian Conspiracy, Sittius decided to push me back to Italy. Where Caesar neatly caught me and made me a quaestor. And I decided to give up."

Apuleius looks at him thoughtfully. "The decision in the Senate today was that Caesar's decisions regarding appointments will be upheld. You are in fact now quaestor. Technically, some of Caesar's assassins hold high office and are going to govern provinces."

"I'm not staying in Rome," says Lucius wearily. "I shall go to Syria with Cassius. He has asked me to serve on his staff and I can't stay here and watch Cicero and Antonius fighting it out." He looks at Albinia. "I don't want to tell Father."

"No," says Albinia, very decidedly. "No, don't, if you can possibly help it, Lucius. There isn't much point and it would be terrible for him. He would have to face the fact that Cicero bears some of the responsibility for Caecilius' death – even though I suppose we can hope that Cicero won't have had any part in the decision to kill Cornelius Rufus."

"He made sure that Caesar recalled Sittius to Rome, knowing perfectly well how the two of them would solve any problem," says Lucius. "He gave them information about our family, while pretending to help us. And he has been helping them to cover up their role in the conspiracy for twenty years. He has been in touch with Sittius all this time. I wish I could tell Sallust. I don't think he will be prosecuted anymore."

"I'm sure someone can drop a hint to Sallust," says Albinia. "It hardly matters what he says about Caesar and Sittius now."

Lucius stands up. "And now I must go home. I have a lot to do before I can go east. And I shall have to go soon, or I shall not be able to avoid seeing Cicero again. Do I tell Marcus or young Quintus Cicero?"

"I don't know," whispers Albinia. "Do they need to know?"

"Quintus Cicero deserves it," says Lucius. "He already sees his uncle far more clearly than we did, and he even warned me not to trust him. If I see him before I leave, I shall tell him. Oh, and you two need to come to dinner tonight. It will be a special occasion."

That evening, the slave Decius becomes the freedman Decius Sestius Quirinalis when his ex-master invites him to dine with the family. The whole household rejoices, especially as they are also celebrating the return home and new promotion of the son of the house, Lucius Sestius Quirinalis. There is talk that he will go east to serve the praetor, Gaius Cassius Longinus.

It is the start of a very promising career.

·